MY DEAD BROTHER

MY DEAD BROTHER

REX ANDERSON

ST. MARTIN'S PRESS NEW YORK

Library of Congress Cataloging-in-Publication Data

Anderson, Rex.
    My dead brother / Rex Anderson.
       p.   cm.
    ISBN 0-312-03898-4
    I. Title.
    PS3551.N379M9   1990   89-24100
    813′.54—dc20   CIP

First Edition

10 9 8 7 6 5 4 3 2 1

For everyone at Houston's
Murder By The Book,
with special thanks to
Barbara Douglas.

MY DEAD BROTHER

CHAPTER 1

"**Y**ou wouldn't remember me, Mr. Morris."

He was right. Almost. I had the feeling, though, that if I took some time and worried over it, I'd place his face, at least. But he didn't put me to the trouble.

Flipping open his wallet with a gesture that proved that he'd done it a time or two before, he flashed I.D. "I'm Bob Gould—Police," he said. And in a moment added, "Homicide."

That did it.

"Come in," I said.

He did and said, "Sorry to stop by so late and disturb you."

He wasn't disturbing me. Writer's block is something that is hard to put your finger on, but when you're in the middle of it, there's no such thing as somebody disturbing you. And it was after ten o'clock, but I wasn't sleepy yet, so it wasn't late.

I motioned him to the sofa and sat down across the coffee table from him. "You talked to me three years ago," I said.

He hadn't changed much since then. He was still short

and chunky, and his face was still red enough for him to play "Before" in an "Eat your oatmeal and ZAP cholesterol" ad. When he smiled, I was sure that he'd show teeth that were ultrawhite and healthy, but crooked as hell. If he smiled.

He said, "Right. Three years ago. We talked after your brother was killed, Mr. Morris."

I hadn't pretended that that was the tragedy of my life for a long time. I didn't now. "I do remember you, Sergeant Gould."

He smiled, and I got ready for those crooked teeth. But what showed was braces. "Lieutenant now," he said proudly.

"You got a promotion and braces."

He looked at the ceiling and got just a little redder. "The wife kept after me."

I had a flash picture of "the wife" feeding him scrambled eggs and fat nuggets and shoving him out of the doorway to the orthodontist so that, when they knocked him out so they could try to balloon the crud out of his arteries, his teeth wouldn't look funny. "What can I do for you, Lieutenant?"

He was looking around. First sweeping the coffee table. Then the tables at the ends of the sofa.

It's the standard glance these days when you're in some- body else's house. I bent forward and opened a drawer in the base of the coffee table and set out an ashtray for him. "Go ahead. I hide 'em to try to kid myself." Then I pulled a cigarette out of the pack in the drawer and had it going before he got to his.

When he was stuffing his lighter away into his jacket pocket, he said, "I need to talk to you about your brother."

"Why?"

He chuckled and gave me a shot of the braces again. "I told myself that's what you'd say, Mr. Morris. Roy Purdy was tried and convicted, and he's in prison for Life, going on ten-twelve years with good behavior, so why bother?"

I hadn't thought about Gene for a while. Or about my

reaction to his death. The first thing I said, when I got the news, had been, "Well, somebody was going to kill the schmuck sooner or later." I had felt guilty for saying it. But I knew Gene probably better than anybody else—and certainly longer—and the guilt couldn't stand up to the facts.

My next reaction had been chill over wondering whether I was a suspect because, if I was running the cops, I sure as hell would be. But I had lots of company, I realized—practically everybody Gene had come into contact with since he was five years old would want to kill him. As it turned out, the time of his death was pinpointed within a couple of minutes, and it was easy for me to verify that I was at home, on the telephone, hassling with my editor about corrections to the galley proofs of a book for about an hour on both sides of that.

"We built up a good, solid case against Purdy," Gould was saying. "He was your brother's partner and had just been screwed out of the company and a hell of a lot of money—by your brother. And he'd made threats. The gun was his, that he kept in his desk. It still had his fingerprints on it when we found it in the Dumpster down the street. The clerk at the convenience store across the street saw a car that looked like his at about the time of the shooting. Purdy said he was at the bank, cashing a check at ten A.M. when your brother was killed. But the teller couldn't verify the time."

I remembered that from the trial. The teller was a fifty-year-old woman who looked as if she had spent a month's pay trying to look forty and beautiful for her Fifteen Minutes of Fame. She swore Roy Purdy was at her teller's window, eight miles of rainy-day Houston traffic away, when my brother was murdered.

She was a good witness for Roy as long as his lawyer was running things. But the prosecuting attorney turned her into dogmeat and showed that she actually couldn't establish what time she cashed Roy's check. And some $3.35-an-hour trainee banking executive hadn't remembered to load the surveillance camera that morning, and there wasn't anything to back her up.

That took care of Roy Purdy. I had been sorry that he was the one. There was a bunch of candidates, and I would more happily have picked out any of two or three of them.

I put out my cigarette and pushed the ashtray across toward Gould and wondered what this was all about. Maybe every three years the homicide detectives took a day off from the orthodontist and went around reliving the glories of their successful cases.

"Interesting," he said, nodding toward the object that dominated the coffee table.

"Stainless steel," I said. "Solid. A stainless steel ostrich egg. My ex-wife's an artist—maybe you remember—and she gave me that for my birthday once."

"Ex-wife?"

"Since eight or nine months after my brother was killed."

"Sorry to hear that, Mr. Morris. She seemed nice."

"She was," I said, and couldn't help amending it to "She is."

Gould clucked with the mild sympathy you work up for a near stranger. Then he looked curiously around with the patented expression of the once- and terminally married man who wouldn't even think of himself in such a situation, but still wonders just how it is to be divorced. And wonders why the place looks pretty much the same as it did three years ago—shouldn't the divorced man be living in an efficiency and riding around on a bicycle?

"Everything worked out pretty amicably," I said in explanation. "I got custody of the townhouse."

He looked surprised and worked out an explanation of his own. "Well, you didn't have kids, did you?"

"No. No kids."

He looked at the egg again. "She did that big thing down

in front of the Wortham Theater Center a couple of years ago, didn't she?"

"Yeah. 'The Dead Pullman Car,'" I said, repeating what somebody who wrote cutesy local stuff on the editorial page of one of the newspapers had dubbed it, saying it before Gould could, because it wouldn't irritate me if I said it. The critics loved it, but I wasn't exactly crazy about it myself. I was even less crazy, though, about hearing it knocked.

Gould spotted another piece that sat alone on a black-lacquered table against the far living room wall. It was from her "stainless steel period," also. It looked like a free-style Gordian knot.

He didn't comment on that one. It probably reminded him of his braces.

Art Appreciation time seemed to be finished, and he stubbed out his cigarette and glanced around some more. "Do you have a VCR, Mr. Morris?"

"A VCR?"

He nodded and sat back and pulled a cassette from his inside jacket pocket. "Right."

Maybe they showed those successful investigations in living color, I thought, but I stood up and motioned toward what I call my office when I'm being serious. "Yeah. Back here."

I opened the door, and the computer was sitting there humming and glaring its screen at me, waiting for me to renounce the freedom of writer's block and return to it. I ignored it and turned on the light.

"Wow!" Gould said. He had said it in exactly the same tone of voice three years ago. But now he added something new. "My kid's crazy about science fiction."

I figured he was just being flattering. But maybe not. Maybe the kid hadn't been old enough three years ago. Maybe she really did read it, since he didn't make the boo-boo of calling it "Sci-Fi."

Clutching the videocassette, he walked around, staring at my collection of framed artwork from my stories and book covers—obviously, I still get kind of excited about it myself. "Isn't this impressive!" he said. "She'll be crazy when I tell her I talked to you. She'd give anything to see some of this stuff."

The kid was sounding more real. But I didn't bite. I figured that after I'd blasted off to that Big Library in the Sky and they were displaying my memorabilia in the Smithsonian, his kid could go stand in line to look at it just like everybody else. "The VCR," I said, tapping the top of it.

Gould tore himself away from the original photomontage that *Omni* had butchered to size and splashed print across the best parts of to use to illustrate my short story, "The Storm Skater," and handed me the cassette. "Would you mind playing this?"

"Anything for the father of a fan," I said, and stuck the cassette into the machine and set things going.

Then we sat and waited for a moment. Both silent. I'm sure I was supposed to ask what we were going to see, but I didn't.

I spent the warm-up time calling up the only kind of mourning that I've ever been able to do for Gene. And it's not mourning at all. Just regret that things weren't different. I remembered how it was growing up, knowing that I had a big brother and trying to act around my friends as if my big brother was just as great as theirs. But knowing, also, that he wasn't. And worse, that they knew it, too. Regret. And a poor enough grade of it that, technically, it shouldn't even be capitalized.

The picture started.

Black-and-white.

It took me a moment to realize what I was seeing because it wasn't Supercop Gould in some moment of triumph.

It was the inside of a bank. Just like those cuts they show

on the six o'clock news of somebody with a gun and panty hose over his face.

There were numbers all along the bottom of the frame, and I was trying to figure them out when Gould picked up the remote and froze the picture.

"You remember her? From the trial? The teller."

Now that he said that, I did. She looked better in black-and-white. "Yeah," I said.

He started things moving again. On the screen a customer stepped up to the window and pushed a check across the ledge to the teller.

Once more Gould stopped the tape.

I stared at that customer. There was no mistaking him. Black bushy eyebrows that almost met in the middle. Dark, brooding eyes. With just a little work in either direction, he could be a werewolf or a fairly good-looking guy. At the moment he was leaning toward werewolf because he was my brother's latest sucker.

"That's Roy Purdy!" I said.

"Right—Roy Purdy!" Gould said. "See those numbers?"

I did. Part of them didn't make much sense. But "27 Oct 86" did. And so did "AM 09:58:23." I turned to stare at Gould. "Where the hell did you get this tape? They said the bank camera was empty."

He wasn't going to explain the minor details and skip his big, dramatic moment. "That bank teller was right," he said.

And after one last big pause, he showed me all his braces and announced, "We convicted the wrong man."

CHAPTER 2

Jane didn't act any more impressed with me tonight than she had when we were deciding that we shouldn't be married any more. And she certainly didn't look like somebody who used welding equipment and cutting torches on chunks of steel for a living.

"I saw your lights," I said.

"That's what you always say."

"So do you. Can I come in?"

"It's late, Mel."

"That's what you always say."

She smiled. "So do you."

She closed the door behind me, and I said, "Don't hassle me."

She kissed me. Somewhat. And then stepped back. "Let me guess. Is this a 'Don't hassle me, I just finished a book and I'm lost,' or a 'Don't hassle me, I'm stuck in the middle.'?"

"It's just a 'Don't hassle me, please,'" I said, moving in and getting her to hold me.

She did. With her usual skill.

I used to spend these moments kicking myself in the ass

and wondering why we'd split up. Then I came around to the only explanation I could live with—we hadn't split us up—marriage had—and if that had had to happen, divorce was the best thing that ever happened to our relationship. Now I spent them smelling her hair and holding her and being held by her.

We dropped in on each other sometimes when we needed to—like tonight. To avoid awkward situations, we had our signals that we never talked about. If I turned off the walk light, she wouldn't stop. Hers was, if there was a car in the guest parking spot in front of her apartment, I didn't stop. If he didn't have a car, she parked hers in the guest parking spot. Not more than five or six hundred times—it seemed to me—had I sat in my car in the dark and talked myself out of blowing out somebody's tires with the .38 I kept—illegally, of course—in the glove compartment.

"I was about to go to bed," she said.

"I didn't think you'd ever ask."

It didn't mean anything at all to me when she said, "Where'd you park?"

"In your guest parking spot."

"Okay."

We always liked undressing each other.

"Not a bad body for a welder," I said.

"You're getting fat, Mel."

I said, "The left one feels like it's sagging more than the right one."

She giggled. "I didn't shave my legs, either. That rechargeable thing doesn't recharge worth a damn."

"Christ! If I wanted hairy legs, I would have gone over to Montrose."

"Hmmm. This is getting fat, too."

"Forget about Montrose."

"I thought you'd say that."

I said, "Olympic-class butt. How the hell a woman your age maintains an Olympic-class butt, I've never figured out."

She was purring. And doing nice things with her hands. I used to gig her by telling her that, when she stopped working with gloves on, we were through. She hadn't yet. "This isn't Olympic-class," she said. "Except maybe Special Olympics."

I held her tighter and scuffed out of my shoes. We were going to need to get to bed pretty quick. That's why I always wore loafers when I dropped in on her. Shoelaces were hell at moments like this.

"But Gold-medal Special Olympics," she said, really purring now.

I was doing some purring, too. "Pommel horse," I said. And gave up and made the first move toward the bed. I usually did.

She giggled. "There's just one little problem. I'm out of balloons."

That was a rule we set up the first time we got together after the divorce. We talked about AIDS. Being an artist and a writer, we'd lost gay friends to it. We'd also lost a few straight ones. One or two of them, it could be blamed on blood transfusions. But it was getting more and more obvious that, whatever you did in bed, whoever you did it with, it was damned stupid to rely on luck. So we talked about condoms and voted them in. Except Jane always called them balloons.

"Out? Oh, shit!"

"Don't you have one in your wallet?" she asked.

"If I did, you'd think I was just coming over to get you in bed."

"Oh, shit."

"You're kidding. You're completely out?"

She nodded against my throat.

"Saran Wrap."

"Mel!"

"Don't act so shocked. There were a couple of times we'd have used emery paper if we'd had to. Besides, it was your idea. You were skipping Home Ec, and your mother was due home in an hour."

"I never took Home Ec."

"Skipping shop, then. Whatever. It worked."

It worked now, too.

It was kind of fun.

More than fun. Kind of like doing it in a Honda. Not exactly optimum, but kind of kinky, and a lot of fun. Memorable.

"I can't believe we did that," Jane said.

"Yes, you can."

We smoked a cigarette and, in a little while, she went to sleep. I held her nestled to me and silently apologized to her—neither one of them was sagging at all.

It would have been perfect except that I woke up about the time it was starting to get light outside, thinking about Gene.

Not so much thinking about Gene as about Gould's visit.

I could sure as hell have done without that.

"We convicted the wrong man," he said.

"Shit! Where'd you get that tape?"

He shrugged. "The Feds had it. A week, ten days before the killing, the bank was robbed. The Feds grabbed that day's tape for evidence right then. And then, two or three days after your brother got killed, they got around to picking up the ones for thirty days prior to the robbery. They check those to see if they can pick up the robber standing around casing the place beforehand. They should have picked up September 19 to October 17, or something like that. But the bank gave them a box that October 27 had got mixed into. Sloppy."

"So there was a tape in the camera that day, after all," I said.

"Yeah. The Feds just now got around to releasing those

tapes back to the bank, and somebody noticed the twenty-seventh of October was with 'em."

"It gets Roy Purdy off."

Gould waved a pudgy hand as if that wasn't very important. "Yeah. Pretty soon."

"Pretty soon? For Christ's sake, the man's innocent."

"They got to go through channels. Throw out the old trial. Have a new one. Dismiss the charges."

"He could be eligible for parole by the time they get around to all that."

"Aw, they'll probably let him out on bail—personal recognizance—something like that, pretty quick." He cut off any more of my outrage by adding, "Listen, I just put 'em in. I don't have anything to do with getting 'em out. That's somebody else's problem."

"Fine. All right."

He put on a very solemn look. "What all this means is that your brother's murderer is still on the loose."

"Who the hell cares?" I said.

He giggled.

Those goddamned braces! I wondered suddenly why Gene had never thought of braces when I was a little kid. A scenario sprang full-blown into my mind. It was wholly fictitious, but there were enough real ones that it was easy to construct.

We're at the breakfast table. Gene's about fifteen and I'm about ten. He's starting to sound froggy and making a big deal about having to shave every day, but mostly he fakes it. He looks across at me with those cold, scary pale gray eyes and gets that look that always told me I was about to get it one way or the other. And he stares at my mouth and says, "Look at the kid's teeth! Are they crooked or what?" and ten minutes later I'm strapped down, and Godzilla the Dentist is arc-welding an Oldsmobile into my mouth.

Gould was saying, "I told myself that's what you'd say.

But seriously—you got any ideas of who might really have killed him?"

"Me? You're the one that puts 'em in, aren't you?"

"I mean, anybody you noticed acting funny? Anybody that seemed too relieved when Purdy got convicted?"

"There were some people who were relieved that the cops wouldn't be hassling them any more when he was charged. But that's only natural."

"I guess so. That all?"

"Yeah," I said.

He stared at the computer screen as if he were trying to get himself hypnotized.

I interrupted. "What are you going to do now?"

He shrugged. "I just did it."

"You just did what?"

"Checked things out."

"Checked things out by asking me if I wanted to rat on somebody?"

"Is there anybody you could rat on?"

"No."

"Well, that's about it, then. I checked things out. Most of the people we were looking at then aren't in the phone book any more, or they're out of town, or something. You're here. So I checked."

"That's it?"

"As far as we're concerned." He gave me a flash of braces again. "Unless somebody raised hell, of course. Went on TV and stirred things up, say, trying to pressure us into acting like we were reopening the investigation so as to avenge your brother's death."

"I don't think there's anybody that wants his death avenged very much," I said, feeling that old twinge of regret, but certainly not the slightest glimmer of a thirst for vengeance.

"It's a cold trail," Gould said. "Nothing else's come up

that we could tie to it. We used everything we had when we hung it on Purdy."

"That's about it, then."

"That's about it," Gould said. "It's election time. We got drugs and dirty bookstores to worry about. Three-year-old cold trails don't get very much priority." He stood up and started toward the door. "Of course, if you happened to think of something, you could give me a call."

"Sure."

He took one last, longing look around. "My kid's just gonna freak out when I tell her who I talked to. She loves your books."

"Aren't you going to take your cassette with you?" I asked.

He giggled. "Oh, yeah. I guess I better."

I pulled it out of the VCR and handed it to him, and he went off to try to find a Dunkin Donuts that was still open.

Then I drove by Jane's, and her guest parking spot was empty.

She shifted more onto her back and started to snore. That was one thing I had never told her, through thick and thin—that she snored like a piece of farm machinery. When it got too obnoxious, I just shifted her around until she stopped.

It was pretty obnoxious now, and I played spoon, and her cheek turned to the pillow and she was just breathing again.

I tried to think, "Poor Gene," but it was really "Poor Roy Purdy." It was bad enough that he had to serve time for killing Gene. It was a damned crime that he didn't even do it.

Jane woke and turned to face me, snuggling. "You're awake, and you didn't even wake me up."

"A woman your age needs all the sleep she can get."

"Fuck you, darling."

"Did you bring the roll in here?"

"Of course."

"Where is it?"

"By the bed," she said, giggling like the high school girl she was fifteen years ago. "And we've got to hurry. My mother's going to get home at any second."

We didn't hurry.

Afterward she said, "You know, I'd completely forgotten about the Saran Wrap."

"I didn't."

"I remembered you, but not the Saran Wrap."

"I remembered both," I said.

She started a cigarette going for us.

I took a drag and said, "This cop came to see me last night."

"What in the world for?"

"To tell me Roy Purdy is going to be released."

"Released? How can they release him?"

"It turns out he didn't kill Gene, after all."

"Oh, God! Are you serious?"

"Serious as Duluth."

"God! That poor man."

I didn't ask her which one she meant. I told her what had happened.

"So that's it," she said when I was through.

"Yeah."

"They're not going to look for somebody else?"

"I don't think they even want to go through the motions. Three years is a long time."

"Good. They shouldn't. They shouldn't ever have tried to find out who killed him."

She sat up, killed the subject. "Coffee?"

"Sure."

But she didn't get out of bed. She leaned down and kissed my forehead and then said, "You didn't even hear what I said, did you?"

"'Coffee?'"

"No."

"When?"

"Last night. When I asked you where you left your car."

"My car?"

I wasn't catching on quickly enough.

She gave up and helped me. "I have to tell you some things. You're not the only one who knows when to stop, and when not to."

I stared at her for a moment, and then got up and started looking for my clothes.

"Mel . . ."

"You snore," I said, telling myself that I was angry, not hurt. "Did you know that? You snore like a John Deere tractor."

When I left Jane's apartment, we were getting the kind of rain that the word "drizzle" was invented for. But that was nothing new. It always rains in the fall in Houston. That's so you'll feel right at home when it rains in the winter. And in what passes for spring around here. But no big deal. We're all just toughing it out and trying to keep from getting mildewed too much until they build a dome over the city.

I had breakfast on Fountain View in a place that used to be a Savings & Loan. Now you get scrambled eggs and bacon instead of a passbook, and it's a better deal.

The eight-to-five crowd had already gone off to work, and the true Yuppies were having their power breakfasts in more auspicious places than failed S&Ls and I had the place pretty much to myself, so I decided to have a second cup of coffee and do some thinking.

Jane.

Why the hell had we broken up? How come I could neither answer that nor get it out of my mind? And then there was "You're not the only one who knows when to stop, and when not to."

Damn!

That wasn't the kind of thinking I wanted to do.

I cut to Gene. "We convicted the wrong man," Gould said.

Double damn!

Maybe any thinking at all right now was too much to ask of myself. So I started another cigarette and went farther into the morning paper than the Sports section.

For once I was glad that I did. There was some good news there, along with the drug stories and the child-abuse stories and the world-going-to-hell stories.

Houston, it seemed, was getting back onto its feet. Unemployment was down. Retail sales were up. Buildings were filling up. Tax revenue was finally getting back up to the point that somebody besides the mayor and the city council might get a raise. Nobody was saying we were booming again, but it sure as hell looked as if the Bust was definitely over with. What would the big Eastern papers write about now if Houston wasn't going into the toilet anymore?

Looking through the rain-smeared windows, I discovered that I could verify the upturn with my own eyes. Down the block a four- or five-story office building was under construction—the first time I'd noticed anything like that in a while. I couldn't see a single "For Lease" or "Going Out Of Business" or "Closed" sign in the windows of the shops along the street.

This was good news, indeed. I hadn't been affected very much personally by the downturn because, if people can't afford books in one place—even your own hometown—they can in other places, but lots of people I knew had gone through hell.

I decided to have a third cup of coffee to celebrate. But halfway through it, I got back to those two fatal sentences: "We convicted the wrong man," and "You're not the only one who knows when to stop, and when not to." And what had followed.

Damn it, Jane.

I went back out into the drizzle and drove toward the Galleria until I found a Walgreen's.

Writers—this one, at least—are a little peculiar when they go into a place that has a book rack, no matter what they're shopping for or what's on their minds. I wound around through Cosmetics and Candy and Greeting Cards until I found the magazines, and stopped to check them out. But what I was really interested in was the paperback display, right next to the rock music and TV heartthrob magazines and, after a couple of casual moments, casually moved over that way and gave it a casual look. Other things might be bothering me, but what I really wanted to know at the moment was whether I was still real.

I was. Just barely. Two copies of the paperback of *Shuttlemaster*, by Mel Morris, nestled tidily in the rack.

Warmth.

It's stupid, but seeing one of my books out for sale, no matter where, always made me feel good. Even on a day when the ghost of my big brother, Gene, was suddenly out running in the rain, and Jane had whammed a big one right in there below the belt, it gave me a lift. My new book might be stalled cold, but some of the old ones were still out there.

But the bottom row?

No way.

Glancing around to make sure nobody was going to catch me at it, I plucked the two books up and set them in the rack, right at eye level.

Yeah—warmth. It might not exactly knock the socks off the average guy, but it did okay for me.

Feeling a little better, I went on back to the drug counter.

It was getting close to Halloween and, while I was waiting for the cashier to get tired of talking to her boyfriend on the telephone and take my money, I checked out the display of masks and costumes. Batman and The Joker were big items this year. So was Barbara Bush. But among the topical stuff, there were still lots of Frankenstein's Monsters and vampires and assorted ghouls.

And I found myself absurdly wondering why there wasn't a Gene Morris mask.

That made me rude. I growled at the cashier and forced her to take a break from her love life and accept my money.

As I drove on toward the Galleria, the downtown skyline loomed ahead in the rain. As a Houston native, who remembered well when there was no skyline at all, I was still astonished at the realization that I was looking at the seventh, eighth, and fourteenth tallest buildings in the country.

With the unenthusiastic rain blurring details, hiding the bizarre gewgaws with which the buildings had been inflicted by the thoughtlessness of the early eighties Boom-time builders, they looked great. Maybe the buildings that would come along now, in what looked to be just prosperity and not Boom, would be better and cleaner—impressive even when it wasn't raining and you could see them clearly.

The closer I got to the Galleria, the more evidence there was of recovery, now that I was looking for it. Even Sakowitz looked great again, with new paint and a busy parking area. Time was when Sakowitz Department Store was the Spirit of Houston Incarnate. You could walk in and walk out with a bathtub full of diamonds for your sweetie, or a full-length sable for her to wear to the luncheon meeting your ex-wife was helping to host tomorrow. Then came Bust and Bankruptcy. But things were looking lots better now.

I helped out their cashflow a couple of bucks. Pulling into the parking lot, I went in to the gift-wrap counter. The blue-haired old lady there didn't bat an eye while she wrapped and ribboned. I guessed that word must be getting around, after all. Or maybe she just didn't know what she was wrapping.

Next stop was a flower shop that had opened recently in

what had been the lobby area of a failed bank. I ordered a dozen yellow roses to be sent to Jane with the gift-wrapped present in the box. I had never sent her flowers—or anything—after one of those nights before.

But this was the first time that she had told me that she was getting married.

Waiting for the left-turn light at Westheimer Road and the Loop, I stared through the drizzle at the Galleria and got more prosperity. The Galleria hadn't suffered all that much; it had just gotten quiet. Suburban strip shopping centers had closed completely. Office buildings had stood vacant all over town. But the massive, crystal-roofed agglomeration of specialty shops and famous department stores and hotels and restaurants, including even an ice-skating rink and a health club, had experienced only a downturn. That was largely finished now, though, judging from the crammed parking areas and the murderous traffic on Westheimer and Post Oak Road.

Sometime soon I'd elbow my way into the place to buy Jane's wedding present and then go by Waldenbooks to look for warmth and then make a stop at the Oaks cocktail lounge for six or ten overpriced drinks to toast her health and happiness.

When I got inside the Loop, heading toward home, it started raining harder. Obviously, wet was the plan for the day.

It looked like a hell of a good day to be inside, working on the book.

That was a bright thought! Maybe it meant that I was finally about to get some work done again. And I celebrated by letting a hundred-year-old lady ram her BMW down my throat and not ramming back.

But I didn't go straight home. This had turned into a magical mystery tour and there was no point in ending it now.

I cut over to Bissonnet and drove past the place where my brother and Roy Purdy had opened their business.

When Gene and I were growing up a few blocks away on North Boulevard, there were a dime store and a couple of doctors' offices and a TV repair place here. But in the early eighties, when the very craziest of the real estate speculation was going on, somebody had bought the property, poured a concrete parking lot in the front, and remodeled the buildings into a style which can most kindly be referred to as Nicaraguan Gothic. When Gene hooked up with Roy Purdy, they leased the middle of it.

Six months later Morris, Purdy Properties, Ltd., and Roy Purdy were broke, but Gene wasn't, of course. The help had been let go by telephone on Saturday morning, and Gene was in his office, probably trying to figure out if there was another dime or two he'd overlooked in his screwing of Roy, and a gray "Oldsmobile or Buick or Caddy," in the words of the clerk at the convenience store on the cross street, turned off Bissonnet and parked, and someone in a gray raincoat got out and hurried through the rain to the back door of Morris, Purdy Properties, Ltd., used or didn't use a key, depending on whether the door was locked or unlocked, went inside, slogged water and wet, but indistinct footprints all over the $3.95-a-yard maroon industrial carpeting that Roy Purdy's portion of the partnership had been socked $17.95 a yard for, plus installation, got the .45 calibre automatic that was in Roy's desk, which was slated to be repossessed that afternoon with all the other office furniture, trailed some more water across some more overpriced carpeting into Gene's office, whanged four shots into him, went out the same way, got in the car, and drove off, stopping only momentarily to throw something—the gun—into the Dumpster that stood by the nursery school down the block.

The time of the killing was established by the postman, who walked in the front door of Morris, Purdy Properties, Ltd., with that day's ration of threatening registered letters just in time to hear the shots.

That was just about exactly three years ago. Since then the place had stood vacant with the plate glass growing progressively grimier, and the Morris, Purdy sign, discreet and terribly expensive—to Roy Purdy's part of the partnership, I'm sure—hanging forlorn and unlighted on the orangy-pink stucco wall above it.

Things were changing now, though. The Morris, Purdy sign was gone from the building, but there was a temporary sign at the front of the parking lot that said, "Grand Opening Nov 15—Café Mariposa." And there were people working on the property, even though it was raining.

The plate glass was clean and shiny. Trucks bearing the logo of a restaurant supply company were being emptied of big stainless steel counters and stoves and cartons that probably contained pots and pans and dishes. Near the street sat a huge open-topped dumper of the kind you see parked around construction sites. I eased up at one end of it and stopped the car, not displeased to see that sticking up out of it, along with jagged chunks of sheetrocking melting in the rain, were rolls of that cheap maroon carpeting.

Progress toward recovery was showing its face even here, and I had to grin at the timing of my discovery of it—on the day after I found out that Gene's murder was still unsolved. Because Gene would have hated this; he did his best work in the economic downtimes when people were scared and insecure and foolish. When times were good, even though there was extravagance, Gene had had to work to find his suckers. When times were bad, they flocked to him.

It was beginning to rain harder now, and I took my foot off the brake and started to drive on.

But three husky young men came dashing across the parking lot toward the dumper, hooting laughter at the falling rain, balancing skillfully and precariously on their shoulders the missing Morris, Purdy sign.

Pausing beside the dumper, raindrops running off their

faces, acting in concert as if they were reading each other's minds, they heaved upward all together and tossed the sign—which was fully fifteen feet long—up and over with the rest of the remodeling trash.

In anticipation of the explosion of green-and-white Plexiglas, the young men ducked away from the dumper and then turned gleefully back to watch it, wiping rain out of their eyes and laughing.

I was laughing, too. This was a most fitting end to a magical mystery tour.

I took my foot off the brake and drove home through the rain to write some science fiction.

C H A P T E R   3

I took a shower and confidently asked the mirror, "Who the hell says you're getting fat?" Even so, I promised myself that, just as soon as it stopped raining, I'd do some running. If it didn't stop, I'd just glue some rabbit legs on my face and start posing as Isaac Asimov.

But first I'd get some work done on the damned new book.

Yeah!

The telephone rang when I was halfway across the living room.

It was Jane.

"You bastard!"

"You're welcome," I said.

"I can't believe you sent me these goddamned things."

"You know what roses cost these days?"

"Not the roses, Mel. Damn it, be serious."

"Serious," I said. "I'd just hate like hell for you to have to tell Mr. Right you were out of balloons."

"You bastard."

"How come you can't call 'em anything but balloons? Say 'condoms' just once. Or 'rubbers.'"

"You sent me three dozen gift-wrapped *rubbers*, Mel. And a dozen roses. What kind of pervert are you, anyway?"

"The rubbers were on sale and the roses weren't."

"You really are upset, aren't you?"

"Hell, yes, I'm upset. Why couldn't you just tell me you were going to marry somebody? You didn't have to cute it at me."

"I'm sorry. I didn't know how to tell you. I didn't want you to be upset."

"I'm not upset. I'll get over it. I'm just going to miss you, that's all."

She sounded miserable. "I think I like you better when you're not serious."

"Okay, I won't be serious. Who do you think killed Gene?"

"What? What did you say?"

"Just give me your best guess."

"You bastard! I don't care who killed him, any more than you do."

"Damn it, Jane. Why of all people do I have to love you?"

"Oh, Mel. I love you, too. I just wish we could have figured out how to keep on living together. I just wish we could have done that."

This was getting very close to the old question, and I couldn't leave it alone—"Why couldn't we, Jane?"

Her voice was suddenly small and very far away. "We've been over this so many times."

My voice was kind of small, too. "Without ever figuring it out."

"It was just over. That's all."

"Over. Even though we kept loving each other."

Softly—"Yes. Even though."

"Since the eleventh grade," I said. "Nobody else stays in love since the eleventh grade. Why us?"

We had reached the wall. She signaled it by making herself chuckle. "Maybe because I was the only one your brother couldn't run off."

I lightened-up too. Why not? When you get to the wall, you can beat your head against it or you can laugh at it. I had done my head-beating time. "I guess that's enough reason for me. Why you?"

"Because you were so different from him."

"I wasn't going to mention it," I said. "But that's my second reason—because you say such nice things to me."

"You're still being serious, aren't you?"

"Hell, no."

She laughed. And then said, "Why are you so set on who killed Gene?"

"I'm not."

She laughed again. "This is Eleventh-Grade-Jane. Don't try to lie to me."

"I don't know," I said. "I don't think I am. I sure as hell don't want to be."

"Oh, Mel. I love you so. And I worry about you."

"I love you, damn it. And I'm sorry about the balloons. But not about the roses. And I've got to get off the phone and do some writing."

"Okay. And stop worrying about who killed Gene."

"Stopped. And whoever this new guy of yours is, you ever do Saran Wrap with him, we're through."

"Okay, that's a promise." After a pause she said, "You haven't even asked me who he is."

"Send me an invitation," I said. "That'll be soon enough to find out."

The words "CHAPTER TWENTY-THREE" sat there in the middle of the screen, all by themselves, and stared at me.

"Damn!" I said. Writer's block hadn't just slipped away into the sunrise, after all.

What came next?

I had the story all worked out, and loved it and loved what I had done on it so far. In fact, I thought it was probably some of the best stuff I had ever done—and I don't think that nearly as often as I'd like.

But I didn't have any damned idea at all of what came after "CHAPTER TWENTY-THREE." About another eight or ten thousand words. But which the hell ones?

The hero was heroic, but not overwhelmingly so. And the heroine was heroic, too. The science was reasonably authentic. The aliens were reasonably alien.

What came next?

"Who the hell knows?" I typed, just to see if the machinery still worked. It did.

So I typed some more:

WHO KILLED GENE MORRIS?

Mel Morris—Alibied
Roy Purdy—Alibied about three years late
Grace Morris—Gene's widow/now Mrs. Hugh Rand
David Perryman—Son of Kent Perryman
Elaine Purdy—Mrs. Roy Purdy then/divorced and Mrs.
    Somebody Else now/Gene's last girlfriend
Sallie Lacie—Gene's next-to-last girlfriend
Sam Hauser—Gene's next-to-last partner

I thought about some other people and added some other names. But they were stretching it, and I erased them.

It was still raining.

This stuff on the screen didn't exactly read like award-winning science fiction to me.

I started to blank it, but a name puffed into my mind.

Tom Crenshaw. That's whom I had heard Elaine Purdy had married. Tom Crenshaw of the hardware Crenshaws. I erased "Somebody Else" and typed that name in its place.

Then I went back to the top and erased "WHO KILLED GENE MORRIS?" and typed in a new title—"CANDIDATES LIST."

Why the hell was I doing this?

It made no sense at all.

In ten minutes I had done more work on a list I didn't give a shit about than I had done on my new novel in the last week.

Go figure.

I started to blank it out, but didn't.

If I was going to spend my valuable time on something I didn't care about, I might as well make it complete.

I typed another name on the list:

Jane Morris—Once and now Jane Saunders/the Prettiest Girl in the Eleventh Grade

Then, just to be completely honest, I went back up to the "Alibied" beside my name and changed it so that it wasn't capitalized.

That started gooseflesh skirmishing around at the back of my neck.

So I blanked it all out, except for that damned "CHAPTER TWENTY-THREE," and sat there staring at it for a while longer.

Finally I decided I'd go running whether it was raining or not.

I got as far as the L's in the telephone directory.

When I started writing *Shuttlemaster*, I drove down to NASA and explained that I was a science fiction writer looking for some authenticity, and it worked great. They still kept a pretty close watch on their moon-rock supply, but they were very nice, and they showed me all over the Space Center and answered just about all the questions I had to ask them.

So I thought, since it worked okay once, let's try it again.

I had some doubts after I parked the car and looked things over some, but what the hell?

"Miss Lacie?" I said. "The lady over there at the cash register said you're the owner."

She gave me a look and a beat of pause and a tilted eyebrow. "That's right."

"I'm a writer, Miss Lacie. And I'm working on a book that has some lingerie involved in it, and I was wondering if you could help me out?"

Somehow that didn't come out nearly as impressive-sounding as "I'm working on a book about a space shuttle in the late 1990s, and I wonder if I could ask some technical questions?"

Sallie Lacie didn't think it sounded too great, either. "You're putting me on."

I lifted my hands and gave it up. "I was trying to, but it started sounding dumber and dumber, didn't it?"

She laughed, and it had a very pleasant, low, nice sound to it. Almost a trill. Her voice had a lot of Southern in it, and I realized that I remembered it from the couple of times I had run into her and Gene together.

I remembered how she looked then, too, and she looked practically the same now, except that, instead of wearing ultimately sexy clothes that showed off right up to the legal limit of her championship breasts, she was wearing ultimately sexy, but daytime, clothes that didn't leave much doubt about the championship shapes of her breasts, but covered them all the way up to her neck.

"I just wanted to talk to you for a few minutes," I said.

"What I said before sounded okay when I thought about it, but it didn't come out very well."

Pursing her lips a little, frowning slightly, she looked me over. Maybe she was starting to remember me, too, even though I thought it was pretty unlikely. "I'm Sallie Lacie," she said after a long moment, giving me her hand in a very businesslike manner, considering that we were surrounded by most of the women's underwear in Texas. She retrieved it and leaned against the counter, waiting pointedly.

I had a name ready—Frank Dunne. But I was awfully new at playing detective, and it had been all I could do to mumble out that ridiculous crap I started with. I gave up again and said, "I'm Mel Morris."

She was on the edge of figuring it all out, and I tried to forestall it. "Nice place you have here," I said, turning to look around admiringly.

Looking around a bit suspiciously, too.

This whole place was arousing my curiosity more all the time. The name, "Lacie's Things," had prepared me for the fact that it would probably be some kind of boutique, probably specializing in ladies' underwear. And the address on Post Oak, not exactly in the shadow of the Galleria but close enough, had indicated it was probably upscale stuff. But I was surprised when I drove up to it and found that it wasn't nestled sweetly next door to an Isabell Gerhart or a Palais Royal. Instead, there was a tobacconist on one side and a sporting guns shop on the other.

Looking around the inside of the shop was what was really confusing, though. I realized that the women who probably spent the biggest bucks on lingerie were the ones who have tended to linger over the dessert tables and the birthdays a little long, but even so, I expected the display mannequins, as in every other women's store I'd ever been around, to be modeled after anorexic seventeen-year-olds. Not so, in Lacie's Things. There were a few of those, of course, but most of the mannequins tended to be just a tad bulky. Tad. We're talking pink silk panties with roses embroidered on the crotch, and forty-four-inch waists.

Evidently Sallie had thought it over and decided she couldn't figure out why I seemed familiar, and it wasn't worth the effort. When I looked back at her, there was an amused look on her face. "Your first time in, I think."

"Right."

Her eyes twinkled conspiratorially. "You're looking for a little gift for your wife, or your mother, or your sweetheart, I suppose. And you're just a little embarrassed."

"Well," I said. Then I figured out something else that seemed a little strange—there were five or six customers in the place at the moment; all of them were men.

"Don't be embarrassed," Sallie was saying. "Just make yourself at home and look around all you want. Perhaps, in a while, if you'd be more comfortable, you could take some items into one of our coffee rooms and make your choice in private."

"In private?" I said. "Why in private?"

She pursed her lips and looked at me carefully. "Hmmm. Maybe we should have stuck to talking about that book you said you're writing."

"Maybe," I said.

She was really looking at me now. "Have you always had that mustache? And what did you say your name is? Mel? Mel—what did you say?"

A man about ten feet away was looking at a peignoir that managed to be both silver and nearly transparent. He was fifty-five or so, and wore a suit that would run about eight hundred dollars, and a Rolex that cost ten times that. He was big and strong and bulky and looked as if he probably owned or ran a company that manufactured big, strong, bulky objects. His eyes were half-closed as he tested the feel of the silvery fabric against the back of his hand. The peignoir hung

on a mannequin that was technically female in shape, but
would bulk right up there with Arnold Schwarzenegger.

"Morris," I told Sallie quickly. "No. I didn't have the
mustache then." I took a breath and said it: "I'm Gene Morris's
brother."

She took a half step back and looked me over. "Isn't that
interesting."

"Sorry for acting like such a fool. I just didn't know how
to start."

"Gene's brother." She shook her head as if she weren't
certain whether she should be angry or sad.

"Could we talk, Miss Lacie?"

"Why?"

"About Gene."

"Really why now? He's been dead for—what?—just
about three years, isn't it?"

"Just about."

She was a strikingly attractive woman. Even with those
breasts covered. But at the moment, she had a very ugly
expression on her face. "I'm afraid I didn't send flowers," she
said.

"I did. But it was because I had to."

The ugly went away and she looked sad. "I seem to
remember that you didn't get along with him."

"That's kind of an interesting way of putting it."

She smiled along with the sadness. "I wondered about
that later. We met a couple of times, you know. I remember
wondering how you could be so much trouble to your
brother. When he seemed so concerned about you. Later, of
course, I wondered how much of what he told me about you
was really true."

"Probably not much, as a matter of fact."

She made that soft little trilling laugh. "Talk? Sure. I
haven't had a good heart-to-heart talk about a real son-
of-a-bitch in a long time."

I think she expected some shock, or at least a try at it. When she didn't get it, she laughed and hooked her arm in mine and headed us toward a gold-lamé-padded door that said "PRIVATE" on it in red sequins. "Mel," she said. "As in Gibson. How nice. Come on, Mel. I'm Sallie. This might be fun."

The other side of the door was plain brown wood, and the office, unlike the shop, was very plain and neat and utilitarian. Across the front wall of it was a long window that was mirror on the shop side. Sallie moved behind the desk toward the Mr. Coffee that sat on the credenza and motioned me into the visitor's chair.

While she poured coffee, she chattered. "You had me fooled. I thought it was first-time jitters. You know, you come in and nervous around and finally buy a nightgown for your wife's birthday, and she just happens to measure 48-30-38, even though you're a nice-looking fellow yourself. Or you pick out a darling little sheer teddie, size 18, and stutter that it's for your mother. And then there're the ones who insist that their dermatologists told them the only thing that'll take care of that heat rash is panty hose."

She turned around with filled coffee mugs and set them on the desk and sat down. "Gene's brother. My God."

"I said that myself a time or two."

She played microscope. "You don't look anything like him, you know. You're much fairer—almost blond. And you look like you take lots better care of yourself. He'd have probably had a gut and real love handles by now."

She looked suddenly at the ceiling. "But my God! Those eyes of his!" She looked back at me. Looked contrite, as if she were about to hurt my feelings although she didn't really want to. "You've got very nice eyes. Really nice and sexy. But even so you missed out on the eyes somewhere. I tell you, Gene could have been a rhinoceros, and with those eyes, I'd still have followed him anywhere."

What do you say to something like that? I'd never figured it out. Gene's eyes, so pale that you looked at him and thought you were seeing smoke inside his head, never did anything to me but make me want to run out into the woods and beg Jason to protect me. I'd been hearing this kind of crap from people all my life, though.

"But under those eyes," Sallie was saying, "all there was was the original snake-oil peddler."

I had to laugh at that.

She laughed, too.

I liked her. She was definitely Southern. Not Melanie, thank God. But maybe a combination of Scarlett and Belle Watling.

I wondered, besides his eyes, what the hell she could have seen in Gene. And remembered that I wondered about that the first time I met her.

It was in Gilley's. On a Saturday night, I think. And I was skirting along the edge of the dance floor, trying to find my way back to Jane without getting into a fistfight with anybody—the place never did get completely over its *Urban Cowboy* image. And I noticed a spectacular girl sitting at a table and realized that most of the fistfights occurred over lots less than her. But I had to look again. Smiling eyes. Lots of loose blond hair. And those tits! They weren't huge, but they were outstanding. The real thing about them was that you could tell that she was proud of them and obviously liked and respected them.

Suddenly I realized that the man with her was Gene, and he grabbed me with that phony, backslapping affection he showed sometimes when there were people around and it suited his purpose, and introduced me to her as his kid brother. I liked her, even though it knocked me out that she was with him.

And if you're expecting me to say I was outraged to find my brother stepping out on his wife, forget it. First, it wasn't anything new. Second, Grace and I weren't exactly pals, but I still liked her enough to wish her luck, and if she wouldn't leave Gene, it'd serve the same purpose if he'd leave her.

Laughing along with Sallie over her "snake-oil peddler" remark, and watching her laugh while she was sitting down, I couldn't help noticing that her breasts weren't quite laughing along with her.

Something was making me very uneasy, and I knew I had to move things along. "Other than his eyes," I said. "You knew he was married, didn't you?"

She looked at me as if my nose had just fallen off. "Are you kidding? Of course, I knew it." She rolled her eyes. "I even knew when he was going to file for divorce."

"Oh, yeah?"

"Oh, yeah." She was suddenly looking off into some distant, misty memory. "I think one reason I remember you and remember meeting you—it was in Gilley's, wasn't it?—was because that was the night Gene said he was going to divorce his wife and we were going to get married." Her eyes were very sparkly and close to tearing now, and her voice was getting husky, but she fought it off. "Do you remember that night? Meeting me?"

"Yes."

"Did he tell you we were going to get married?"

"We didn't confide in each other very much."

She was hurt, but fought that off, too. "No, I guess he wouldn't have told you that, would he?" Eagerly—"But you do remember meeting me, don't you?"

I smiled because you remember happy, striking people, no matter whom they're with, even if you don't remember where or when you saw them. "Sure I do. You had on this red dress. Kind of gingham, and kind of cowboy, but silky, too." Unconsciously, I brought my hands up to my chest in demonstration. "Cut way down, but nice."

Her face went very still. For some reason she needed a

break from all this. She glanced through the one-way glass. Glanced at me. Then at the cigarette pack in my shirt pocket. Suddenly she looked apologetic, but grateful also, because she had found a diversion. "I didn't say you could smoke. Go ahead. I keep forgetting how guilty we've all gotten about smoking." She reached into one of the desk drawers and came out with a cigarette and lighter.

I hadn't thought about it before, but I was glad to smoke now. For some reason I needed to.

She blew smoke at the ceiling. "He was going to divorce his wife and marry me. But first, we were going to set up our company."

"Company?" I said.

She smiled. "I thought that'd get your attention. I followed that trial. I saw what he did to that poor fool that killed him. Set up that company with him and robbed him blind. Well, that was the company that Gene and I were going to set up."

"I don't know how it happened," I said. "But you had a lot of luck. And you must have had some money, if he was trying to set up a company with you."

"Oh, lots of luck," she said. "Yes. I had some money." She tapped her cigarette into the ashtray and turned businesslike. "All right. We've had lots of nice heart-to-heart. Isn't it time you told me what this is all about?"

"Are you feeling strong, Sallie?"

She smiled. "Tall buildings. The taller the better."

"Okay. When Gene was killed, you were a suspect."

Less smile, but no cowering. "Yes, I was, wasn't I? But not for long. I was having some medical problems at the time. I was just learning how to brush my hair again. There wasn't much doubt that I couldn't be out gunning people down, and the police gave up on me right away."

I waited, wondering if she would explain.

She didn't. She waited, too.

I gave up first. "The man who was convicted of the killing and went to prison—Roy Purdy. He's about to be released."

"Released?"

"Released."

"Well, good for him. Why, though? Isn't it kind of early? Don't tell me the prisons are that overcrowded."

"Because they've finally figured out that he couldn't have done it."

She made a surprised face. "That's interesting. That's good luck for him. But I was hoping he'd get what he deserved—a pardon and a medal."

"Not quite. It's just that he didn't do it."

"Well, who did, then?"

I raised my hands. "Who knows? The cops aren't very interested, and I was kind of curious."

"Why?"

"I didn't have anything else to do."

She laughed that nice, soft Southern trill.

I said, "Why is it that, out of all his girlfriends and his prospective victims, you were the one who got away?"

She flicked the question aside with her cigarette and then determinedly stubbed it out. "If Roy Purdy didn't kill him, then who did?"

"I don't know. There's a pretty good list of possibles, but it looks like you're off it now."

"Did you do it? From everything I remember, you would have had reason to."

I shook my head. "I was off the list right away. I was home on the telephone when he was shot."

"Is this what this is all about? You're going to run around playing detective and then run to the cops? I don't think I'm very interested in chatting along with you if something I said—and I don't know what it'd be—was going to help pin Gene's murder on anybody."

"It's just curiosity. That's all. I don't think there's anything you could tell me that would pin anything on anybody. But you're fun to talk to. And you're clearing up some personal curiosity."

Promptingly—"Curiosity."

"About how you're the one that got away. Evidently you got away, and he went to the next one on the list—Roy Purdy."

"Something like that. Close, but not the way you think."

"Then how was it?"

She looked off into somewhere else again. I think she remembered Gene's eyes for a moment—her version of them. Then she went on to remembering other things. "First," she said, "I didn't get away—not exactly."

"Okay."

"Gene was going to marry me. He was probably lying, but I still like to think that he really meant it. Anyway, he had to do some things to keep his wife from breaking him in the divorce—so he said. That was the company we were going to set up. I told you I had some money. I grew up the daughter of a machinist in Natchitoches, Louisiana. He had some ideas for oil tools, and they worked out very nicely and we got kind of rich. I married somebody that was kind of rich. About six years ago my daddy retired and sold out before all the oil tool companies busted. About four years ago my husband and I were divorced and then my daddy died, and I had some money—about three million dollars. I came to the Big City."

"And met Gene, and he loved you for yourself, of course."

Anger flashed in her eyes. "Don't be sarcastic about him. Not with me. I almost wish I'd killed him myself, sometimes. But I don't want to hear him put down."

"Go on," I said.

"The way we were going to keep Grace from bleeding him was we were going to set up this property development company. We were both going to put up about three million. That was about all Gene said he could beg or scrape or steal."

"He left an estate of almost thirty million dollars," I said.

"Don't interrupt," Sallie snapped. "I know that now. But then I thought he was scraping up everything he had."

She made her lighter flare and started a new cigarette. "There was also a dummy corporation we were going to set up. We'd start our business, work it for a while, and then, just before he left Grace, this dummy corporation would raid the first one and break it. When it came time for the divorce settlement, all there'd be for Grace would be half the bankruptcy papers. A while after that we'd get married, go to work for this dummy corporation, and just gradually take it over— or we'd make it look like that was what we were doing, even if it was already ours."

"Neat," I said. "But didn't you see all the stuff about Sam and Bella Hauser's scam that was all over the papers and TV then? Gene squeaked out of getting involved in their legal problems, but anybody could tell he was dirty as hell in the deal. It looks like you'd have gotten suspicious of him."

"Not my Gene," Sallie said vehemently. "They were just trying to find a scapegoat." She relented. "At least, that's how I saw it at the time."

"What about Grace, then? Didn't you feel kind of bad about what you were doing to her?"

"Not for the ittiest-bittiest heartbeat. She deserved everything she got, as far as I was concerned."

"Why was that?"

Sallie smiled across her desk at me, giving me warning that I should probably start hanging on to my chair. Mentally, I did. Then she said, "This gets us to your story. Among other things, besides being the kind of heartless, sexless woman you read about every day in Ann Landers, Gene told me she was having an affair with his little brother."

That made me glad I was sitting down.

"Gene told me lots of stories about you, you know. Things you did to make him look bad to your folks while you were growing up. And the fact that, every woman he'd ever been interested in, you'd gone after and either took away or turned against him. Except Grace—the one he wished you would take away.

"That was one of the nicest, saddest nights I'll ever have, you know. That night after we ran into you in Gilley's. Gene broke down and cried in my arms because he was afraid you'd try to take me away from him."

I didn't say anything. What could you ever say when you heard about some new way Gene had gotten you in the ass, and you didn't even know about it at the time?

"I swore I wouldn't ever let that happen," Sallie said. "He told me about the first girl he ever really loved. Really loved. And you took her away from him and, to make it hurt him all the worse, you even married her."

It took a moment for that to hit. When it did, I said, "I wish I had killed him."

"Get in line."

"Fine," I said. "Let's get off this stuff. How come you broke off with him and didn't go ahead with this company?"

"This new company? And this dummy corporation that one day I was going to wake up and figure out Gene had entire control of, and he was still married to Grace?"

"Yeah. That one. The same one that he rammed down Roy Purdy's throat."

"I didn't break off with him," she said.

"Gene never stopped any other time while somebody still had a dime left."

She smiled. Very bitterly she smiled. "It was that luck that you were talking about a while ago."

"Gene dropped a copy of the paperwork, I suppose, and you looked it over and saw that you were getting the shaft."

"No. If that had happened, he'd have talked me out of worrying about it. I'd have begged him to talk me out of worrying about it." Her face became very cold now. "What happened was that I found a lump in my breast."

There was a lot of silence.

On the other side of the one-way glass, a beefy man with red embarrassment flush splotching his neck like hives was trying to act as if he was invisible while he bought a brassiere that looked as if it were made of spun candy and would fit the average duplex. I recognized him as a wheel with one of the Houston sports teams.

His timing here, as during the season, was about as bad as it could be.

Maybe Sallie didn't see him. She wasn't exactly looking at anything.

She said, "The doctor found some more. In both breasts. There was a bad biopsy. Terrible."

I couldn't help myself. I shifted my chair and bumped the corner of the back of it against the one-way glass damned near hard enough to break it.

Sports-Guy jumped and looked around as if somebody had just started interviewing him about his trade philosophy. He dropped the brassiere. And hiked out of the shop, going almost as fast as the guys he liked to trade away.

Sallie shook her head at me. "You can be a shit, can't you? But thanks. I needed that."

"I did, too."

We smiled at each other for a moment.

Then she said, "I still have that red cowgirl dress some-where. With my other keepsakes. And yes, moving along—that wasn't a very nice time for me after the biopsy and all. I grew up in tit-time, you know. *Playboy*. Jayne Mansfield even died in Louisiana. When I was a little girl and we were poor, I knew all about tits. They were a way for a poor little girl to make it big.

"So I didn't like it very much when I found out what was going to happen. And what did happen, to cut the damned suspense, is Mastectomy. Capital *M* Mastectomy. Plural capital *M*.

"What a woman needs most in a time like that is to be reassured that her man is still going to love her. You can go out and march for ERA and female coal miners, but when it comes time for something like that, you want your man to love you and stand by you."

There was too much silence, and very softly I said, "I don't think Gene was ready to do that, was he?"

Very, very softly—"Not even long enough for our little plan to get working. I finally got up nerve to tell him about it the day before I went into the hospital. And those eyes of his that I always loved just turned into nothing when I told him, and I wanted him to hold me and comfort me, and he looked at me like I had leprosy. Or worse. He couldn't even touch me."

She looked through the one-way glass, shaking her head at herself. "It wasn't luck that saved my money. It was lumps. Just like that."

"So then Gene went after Roy Purdy instead of you."

"Right. For all I know, he used the same paperwork. When he got killed, it was a while after the operation, but I told you it was a capital *M* didn't I, and I was still pretty sick. They did follow-up radiation. And then they had to do some follow-up chemotherapy. That hair that I was trying to learn how to brush—with a whole lot of different muscles than I'd ever had to use before—when I wasn't throwing up—wasn't even attached to my head. I wasn't much of a suspect. Later on I got myself busy and opened this place. It's fun. I'm not hurting anybody. I make it more comfortable than it usually is for men who want to curl up in something nice in the privacy of their own homes. There's nice money in it. And don't get going on any psychology theories about me selling lingerie I can't use very well any more to men who don't want me."

I said, "A lot of them probably do want you, Sallie. You're

a damned nice and damned attractive woman. Don't put yourself down."

"You're sweet," she said. "Just for your information, I figured out a long time ago that practically everything Gene told me about you was a lie."

I put out my cigarette. "I have just one last small question. Are you sure you didn't prune this story just a little bit? I knew Gene better than anybody. He may have reacted badly out of shock when you told him. But I can't believe that about ten minutes later, he didn't start thinking about that three million bucks of yours and go kind of crazy that it was getting away from him."

"I was hoping you'd skip past that," Sallie said. "But you're right. He came back. That same night. With those eyes of his just brimming with tears, telling me how he'd never forgive himself for acting like that. He told me how much I needed him. And he'd take care of me. All I had to do was go ahead and sign the papers, and he'd take care of me."

She looked at her hands. "That was when I damned near did kill him. I emptied the whole damned gun at him. But I missed. Sometimes I'm sorry. Sometimes I'm not."

CHAPTER 4

I wasn't overly impressed with the detective profession when I left Sallie. But I was already close to River Oaks and figured one more try wouldn't hurt.

The Crenshaw place would have rated only about a three on a River Oaks scale of one to ten. No wall. No gate. And it sat in what practically qualifies as slum housing, River Oaks style, because there were four other houses on the block.

It was no dump, though. Wide, sloping lawn of closely clipped, faintly bluish St. Augustine grass. Ancient oak trees with thick, far-flung limbs that begged for rope swings, except that the deed restrictions would have strangled you for hanging one. A pillared verandah, instead of a front porch, and lots of white-painted brick.

I expected a maid, but it was Elaine Purdy Crenshaw herself who opened the little slide set into the front door and peered at me through tiny brass bars. "Do I know you?" She frowned at me. "I do know you, don't I?"

"Mel Morris, Elaine."

She thought about popping the slide shut and ending my

visit before it began, but the sudden appearance of a ghost out of your past can make you curious. "Good Lord. Mel. What in the world are you doing here?"

"Could we talk for a few minutes?" I asked.

Her fascination with old times was quickly fading. "I can't imagine what there'd be for us to talk about."

"Roy and Gene," I said.

I figured that would end things, for sure. She would say something completely unrevealing about her ex-husband being innocent, after all, and I could drive back home and sit and stare at that accusing "CHAPTER TWENTY-THREE" until I thought of what came next. Or it stopped raining, whichever came first.

She surprised me. "All right. Come in," she said, and opened the door.

She made some forgettable remark about the rain and stood watching approvingly while I rubbed my feet around on the mat in the entryway.

I had done a little arithmetic driving over from Post Oak. I was thirty-one. Gene would be thirty-six now. Roy Purdy was a year or two older than Gene. And Roy's wife—then-wife—Elaine, was about three years younger than Roy. That would make her thirty-four now or thirty-five, but she looked older than that. Obviously, she hadn't been expecting company. Her hair was neat, but she hadn't made up her face at all, and she was wearing a dress that looked as if it was probably expensive, but still was just a shapeless, ordinary housedress.

When my feet were passably dry, she led me into the living room, where she excused herself for a moment to go to a doorway on the other side. "Maria," she said, into another room, "we're going to the sunroom." She pointed off to her left and enunciated aggressively. "Sun-room."

That was good news to me. This place was big and

obviously expensive, but it was gloomy as hell. You'd think that somebody who owned a chain of hardware stores could install a window or two and bring a couple of light bulbs home with him once in a while.

Elaine was still talking into the other room. She pantomimed holding a tray. "Would you bring some coffee?" She looked questioningly around at me, and I nodded. "Cof-fee," she said into the room, and held up two fingers.

"Thank goodness you wanted coffee," she said when she came back to me. "I haven't taught her 'tea' yet."

We went down a hallway that must have been practicing for Halloween and finally got to the sunroom.

At the doorway Elaine paused. "Just make yourself comfortable." She fluttered her hands over her face. "I must look awful. Just give me a minute." Then she waved me on and hurried off.

The sunroom wasn't much relief from the gloom. The ceiling and two walls were glass, but they were streaked gray with rain, and the place was crammed high and low with ferns and orchids.

Many orchids are extraordinarily beautiful when they're in bloom—which these weren't—but most of the foliage looks like something you'd find in a leper colony. And when I get in a place where there's more ferns than air, I always wonder what's about to crawl down my neck.

Almost hidden among the foliage, I found a grouping of rattan furniture that had cushions covered with fabric in—of course—a gigantic fern-leaf print, and sat down to wait.

I was a little puzzled about something—why hadn't Elaine mentioned Roy's release? Wouldn't that have been a lot more interesting to comment on than the rain?

Mentally shrugging, I looked around for an ashtray. I couldn't find one, but with a little surprise, I saw what could only be one of Jane's sculptures half-hidden behind banks of ferns over toward a corner. It wasn't stainless steel, but one of her more recent, "more extemporaneous works," as the critics put it, made of rough, tortured steel rods and chunks, cut and twisted and welded into shape. It looked as if it might be a nice piece, but I decided I wouldn't mention it because I wasn't exactly ready to chat about Jane too much at the moment.

After about ten minutes Elaine came back all gussied up—an ancient and unoriginal phrase, but entirely appropriate. She had changed into a jumpsuit made of some kind of semi-shiny denimlike fabric. The zipper was pulled very low to show off not only her bosom, but also a massive free-form pendant of gold on silver with two arrowlike protrusions which, by design or coincidence, pointed precisely at her nipples which showed clearly and proudly through the thin, stretchy, denimlike fabric. She had done makeup and looked younger now. And she was wearing wedgies. Real wedgies, covered with brightly colored little straw braids. Joan Crawford would have killed for them.

"I feel so much better," she said, settling into the ferny cushions of the armchair across from me, crossing her knees with a movement that was so determinedly demure that it looked obscene. She smiled brightly at me. "You're still writing those books, aren't you? Sometimes I see something about you in the newspaper."

I nodded, and we sat and stared uncomfortably around for a few moments. I think I should probably have said something complimentary about the room or the plants but, feeling as if my hair was going to turn green and sporey and droop down over my forehead at any second, I didn't.

I did the Glance, and saw no ashtrays.

"Oh. Smoking," Elaine said, smiling happily for the first time. "It's all right. I'll have one with you." She pulled herself sideways in the ferny cushions and reached—very bravely, I thought—into the green jungle on a plant table and pulled out a clay pot saucer with black smudges in the bottom. The diamond in her engagement ring was huge. Even in the dim gray daylight it cast brilliance as she set the saucer on the coffee table. On that wrist she was wearing a thick silver-and-gold bracelet which was probably a mate of the pendant. There were diamonds at her ears now, too.

I got out a cigarette and my lighter and waited to give her a light. She looked nervous, but didn't produce cigarettes. Finally she said, "I'll just wait until we have our coffee."

I translated that to mean that the maid, Maria, might not know "tea" yet, but was somehow able to communicate, "The Senora's been smoking cigarettes again," to Mr. Crenshaw.

I lighted my cigarette. We stared around for a few more moments. And I picked up some interesting things about Roy Purdy's ex-wife.

I hadn't met her in some chance running-into Gene and her, but in what passed for a family get-together. There hadn't been too many of those, of course, since I'd had about enough of my big brother during the years of growing up when I didn't have any choice. Once in a while, though, Jane and Gene's wife, Grace, would get together and make yet another big push to "heal the wounds" and make us all over into one big happy family. Or so they justified it.

Privately, I felt that their motives were somewhat different, particularly Jane's. Her real reason for pushing me together with Gene, I was certain, fell into about three categories. One was when she felt I was getting too soft on the world in general and she knew an evening around Gene would certainly shake me up. Another was that she did, actually, hope that we could somehow make that magic, highly overrated American thing, "The Family," come into being, after all, even though she should sure as hell have known better. The third category was when she was pissed-off at me about something and didn't want to handle getting even with me herself.

There were some required times, also. My grandmother was still living then—she died about a year ago—and she insisted on our periodically getting together and playing family—Christmas, Thanksgiving, her birthday, and Mom's and Dad's wedding anniversary, an occasion she observed even though they had been dead since I was seventeen. These stiff and horrible social events, the ones which could not better be conducted on neutral ground at some restaurant, were rotated between Gene's house and Jane's and mine because Grandma lived in a rest home.

At the events which were not strictly for Grandma's benefit, there were almost always other people around. With enough other people, Jane and Grace could keep Gene and me from confronting each other for, sometimes, the whole evening, while maintaining the fiction that we were "healing old wounds."

These get-togethers with Gene were always times of tension, of course. Not just between him and me, but among the other people as well. Surely they didn't know it in advance, but there must have been something in the air that told them that someone was being considered as his next victim.

At one of these dinner "parties," Jane and I met Elaine and Roy Purdy, who were, we gathered, relatively new acquaintances. I remember the meeting because we argued about Roy Purdy's nearly bizarre looks. I opted for werewolf; Jane voted for the young Rory Calhoun.

At that first party Elaine was an attractive but restless-seeming woman, smoking one cigarette after another, the expression on her face saying that each one tasted worse than the last, and no improvement was expected. She and Roy seemed cordial enough with each other in my opinion, but Jane defined their situation more specifically—"probably just a tad too settled for their own good, which I'll translate to 'she probably gets him into the sack with her about once a month.'" I remember feeling sorry for Elaine when Jane said that because she was obviously a very sexual woman.

A few months later we saw them again. This time, when we discussed Roy, Jane voted werewolf and I talked up young Rory. Elaine seemed different at this party, and soon I became more interested in wondering about that than worrying how Roy spent his time when the moon was full.

The big thing about Elaine on this second occasion was that she didn't look bored any more; she looked, rather, as if there were going to be a door prize and she had just gotten through writing her name on all the tickets. She was smoking differently, also, savoring the smoke. She was wearing a very simple-appearing off-the-shoulder, barely on-the-breasts dress made of some kind of soft, clinging peach-colored material which was perfect with her strawberry-blond hair and pale, pale orange complexion. Probably a whole army of engineers had worked months to perfect the basic design of dresses like this, but it appeared so artlessly simple that it gave the impression that it had been draped around her just moments ago. She wore it as if, at any moment, there would be a striking of unseen harp strings and she would shrug a shoulder and it would fall away and Titian would appear with his paints and brushes.

My first thought was that Roy had been taking hormone shots or something. But then he arrived to bring Elaine a fresh drink.

She took the glass and chilled the fingertips of one hand against it and then drew them sensuously up the inside of her other arm. During this, she glanced at her husband for about a tenth of a second and said something which, judging from her disinterested expression, was probably, "You can bring me another one in fifteen minutes, waiter."

So much for the young Rory Calhoun or the hormone shots, or both.

I was really curious now and stood where I was, watching her, even though I was trapped by a sweet lady whose perfume smelled like apricots rotting, while she chatted to me about how much she loved "Sci-Fi," and that she had wonderful ideas and someday was going to take a few days off and sit down and write a book herself.

Roy moved on, leaving Elaine alone inside her bubble of satisfied sensuality.

The apricot lady was getting to be a bit much. At any second she was going to demand that I give her Isaac Asimov's unlisted telephone number.

I began to extricate myself, but then Elaine took care of my curiosity. You could almost feel the air around her crackle with electricity.

I followed her gaze and stared for a moment.

Then I gave the apricot lady a couple of quick, helpful hints and introduced her to a man who wrote book reviews for the *Houston Post* and hated science fiction passionately and mine rabidly, and went to find Jane.

I reassured myself that she smelled nothing like apricots, rotting or otherwise, and said, "She's screwing Gene."

"Are you serious?"

"As Ponca City, Oklahoma."

She giggled tipsily. "Maybe he'll mess up. Maybe he'll go sneaking around their house to meet her some night, and it'll be a full moon."

We both thought that was very funny at the moment; we both remembered the remark later, after Roy Purdy was arrested and charged with killing Gene.

Shortly, Jane went for more booze, intending to get a closer look at Elaine, and at Grace, to see if she suspected.

I waited for her, wondering, not so much about Grace, because she had to be used to things like this by now, but about the woman who had been with Gene at Gilley's. Elaine was definitely attractive, but I couldn't imagine her competing with the wholly striking girl in the low-cut cowgirl dress.

Jane returned without the booze, her eyebrows about to fly off her face. "You're right about Elaine," she said. "And Grace knows. But you know what else? Roy Purdy's just inherited this huge pile of IBM stock, and Gene's after him."

"Let's get the hell out of here," I said.

She said, "It'll be me, right behind you, stepping on your heels and watching your buns."

We saw them one last time before the trial, at a party we wouldn't have attended had we known its real purpose was to announce the formation of Morris, Purdy Properties, Ltd.— we didn't like to see lambs slaughtered. We both thought Roy looked like a puppy dog now. A full moon wouldn't have done anything to him but make him shake his ass and whimper for another Puppy Treat.

Elaine was different also. "Gene's not screwing her any more," I told Jane.

"She wishes to hell he was," she told me.

Gene climbed onto a chair about then and announced that he was making an announcement, and Jane and I got the hell out of there before he could. We read about it in the Sunday Business Section the next morning.

"That must be why he dumped Elaine," I said. "Screwing her and Roy at the same time would mean a lot of complications, even for Gene."

Jane laughed and poked her finger at the newspaper. "Why Business? It ought to be in the Obituaries." We were going to remember that remark later, also.

You're thinking, of course, that we should have warned Roy Purdy. Well, we knew better than that. The way Gene worked over his patsies, any warning from anybody would only have made them crawl faster up his ass, dragging their money with them. That's how good he was. If you want to experience what I'm talking about, the next time you see a meteor, try yelling yourself hoarse warning it to get out of the earth's gravitational pull before it gets sucked-in too far. You'll have exactly as much luck.

The next time we saw them was at the trial. They weren't pretty. Elaine was playing the Supportive Wife of the Falsely Accused Man, but wasn't doing it with any effort or conviction at all. "Damned fool," Jane said. "The women Gene went after never got over him."

"Except for you," I said.

"Except for me," she said.

A rather odd thing was that Jane's and my divorce came through in the same week that Elaine's divorce from Roy was final.

Sitting in that awful sunroom with Elaine Purdy Crenshaw, waiting for coffee, wondering exactly what I was doing there, I saw that she now more closely resembled the Elaine of that third meeting, after Gene had dumped her in favor of Roy's money.

She was not a happy woman. And it was pretty obvious why. Whatever she was getting from Mr. Crenshaw, the hardware magnate, besides a big, gloomy house and a maid she didn't trust and couldn't communicate with, big diamonds and Paloma Picasso jewelry by the pound, and most of the ferns in the Western Hemisphere, she wasn't getting any sex.

She was far too aware of me. Physically. While looking pleasant and rattling on with the complex name of this ruined-looking orchid plant or that one, she was stealing glances at my hands and arms, at my throat.

That can't help but get to you just a little. I stubbed out my cigarette in the plant saucer and felt her look running flowing hot over my belly and down into my lap and, for a moment, I saw us crawling back in among the ferns and pulling at each other's clothing and . . .

One quick thought of Gene took care of that.

One quick reminder that she'd screwed Gene turned her into Typhoid Mary, as far as I was concerned.

"You know, I never thought you resembled your brother at all," she said, almost purring. "You still don't."

Out of gratitude, I upgraded her to Mother Teresa, but she was still forever out-of-bounds.

I said, "We used to joke that one of us was adopted."

She laughed nervously and stole a glance at my crotch.

I crossed my legs and thought about that adoption "joke."

When I was in the first grade, Gene told me that I was adopted, but that if Mom and Dad ever found out I knew about it, they'd send me back. It damned near killed me, but I never let on about it to them. Once in a while Gene would threaten me with telling them that I knew, or he'd seem about to let it slip in front of them that he'd told me, and I'd do whatever he wanted me to do to keep him quiet—filch money for him out of Grandma's purse, provide alibis for him, stand looking dumb and innocent in a store while he stuffed 45 RPM records or bags of candy in my clothing because I was too little and innocent-looking for the clerks to suspect me of shoplifting.

Finally, though, it occurred to me that I liked it a hell of a lot if I really was adopted because that meant I wasn't related to him. When he figured that out, he "confessed" that he'd lied; I wasn't adopted; I was his real little brother. I'm still not certain which "revelation" distressed me more.

Maria finally brought the coffee.

Correction. That wasn't precisely how it worked. I glanced toward the doorway and saw her standing there holding the tray and watching us intently, fern fronds shivering around her. When she realized I had seen her, she put a vacuous smile on her face and bustled in.

She was young and very pretty. And very, very Mexican.

Indian, probably. Very dark, smooth skin. Long, black, wild hair. Thick nose. Face like a Toltec face. Deep, dark, secret eyes. She was dressed in a white maid's uniform that she hated.

She set the tray on the glass top of the rattan table. As she did so, she tilted just a little to her right so that she could definitely check out the clay pot ashtray and make certain that there was just one cigarette there.

"It's mine," I said.

She flinched. Then she turned that vacuous smile on me. But not before I had verified a suspicion—Elaine might not have taught her "tea" as yet, but she definitely had understood what I said.

"Thank you, Maria," Elaine said. "That will be all."

Maria stared stupidly at her, didn't move.

"Go," Elaine said, semidesperately. "That's all." She fluttered her fingers. "Adios."

Maria couldn't fight "Adios." "Ahhh!" she said, smiling, and then backed away.

"I feel so sorry for her," Elaine said. "She has nowhere else to go. We try to help them out, you know. Until they can get settled." She lifted the pot to pour. "I hope you take it black. She doesn't seem to have learned 'cream and sugar' yet."

"*Leche y sucre,* I think."

"Oh?"

"Black's fine."

She handed me the cup and saucer and poured her own.

I set them on the table near me and got out another cigarette.

Elaine stared at the pack. "May I . . ."

I raised my hand and stopped her. "That orchid?" I said, motioning for silence, setting lighter and cigarette on the table. "Oh. Over there."

I stood up and walked to the doorway and then said, "This one? Yes. It's very nice, isn't it?"

The suddenly close sound of my voice startled Maria, and she backed quickly away from the doorway out of sight.

Pretending not to notice her, I called out to Elaine, "But the door's blocking the light. Had you noticed that?"

I closed it.

When I got back to the little rattan conversation area, the zipper on Elaine's jump suit had dropped about four inches, and she was smoking my cigarette. "I hope you don't mind. I must have left mine inside. What in the world were you doing?"

"Maria can get her English lessons some other way."

Elaine looked perplexed.

I let it go. If she hadn't figured out by now that Maria was spying on her and probably knew more English than she did, it was her problem. Maybe it was no big deal. Maybe all it was was that Surgeon General Koop had sent her over to check on whether Elaine was keeping off the butts. But I doubted that.

Inhaling orgasmically, showing off her newly revealed cleavage, Elaine said, "Roy and your brother. I was stunned when you said you were here to talk about Roy and your brother."

I was suddenly kind of stunned myself.

It was obvious that the reason she hadn't mentioned Roy's being cleared and getting out of prison was that she didn't know about it.

Damn! I hadn't figured on that at all.

"It was terrible," she was saying. "I felt so guilty divorcing Roy. But there wasn't anything else I could do."

She blew out smoke and set the cigarette into the pot saucer, as if by separating herself from such a vice, however momentarily, she could achieve a moment of purity in which to emphasize a truth—or untruth. "I was desperate. All the money was gone. Everything. Even our house—it went to the lawyers. And Roy had squandered everything he inherited from his father in his effort to undermine and break your poor brother."

"What?" I said.

"Why does coming into money make people so reckless and greedy? He should have worked with your brother, not tried to ruin him."

I stared into the ferns, wondering if she and I had attended the same trial. Half of it had been taken up by the prosecution's establishing how Gene had skillfully, underhand-edly, and completely—if technically legally—ruined Roy so as to make it crystal-clear to the jury that there was a suitable motive.

Then I reminded myself that Gene was involved. His victims always believed what he wanted them to believe for at least as long as it took him to take them. Good, old, spurned Elaine must have just been more gullible than most. Probably, when she was sitting there in the courtroom, trying to look like the faithful, supportive wife, instead of listening to word about Gene's swindles she had been telling herself again and again that he was the only man who had ever caused her to orgasm.

When I came out of my preoccupation, she was stubbing out her cigarette and smiling sweetly and entreatingly and hungrily, saying, "Would you mind giving me another one? It's so much bother going in to look for mine."

I did.

She said, "I had to think of little Gerald, you know. His future. With his father in prison, there was no future for him at all. Unless I did something with myself."

"I understand," I said. I did. In the business world it's called cutting your losses and moving on. But most businesses probably do it with a bit more compassion than Elaine was showing me.

She leaned forward, giving me a good and quite deliber-ate view of her quite competently maintained breasts.

I thought of Sallie Lacie. Sent her an impossible wish.

Elaine said, "After he lost all our money so stupidly, I would have left him, anyway, you know. Even if he hadn't gone to prison."

I'm a science fiction writer, not a detective. I wondered if I would attach so much importance to her phraseology if I really knew what I was doing. As it was, I couldn't help marking down in my head that she had said, "Even if he hadn't gone to prison," instead of "Even if he hadn't killed your brother." Wouldn't a wife, pissed-off because her husband had not only lost their money and killed the one lover she couldn't live without but, on top of that, had gotten caught for it, say the worst possible thing about him?

Some homecoming Roy Purdy was going to have.

Elaine said, "But I'm still doing all the talking. It's your turn," and started to pour more coffee into my cup.

I'm no hero. I shook my head to cut down on the amount of hot liquid near my person, and waited until she had set down the pot and started to take another hungry drag on her cigarette.

Telling myself that I didn't mind being a sex object for a good cause, and that women had been doing things like this to put men off guard for years—hiking up their skirts, or showing off their boobs, as Elaine herself was doing rather well—I did my bit for Equal Opportunity and leaned back and gave her a really good crotch-shot.

When I definitely had her attention, I said, "Elaine, who really killed my brother?"

She choked on smoke, coughed, went red- and teary-eyed, dumped her cigarette into the pot saucer, finally caught her breath, and daubed at her eyes. "Oh, that went down the wrong way," she said. Then she smiled at me but, curiously enough, seemed to have forgotten completely about my crotch.

"What were you saying?" she asked, as if she had just walked into the room.

I can do a little dissimulation myself. I moved my knees apart and gave her another shot.

She forgot she'd forgotten about such things, and I asked her, again, "Who do you think really killed my brother?"

She found her cigarette and started looking only at the ferns. "Is this a joke, or something?"

"If you thought it was a joke, you wouldn't have reacted like that."

"I don't know what you're talking about."

I lighted a cigarette and didn't offer her one. I also didn't say anything.

She finally did. "It must be a joke. Everybody knows who killed him."

I had all day to waste.

"Roy did it," she said. "You know that."

I gave her the eyebrow of disbelief.

"What are you trying to do?"

More waiting.

"I don't think I want to talk to you any more."

"Fine," I said. "Don't." I shook a couple of cigarettes out onto the table for her and stood up and walked away.

"Where are you going?" she said.

I didn't answer.

"Wait. Please."

I opened the door and found Maria hovering near, her broad Toltec face pursed with frustration because she hadn't been able to see or hear us.

I closed the sunroom door behind me.

Then I winked at Maria and pulled the door open again and walked back out among the ferns to hit Elaine with the news about Roy.

But instantly I knew I'd missed my chance. She was

sitting up straight and stiff. The zipper was pulled all the way up to her neck. Her face was cold.

My timing was way off.

All I said was, "Remember. *Leche y sucre.*"

Then I really left.

CHAPTER 5

It was still drizzling rain and the air smelled like fish sweat, but I felt better that I was getting back into my part of town which, if you described a circle with the Galleria, the Astrodome, the gingerbready downtown buildings, and River Oaks on the various edges, would be right in the middle, economically, as well as geographically.

I met Zoe Zimmerman at Houston's Restaurant on Kirby Drive. And that was really the name of it, no matter how generic it sounds. Beams. Brass. Well-padded booths. Waiters and waitresses who were efficient and pleasant, but didn't try to create a permanent relationship with you. It was too noisy, with all the beams and brass, but the food was pretty good. And in a place where trendy restaurants open and close before a lot of the menu items have a chance to get cooked all the way done, the fact that it was well into its second year made it practically an institution.

Zoe and I sat in the back corner in Smoking. She was sixtyish, going on thirty, and worked on one of the newspapers, where she wrote a society gossip column—but don't ever call it that in front of her. When Jane and I were still married, we got mentioned a few times. Usually it was Jane:

> Gorgeous our-town sculptress, Jane Morris, who works in raw steel and does things to it that construction workers don't even dream of, opened her new show Wednesday night at the posh Hayes Gallery.

Zoe had a tendency to lush-out when the opportunity arose, and a couple of years ago, not long after Jane and I were divorced and I had won a national award and for a while was getting invited to society parties, she lushed-out in the game room of a trash-disposal heiress's house and I helped her out and drove her home. It happened again a few weeks later and we became friends, with her inviting me to escort her to enough places often enough that I guess a lot of people must have started thinking I was queer.

I think Zoe thought I had a secret yen for older women. The truth was that I enjoyed her company and also that she bore more than a passing resemblance to my grandmother. But that last I'd never tell her. Today I had called and asked her to lunch because she was the best possibility of getting information in the most pleasant way I could think of.

She raised an eyebrow and tilted her head. "Good grief. Brad Timmons and his secretary. Again. You'd think he'd have more sense."

I looked over the sunken table section at a booth across from ours and saw a rich man. How'd I know he was rich—other than the fact that Zoe knew all about him, automatically qualifying him as one? Because he was fat and ugly and fifty and was with a gorgeous young blonde, who was doing everything for him, up to and including scraping tomato sauce off his tie.

The waiter brought Zoe's Bloody Mary and my beer.

She tested it, found it nice, and looked around some more. Brad Timmons she wouldn't write about. Her column was about exciting things, not downers, except for divorces—consummated ones, not rumored.

It's official splits for stunning sculptress Jane Morris (Saunders again) and hunky Mel Morris, the writer.

At the moment she was glancing around to see if, against the odds, there might be some material for her column kicking around in the restaurant.

I just sat for a moment. I was still coming down from my visit to Elaine Crenshaw and trying to decide if it had been a big triumph or a total waste of cigarettes. Only time would tell. I wished for a moment that I could be a mouse hiding in those ferns when she finally got the news about Roy's being innocent and sprung. Then I thought about what else was probably crawling around in that place and dropped the idea completely.

"Any new books?" Zoe asked.

"Working on one," I said, not stretching the truth too far, I hoped. Then I said, "What do you know about Tom Crenshaw?"

"Tom Crenshaw," she repeated, and looked into her drink.

Somebody said once that she had a card file in her head on everybody in Houston who made over $500,000 a year, had a net worth of $750,000 or more, or had been to bed more than once with any actor or actress who had had at least feature billing in three major motion pictures or more. She seemed to be consulting that card file now.

"Crenshaw Hardware & Appliances," she said. "Third generation money."

"The dirt, Zoe."

She did eyebrow again. Most of her eyebrows were penciled on. But they could have been constructed of sheet metal and they'd still have been the most expressive ones in town. With the possible exception of Jane's of course. "What kind of dirt?"

I chuckled. "What kinds are there?"

"Two—personal and business."

"Try personal."

"Hmmm. I've heard he likes the women, if you know what I mean."

"What do you mean?"

"Girlfriends. But not public, like Brad, over there."

"'Not public.'"

"Mexican women is what I hear."

"Oh, really?"

"Divorced a few years ago. He was married to one of the Sprague girls, and I seem to remember hearing then that he'd been keeping a Mexican girl or two on the side. Mary Ann—the wife—had an awful time with the divorce—there was some kind of prenuptial agreement—and she had to threaten him with dragging the Mexican girls up to get a decent settlement out of him."

"The Spragues have already got more money than God, haven't they? What did she want with a settlement?"

Zoe fixed me with her sharp dark eyes. "Well, pride, of course, my dear."

"Oh."

Oh, something else. Oh, yeah, now I understood the Maria situation. Very interesting people these were, except "interesting" isn't quite the right word.

The thing was that Tom Crenshaw was definitely River Oaks, but not anywhere near to being *River Oaks!* He had a bunch of hardware stores in Texas and Oklahoma and Louisiana, and that can make you River Oaks. But *River Oaks!* takes the real thing—hardware stores everywhere, rivers of oil, mountains of trash-collecting facilities. It's the difference between the rich and the Very Rich.

He evidently had another little problem, too. He was patterned wrong. Everybody has patterns, you know. Somewhere along the way in growing up, everybody forms a concept of what really turns him—or her—on. Some people have very wide patterns—all they're interested in is fairly regular breathing. Some are somewhat less broadly patterned—good old Brad Timmons, for example. Looking at him across the restaurant, I'd guess that his pattern was the four *B*'s—Blonde, Breathing, Boobs, and as few Birthdays as the law allows. Sometimes I thought my pattern was impossibly narrow—Jane.

Tom Crenshaw's pattern was Hispanic women. And for somebody who was only River Oaks and not *River Oaks!* that created a problem or two.

Someone like Ross Penrod, for example, who was probably about as ultimately *River Oaks!* as you could get, could set up housekeeping with a herd of Grant's gazelles and nobody would look cross-eyed—his buddies would tuck choice bales of hay into the trunk of the Rolls for him when they were on the way back from the ranch.

But Tom Crenshaw couldn't have anything to do with a Mexican girl because he was afraid he'd get laughed over onto the other side of Shepherd Drive. Things had progressed enough so that he could have just barely gotten by with marrying a nice Yankee girl, but no Mexicans yet, please. He was even in trouble over having Mexican girlfriends if it got out. Girlfriends, yes—why the hell not? But Mexican? Snicker, snicker. And when you're only pretty rich and not Very Rich, snickers can be very important to you.

Zoe was saying, "Why in the world are you interested in Tom Crenshaw? What kind of science fiction are you writing these days?"

"Maybe I've gone over to fantasy," I said, wondering if

that was getting closer to the truth than I really cared for. "Go on. What about his present wife?"

Zoe confirmed a lot of what I had just been thinking. "Well, he's only hardware, and there may be three generations of it, but they're not really all that important. She's active—more or less—on committees, but never chairs them. That kind of thing."

She looked into her drink again. Then suddenly the eyebrows really went, and she stared across at me. "She's Roy Purdy's ex-wife! That's why you're asking, isn't it?"

"Right."

"Surely not for yourself! She must be ages older than you are. And . . . well . . . a bit heated, if you know what I mean."

I had to chuckle at her flattery as well as the tactful phraseology. "Not for myself. And yes, I know what you mean."

"What in the world are you up to, Mel?"

"Why do you suppose somebody like Elaine and Tom Crenshaw would be married? He likes Mexican women. And Elaine's . . . uh . . . heated, as you say. Seems like kind of a mismatch to me."

"Well, what's wrong with a little mismatch now and then? Let's march around this restaurant and I'll find you enough mismatches to make your head spin."

"This mismatch. Her husband gets convicted of murder and, about ten minutes after her divorce from him is final, she jumps into this mismatch."

"Money."

"Couldn't it be more than that?"

"What?"

"I don't know. You're the expert. Maybe you could check into it for me a little."

"Why?"

"I thought maybe you might have already heard something about it down at the paper."

She was getting interested now. "Heard about what?"

"Roy Purdy's been cleared. He didn't kill my brother."

"Really?"

"Cross my heart."

She leaned back and considered. "No. I haven't heard a peep. Are you sure about this?"

"Convinced."

"My word! Am I supposed to keep this a secret?"

"When you drop it on somebody at the paper, just keep my name out of it. That's the only secret."

"How interesting."

I watched the waiter set out her salad and my broiled flounder. Then I said, "Do you know of any men who like women's underwear?"

She didn't turn a hair, damn her. She never did. "Of course. Why?"

I was tempted to drop Sports-Guy's name on her. But I didn't. First, she'd probably just say she knew already about it—and be telling the truth. Second, they might surprise the entire universe and go all the way next year, and even though she would never print something like that, I'd still feel like albatross crap.

"Just curious," I said. And changed the subject. "Back to Roy Purdy. If somebody down at the paper really did want to check it out, and wanted to have some fun doing it, I'd suggest hitting up Tom Crenshaw first. And then, before he has a chance to call his wife, hitting her up."

"You're engineering something, aren't you?" she asked, looking pleased.

"Who, me? How's your salad, Zoe?"

They told me that Lt. Gould was just back from lunch, and I followed their thumbs and found him sitting behind his desk, hunched over, facing the window, with his back to the big, crowded office.

This was my first view of Gould, the Cop, in his world. It looked like the place where pre-World War II wooden office furniture and old manila file folders go to die, but he obviously made an effort at neatness and order in his personal portion of it. The top of his desk was clear except for an ashtray, a yellow lined pad, a black rotary-dial telephone, and on the right side four or five of those legal-sized manila folders lined up flat and overlapping, apparently so that he could readily leaf into any one of them.

I had a quick flash of him as a kid. Every day, before he went off to school, his bed would be made and his collection of Dick Tracy comic books would be neatly stacked in his bookshelves beside his Hardy Boy books and the textbooks he had saved because they had been his favorites in past school years.

I cleared my throat.

He looked around, and I realized that he had been facing the window so he could get the best light to check out the spinach content in his braces with the aid of a small hand mirror.

"These things are hell," he said, only slightly embarrassed. He stuck the mirror away in a desk drawer. "What can I do for you, Mr. Morris?"

"Well, I had a thought, Lieutenant. Roy Purdy couldn't have killed my brother. So then, how come his fingerprints were the only ones you found on the murder weapon?"

"Careful handling."

I shook my head in puzzlement.

"Let me show you." He wallowed around in his chair and found his holster and pulled out his gun. "My fingerprints would be all over this thing, you know. Because it's mine. Somebody else picks it up, if they're real careful and use gloves, they can handle it just so and fire it without disturbing very many of my prints."

He demonstrated, with the gun pointing safely at the windowpane, holding it with thumb and forefinger at the bottom of the butt, and touching the trigger at the bottom part with just a fingertip.

"Fine," I said. "In theory. But that's a .38. Roy's gun was a .45, wasn't it? You try firing it like that, the kick would be hell to handle, wouldn't it? And Purdy's gun was fired three or four times at my brother."

Gould frowned for a moment. Then he leaned toward his right and checked something in one of those file folders laid out along the end of the desk.

It would be the file on Gene, of course. And I was surprised, not only because the folder was a brand-new, clean one, but because the papers inside looked white and fresh.

Gould kept claiming that the cops weren't interested, but obviously, they were interested enough to have gone to the trouble of making new copies of the case file, rather than just digging it out of storage, dusting it off, and sending it back. Interesting.

"Four shots," he said. "And you're right. It'd be a problem."

"Looks like a lot of Roy's prints would have been smudged."

"Could have been."

I waited.

He said, "We'll never know. All they were looking for was prints, period. And they found his on the gun. Period."

"So you don't know exactly where they were found on the gun."

He glanced toward the file folder again and shook his head.

"And the gun's gone by now, of course," I said.

"Sure."

"Well, that takes care of my curiosity."

"If we'd had that tape from that surveillance camera back then, we'd have known we ought to check the gun better. We'd have been able to tell for sure what happened." He shrugged.

"It does kind of point out one thing, though."

"What's that?" he asked.

"Somebody must have deliberately meant to lay the killing on Roy Purdy. Used his gun. Made sure his prints were still on it."

"Or somebody meant it to look like they were laying it on him to divert attention."

"Fine," I said.

He replaced his gun in its holster and wallowed around in his chair until he was comfortable again.

I stood up, ready to go.

But Gould said, "You were wondering about Purdy getting out of prison."

"Yeah." I sat down again.

"Tomorrow."

"Tomorrow? That's pretty quick, isn't it?"

He looked beseechingly at the ceiling. "These days they make room in the prisons any damned way they can."

"Well," I said. "I'm glad he's getting out."

Gould took another look at the ceiling. I've always suspected that in cop school they teach them that what they're really trying to do is make the world safe for cops. And the only really, totally complete way to do that is to lock up everybody that doesn't wear a badge. Cops are part of a growth industry, too, you know.

"I'm a little surprised at you," he said.

"Oh, yeah?"

"I didn't think you were interested in this."

"I don't know if I am."

"Uh-huh."

"Well, any interest at all would be bigger than the cops' interest, wouldn't it?"

He chuckled.

I said, "Except I'm kind of surprised that you've got a copy of Gene's file sitting right here on your desk."

Another chuckle. "I get lazy. Things pile up. You know."

I stared at the ultimately neat top of his desk for a moment and then took a look around at the other cops' desks, most of which looked as if they'd canceled the Garbage Pickup Department.

Gould started to smile, and then remembered that he hadn't had time to do a thorough check of his braces, and just looked pleasant, instead. "I was right, Mr. Morris. My kid just went crazy when I told her I talked to you last night."

"That's terrific," I said politely. And had a sudden blinding flash of inspiration. "Tell you what, Lieutenant. I'll make a deal with you."

In cop school they also teach them to look stern and unforgiving when somebody says that word. So he did. But they can't teach them how to disguise the interest that comes out in their eyes. "What deal?" he said sternly, while his eyes looked even more sparkly than his braces.

I settled back and got ready to play rough. "Well, you keep talking about that kid of yours. Is she really into science fiction?"

I stopped at a pay telephone at a convenience store that was just far enough away so I couldn't see the Police Building any more. It was still raining, and even in the best of weather that big, ugly, gaunt gray building is depressing enough to star in a Vincent Price movie.

There was a message from Zoe on my answering machine.

I called her.

"They already knew about Roy Purdy in the newsroom," she said. "For a couple of days."

"I read the paper. I haven't seen anything about it."

"Maybe tomorrow, they said."

"Isn't that kind of funny? I'd think it'd be a pretty interesting story. 'Wronged man freed.' Stuff like that."

She laughed dryly. "Not these days. Don't you know what things are like, my dear? Nobody wants anybody freed. The more people they lock up, the better chance that your personal burglar or mugger or rapist or somebody who disagrees with you might be one of them."

"You sound more like Editorial than Society."

She chuckled. "Not quite."

"Well, I guess I didn't give you the Scoop of the Century, after all."

"Lunch was enough, my dear."

"So it'll hit the papers tomorrow maybe," I said.

"'Hit' isn't exactly the right word. It's going to be small news. That's all. They're not enthusiastic right now about publicizing the fact that someone was framed for murder. They're too heavily involved in pushing the death penalty. Something that casts doubt on the wisdom of execution gets set up right under cute little stories about double-yolk eggs. But I did do one thing you wanted."

"What's that?"

"I talked a friend into making those calls. One to Tom Crenshaw. And one right afterward to Elaine Crenshaw."

"Good." At least I supposed it was good. It had probably taken Elaine's mind off how horny she was for a few minutes.

"He said it definitely shocked them both. He said neither one of them would talk about it at all."

"Okay. Thanks, Zoe. You're a peach."

"Oh, please. For God's sake, if you're trying to butter me up, say something that's at least a few years younger than World War II."

I chuckled. "You're a doll, then."

"You're trying. At least you're trying."

CHAPTER 6

"**Y**es. I've heard a rumor or two about Roy Purdy," David Perryman said.

He was set up in his father's old office and, as far as I could tell, nothing had changed since I used to make my periodic stop-ins to pick up checks for tuition and the allowance I got from my parents' trust until I was nineteen, the age they specified in their wills because Dad had always thought that was when the American male became mature.

It was more than a little bit eerie in this place. I don't think I would have kept this office the same if I were David. Every time I walked in here, I'd be seeing my father face-down on this desk with a gun in his hand and the back of his head missing.

"It's no rumor," I said.

David was two years older than Gene, but had finished UT Law at the same time because he wasn't in a rush to get out and conquer the world as Gene was. Then he came home to Houston to work in his dad's firm.

He was thirty-eight now, approximately. I wondered if there was a mold they fitted lawyers in so they could grow up to look like Gregory Peck and be judges, because from his appearance, that was surely where David was headed. He was balding only slightly, and the silver streaks at his temples were so perfect they looked architected.

He said, "Rumor has it that the police don't see much use in looking any further for your brother's murderer."

"That's the rumor I get, too."

He gave me a sardonic smile. "So what's your interest, Mel?"

"I honestly don't know. I'm just curious."

"Curious about what? About trying to bring your beloved brother's real killer to justice? Or curious about whether Roy Purdy may come raging out of Huntsville looking for the man that framed him?"

"Shit!" I said. Because I hadn't thought about that at all. I guess us Science Fiction types take just a little longer to figure out complicated things like that.

I sat back and looked around David's office some more. There was some personal history for me here, too, and I'd think about it for a moment before I got back to thinking about whatever it was I was getting myself more and more mixed up in.

David's dad, Kent, had been my dad's lawyer for ages. I think they were high school buddies, or maybe college. Kent went into law and my dad went into real estate.

When Mom and Dad were killed and their older son was just finishing law school and their younger one was just finishing high school, it was only natural that Kent would be the executor of the will and administer the trust that would expire when I turned nineteen and the estate was turned over to Gene and me. The arrangement looked damned good to me because it meant that Gene, although he was old enough to be the executor of the wills, wasn't.

The estate wasn't any tremendous thing, but it was nice enough. When the insurance on the house came in and their property was sold and taxes were paid, it figured out to be somewhere around $800,000, which Gene and I would split.

He wasn't pleased with it, wondering darkly why they hadn't had more insurance and why Dad hadn't used better sense in his business. But it was okay with me. It would get me through college with no problem and let Jane and me take that year in Australia that I had been dreaming about ever since I wrote a report on it in eighth grade, and still leave us a damned nice nest egg.

I didn't think too much about it when Kent hired Gene after he finished at UT. Kent was that kind of a nice guy that he'd make room for the son of his old buddy.

What I didn't know about was that, because Gene's prelaw stuff had been mostly finance- and accounting-oriented, and his concentration in law school had been taxes and finance and securities, Kent just naturally put him to working on things like our trust.

You've probably already guessed some of the rest.

I turned nineteen, and somehow the estate had dwindled down to about $200,000 because of some bad investments that were made with it while it was in the hands of Perryman, Chase.

Let me elaborate a little on those "bad investments." One of them will be enough to paint the picture: $300,000 had been invested in a drilling company owned by the father of one of Gene's frat brothers. The father retired about five minutes later and the frat brother took over. The drilling company went under. Bad luck. Tough luck. Sure. Except that, about three years later, Gene turned up as the partner of that frat brother in an oil production company. About six months after that, the frat brother found himself holding about 8 percent of the stock, with Gene holding the rest, and shortly the company was sold to Getty Oil for about $10,000,000. Not bad cash for a guy barely four years out of law school.

Anyway, back to when it was time to settle the estate and split the cash. It turned out that most of it was gone. Not that $100,000 isn't nice money for a nineteen-year-old kid, but once again, Gene had put it to me.

Kent Perryman was going crazy over the situation, of course. So was his son, David. And Gene was in for some trouble.

But before they could get too crazy, my thoughtful brother drove up to Austin, walked into the State Bar Association, and in a fit of conscience—so he told them—turned over a twenty-two-page list of ethical violations perpetrated by Perryman, Chase.

The way something like that works is, you're playing golf. Your old golf buddy steps up, tees off, and hits ten trees and decapitates three squirrels. You ask him what's eating him. He tells you that XYZ Oil just shunted 50,000 barrels of salt water into his rice fields and he's ruined. You ask him if there's anything you can do. He says, "What can anybody do?" You say, "Well, shit, don't just stand there, take 'em to court."

Is that ambulance chasing?

It all depends on who's telling it, and how.

Another cute thing Gene had done was get personal with a beer heiress who was using Kent Perryman to get her divorce. Seeing her on the sly, Gene told her how badly she was being taken, although she wasn't at all. After all, she was the one who originally told Kent that she wanted everything amicable—she had more than enough money to go around. At that point, she felt civilized and generous. Gene took her to bed and chatted with her some and she started getting the idea that people were laughing at her and she was being taken. Is she going to blame it on her own earlier noble instincts? Hell, no. She goes after her lawyer.

The State Bar came down ultrahard on Kent Perryman.

He sent everybody home early one day, locked his office door, and sat down at his desk and blew his brains out.

David never completely got over it—who would? The one thing he wanted was Gene's ears nailed to his wall.

But Gene wasn't stupid. He never practiced law—and probably had never intended to, because he could use his law knowledge so much more profitably in other endeavors—so David couldn't get at him through the State Bar. But as the years passed, David did his best to get at him in court. Anybody with a gripe against Gene could find an instant champion at Perryman, Chase.

But Gene definitely wasn't stupid. Nine times out of ten, David lost because, if there was one thing Gene had specialized in, it was loopholes. Often there was a settlement, but even then Gene always managed to make it look as if he'd rammed another big one right down David's throat.

So it was his father's suicide and all those years of crusading and losing that put David Perryman on my list of suspects.

But now I realized that there might be another list—Roy Purdy might have one of his own. With an asterisk beside the name of the person he was going to pay off for putting him in Huntsville.

I asked David, "Okay. So who do you think Roy might be after for framing him?"

He smiled and didn't look like any kind of judge at all. All he looked like was the guy who walks into the little gray room and pulls your plug after the priest leaves. And enjoys doing it. "Who killed Gene? I don't know. I just know one thing—I wish to hell it had been me."

That was probably the best answer I was ever going to get about why he kept the office the same, I realized. In his shoes, I might have also.

"Was it you?" I said.

He laughed. "What kind of question is that? Get serious, Mel. Would I answer that?"

I shrugged. "Well, I had to try."

We grinned ruefully at each other for a moment. Then he shifted around behind the desk and got comfortable. And started grinning like a little kid. "When they buzzed and said you were up front, I thought you were here about something else."

"Oh, yeah?"

He kept on grinning. "Maybe to wish me luck or congratulations, or something, I hope."

My instant surmise was that he'd made judge early, and I was ready to be happy for him. "Well, tell me what it is, and then I will congratulate you."

His expression changed to puzzlement. "She said she told you."

Puzzled-time for me now.

He glowed, damn him, and said, "I talked to Jane a little while ago, and she said she told you we were getting married."

I had a quick, crazy thought about running down to the State Bar Association myself. But I squelched it and squeezed out a big smile. "Gee, yeah. It just slipped my mind. Sure. Congratulations, David."

I looked at my watch and stood up. "I'm late. I've got to run. Congratulations. No shit."

Then I was out of there. I got all the way to my car without breaking anything.

I must really have been looking for depression—I went to see Sam Hauser next.

The Heights is about the nearest thing there is to Old Houston these days. It's not really that old, dating back to maybe World War I, but it's the part that has changed the least. In the beginning it was a nice Norman Rockwell suburb built on the plateau that starts on the north side of White Oak Bayou from downtown and averages maybe five feet higher than the rest of the coastal plain—hence, the name.

There's still a lot of Norman Rockwell left, in broad areas

of neatly kept houses with gingerbread over the porches and even a porch swing here and there. And some parts have become Yuppie enclaves as evidenced by aggressive, if usually plastic, restoration, and BMWs and joggers in Reeboks and designer haircuts.

But I didn't find any of those things in Sam Hauser's neighborhood.

The 1300 block of East Seventeenth Street, just off Studewood, is a hell of a long way from the fabled Lazy-H Ranch, which is where Sam and Bella Hauser lived until they tried to make up for the drop in oil prices in 1984 by using their Texas Legend status to super-sell time-shares in an ultra luxurious resort/marina/retirement community "soon to be built" on Lazy-H Ranch land on the shores of the also "soon to be built" Lake Bountiful.

Their promotion was a gigantic success. They sold time-shares to all of their big-time social and political buddies and to anyone else who had a buck.

Their only problem was that, after they'd collected enough money to fund most countries' armies, it came out that there was never going to be any kind of resort because there was never going to be any kind of Lake Bountiful—the Corps of Engineers had determined years ago that, if you put a dam where Sam and Bella claimed it was going, the best thing you'd get was a swamp.

Big scandal? Not at first. After all, Sam and Bella were part of Texas History, having rubbed shoulders and wallets with practically every politician you could name since World War II.

They'd just apologize for having gotten overenthusiastic—as Texas Legends have been wont to do since the days of Pecos Bill—and give back the money, and everything would be okay.

But it didn't work that way.

Practically all the money was gone. And it started coming

out that Sam and Bella had known all along that the resort idea was phony. Instead of being lovable and misled, they were crooks.

It came out in the trial that their plan had been to pull in a huge amount of money with their fake promotion and have the use of it for a couple of years before they had to apologize and give it back. In the meantime they'd use it to speculate in Boom-time Houston's skyrocketing real estate market and make gigantic bucks with it for themselves.

We all know where Houston's skyrocketing real estate market went—in the toilet.

At the trial Sam and Bella tried to blame everything on a fellow who had come to them as a property investment consultant—my brother, Gene.

He was squeaky-clean, though, as Gene was used to being.

He got lots of headlines for having had bad judgment, but bad judgment was epidemic in those days.

It's a certainty in my mind that Gene came out of the mess with sacks of cash. Why else would he have messed with it?

But nobody could prove a thing.

Sam and Bella got monster fines, the IRS got liens on everything up to and including the gold in their teeth, and their lawyers got the rest, but their sentences were suspended because they were ex-legends and they were old.

Usually what happens when Texas Legends go wrong— and we've had some—is that at least a few of their rich buddies stick by them and let them camp out semipermanently in a guest house, or something. But Sam and Bella made the big mistake of screwing their rich buddies, along with the general public.

They were wiped out of both money and buddies.

So thoroughly wiped out that they didn't even live in the Norman Rockwell part of the Heights. They lived on the 1300 block of East Seventeenth.

I wasn't really convinced that I had the right place when I parked in front of 1311. The neighborhood was more than depressed—in the gray and drizzling rain it looked like eastside hell. The ancient asphalt street was sliding off into the gutterless ditches. The yard of 1315 was being used as a graveyard for old cars—and God knows what else.

1311 was a one-story, one-bedroom house that some-body had tacked an extra bedroom onto in his spare time between FDR's Fireside Chats, and since then it had settled faster than the rest of the house so that it looked as if it would slide away at any moment. The last paint job had powdered mostly away long ago. The lawn badly needed mowing. The sidewalk slabs had each settled into the ground at a different tilt. More than half the width of the narrow steps up to the barely wider and jaggedly cracked concrete slab porch was hidden under an inexpertly nailed-together wheelchair ramp.

But it was the right place; Bella Hauser answered the door.

For a moment I stared. I recognized her face instantly, but still couldn't believe that this was the lady who used to make the grand appearances at the Livestock Show or the Quarter Horse Auction in her Anne Klein chaps and Harry Winston diamonds.

She was old and ravaged and beat-down. She peered at me angrily through the crack between door and jamb that the chain allowed. "Yes. What do you want?"

"I'd like to see Mr. Hauser for a few minutes, please."

"Why?"

"To talk with him, ma'am."

"What about?"

There was a muffled voice behind her. I couldn't make out the words, but the cadences told me it said, "Who is it?"

"Who are you?" Bella Hauser said.

"My name is Mel Morris."

She turned her head and repeated it.

The cadences this time were of cursing.

She pushed the door shut. Then opened it again, wide, while the chain clattered loosely against the jamb. "Come in," she said angrily.

I did, and wished that I hadn't. The place smelled of fried fish and dirty feet. A cheap TV set with a Vertical Hold problem showed surreal glimpses of the nice folk of "As the World Turns." There was an unsteady stack of old photo albums on a shabby chair that probably used to sit forgotten in the attic of the Lazy-H ranch house, along with a sagging sofa that had probably gone there first. Crowding the mantel of the fake fireplace were a dozen or more framed photographs of prize quarter horses.

In the middle of the room Sam Hauser sat in a wheelchair, glaring at me.

He was a caricature of Big Tall Texan Sam Hauser who always used to turn up on TV hosting barbecues for Lloyd Bentsen or acting as if he was really proud of the fact that Geraldine Ferraro was trying not to fall off one of his famous horses during a fund-raiser at the ranch.

Then he said something, and I realized that "caricature" didn't even begin to do the work of the word that was needed. Half his face was dead.

"He said, 'Are you Gene Morris's brother?'" Mrs. Hauser translated.

She was seated on the sofa, staring angrily up at me, I realized.

I hated this! I was in the presence of people who were legends out of my earliest memories, and I didn't want to see them turned to dirt. I wanted to lie and run. But I said, "Yes. I'm his brother."

Sam spoke. Bella said, "What do you want?"

I sure as hell didn't know, at this point. "I just dropped by to talk with you for a few minutes," I mumbled.

She glared at me out of her ruined face while her hands

twisted angrily at each other in her lap. "You're Gene Morris's kid brother that he was always telling us was always in some kind of trouble," she said, continuing to translate. Sam added, and she said, "Why would you have anything to talk with us about?"

I needed to get out. But I was here, and I might as well find out what I came for. "How long have you been ill, Mr. Hauser?"

She didn't bother to translate this time. "Since the nineteenth of February of '86. Right after your brother got through cheating us out of everything we had. Stroke."

"I'm sorry."

"He's sorry," Mrs. Hauser said to Sam.

I said, "I'm sorry I bothered you. I'll be going now."

Half of Sam's face worked with rage. He spewed unintelligible words.

"You're not getting out of here yet," Bella translated. "You owe us eight hundred and seventy-five dollars."

"What?"

"Eight hundred and seventy-five dollars."

"For what?"

She said, "Sam loaned Gene the money to bail you out of jail when you were drunk-driving."

I stared at her.

She listened to Sam and then said, "Gene said you'd been arrested and he didn't have the cash on him to bail you out of jail. Sam did, and gave it to him. He never paid it back."

There wasn't any point in anything. I pulled out my checkbook and wrote a check and handed it to her.

She handed it to Sam. He said something.

"Is it any good?" Bella translated.

"It's good," I said.

"It'd better be."

"I'm leaving," I said.

Before I could get the door opened and get back out into

the drizzling rain, Bella's voice sounded behind me. But this time she wasn't translating for Sam. And her voice was broken, almost wailing. "He cheated us," she said. "He ruined us. He took everything we had."

I turned around. She was broken and huddled over on that shabby old sofa, wringing her hands together in her lap.

Sam wasn't watching. He was sitting in his wheelchair, grinning at my check with the live half of his face. The man who used to love to take Jackie Kennedy on shopping sprees in Neiman-Marcus just because it made her smile was sitting there, tickled to death over my $875.00 check.

Bella raised her face to me. The lines under her ruined old eyes were full of tears. "He stole from us. Why wouldn't anyone believe us?"

I pulled the door open, got a breath of steamy, late October rainy air, and said, "I believe you."

Outside, wanting to run to my car, but making myself walk, I added, "But you had it coming to you." I didn't say it with much conviction, though.

"Well, of all people!" Grace said.

In living black-and-white, her face stared out of the TV monitor set into the wall beside the gate. This was Piney Point, River Oaks' version of River Oaks. It was maybe twelve miles and a minimum $20,000,000 from East Seventeenth Street.

I said, "Let's talk, Grace."

"What in the world would we have to talk about?"

"Old times."

She laughed. "Just what I needed. All right. Close your window and don't get out of the car until you get to the house. The Dobermans are out."

The screen went dead, but the cameras didn't. They didn't want you to be able to wave a gang of robbers or broke, sick old men in wheelchairs into your car and sneak them in with you. A moment later the gate clicked and the right half of it rolled back.

Nice. A half mile of concrete drive winding among massive old pine trees and oaks standing in an expanse of lawn that looked everywhere like a golf green. It was marred only by the seven-hundred-pound Doberman that was defecating on the perfect grass, glaring at me as if I, personally, had installed his hemorrhoids, and his five-hundred-pound mate who came loping out from behind a pine tree and ran hungrily beside the car, her fangs eighteen inches from my shoulder. I wondered how long it would take her to eat through my convertible top. Not long enough.

I took my mind off her and thought about Grace.

The last time I saw her was at Grandma's funeral. But Jane had been seeing her occasionally since Gene's funeral and, although we communicated less and less efficiently as our marriage skidded into divorce, I had the impression that they had gotten rather close for a time.

Even though Gene's death wasn't much more of a tragedy to Grace than to almost anyone else, it still was a hellacious disruption of her life, and I was sure that she needed a friend.

Grace inherited Gene's money, of course. And it turned out that his death came at a rather opportune time for her. Although he still had done nothing that was technically illegal, he must have been afraid that his luck couldn't run on forever and had begun the process of making torturous transfers of funds among some Cayman and Bahamian and Swiss banks to protect the money from seizure. Another six months and Grace—or anyone else—would have had hell tracking down and laying claim to a tenth of it. As it was, she had little problem. She was a very, very wealthy widow. I was astonished at how wealthy she was. But she sure as hell deserved it, after twelve fun-filled years of marriage to Gene.

There were some complications, of course. When he died, there were three or four civil suits pending against him, as there always were. He would have settled them, as he always did, and still come out far ahead. But Grace played the grieving widow very well and settled them for much less.

I suppose you could make a case for her being so nauseated by the way the money was made—if not outright thievery, transparent cheating—that she shouldn't have been able to stand having it. But she didn't look at it that way. If he had scalped half of Rhode Island and then died, she'd have fought for every lock of hair he collected, no matter whether the stuff made her barf or not. All she'd have been thinking about was that it was hers and she had damned well earned it by putting up with the son-of-a-bitch for as long as she had.

I never knew for sure whether Grace and I liked each other or not. There were certainly times when we gave each other support and comfort. But we were never particularly cordial, even in the times of the greatest support and comfort. Maybe it was a little like a friendship I had at college. My buddy and I didn't sit around saying kind things to each other, even though we were the best friends we were ever going to have. But then again, it probably wasn't like that at all.

Gene died. Grace went through some changes which were eased considerably by the fact that she was very wealthy. About a year later she married Hugh Rand, who was about as different from Gene as it was possible to get. He had his own family money that was older than Texas and would probably outlast it, and he was a professor of architecture at Rice. He adopted Gene's son, Brian. They built a palace in Piney Point. And lived happily ever after.

So Grace had it made now. After twelve ugly years of being married to my brother, she lived in a gated estate guarded by insane dogs with a man who probably wasn't very exciting, but evidently made up for it by being devoted to her, and only to her.

Was that a motive for murder?

You figure it out. I'm just a guy who writes science

fiction. With a little lean toward fantasy thrown in now and then, I guess.

The house was incredible. They'd even built a hill to set it on, hills being something you have to import to the flatlands of Houston. It was stone and glass and terraces and fieldstone chimneys. I wondered why it had never made it into *Architectural Digest* and instantly gave myself the answer—it was too great. Run an article on this house, and they might as well shut down the magazine because where else could they go from here?

Grace met me at the front, holding open a door that was one massive piece of smoked glass that must have been three inches thick. There were two of Jane's pieces on the stone shelving at the sides of the steps. One of them I had seen before. The other was new to me. Both were wonderful, jutting, free-form stele of highly polished stainless steel, one of them about eight feet tall, the other six or so. Beautiful! Probably phallic as hell, but who's going to be Freudian about something as beautiful as that in a place like that?

She took me through the house to a sunroom. As we went, I couldn't help comparing it with the Crenshaw house. And there was absolutely no comparison. There were no Halloween hallways here. No dark caverns. The Crenshaw house was straight out of our primitive, cave-dwelling past, I think, where a dwelling place was nothing more than a place in which to hide, luxurious or not. This house had nothing to do with hiding. It was shelter, of course. But more than that, it was a place in which to live and to enjoy living, and to decorate with the fruits of having lived—or inherited—well.

I had glimpses of paintings which had to be Picassos and Chagalls. Even a Renoir, I think. There were expanses of sculptured carpeting that looked like spun sugar. There was a massive fieldstone fireplace beside which stood one of Jane's sculptures, which was a fantasy of jutting, broken steel plates held together by rough steel rods.

In my books I sometimes find myself needing to describe the fantastic dwelling of some powerful and wealthy being of the far future. As I walked with Grace through her house in Piney Point, I took mental notes for the next time I wrote about a place like that.

I saw four servants as we went. Except that one of them, a squarely built, middle-aged woman who looked as if she could be the sister of Mrs. Windom, my fifth grade science teacher, was probably technically not a servant, but Grace's secretary or, at the least, her housekeeper. She came briskly from the room with the fireplace, a leather-bound appointment book under her arm, and paused to smile efficiently as we passed, and then went briskly somewhere else.

Finally we reached the sunroom. The sky was still gray and intermittently drizzling rain, but even so, this sunroom was bright and cheery and would have made Elaine and Tom and Maria eat their hearts out and then start on the ferns and orchids. The nearest rattan was probably in the doghouses.

There were some variegated ficuses and some spectacular dracaenas and some flowering plants I couldn't name inside the sunroom. Past the glass walls there were monstrous magnolias with raindrops glistening on their broad leaves, and then the lawn sloped down to a swimming pool the size of New Zealand and formal gardens beyond it.

"Well," Grace said when we were sitting down. "Old times."

I didn't know what to say. Even Columbo would have been humbled in this place. What was I supposed to do? Say, "Listen, Grace, this is the most fantastic place I've ever seen. Did you kill Gene?"

I didn't think so.

"It's been a long time," I said.

"You look as if you're doing all right, Mel."

"So do you, Grace."

She did. She looked splendid, my former sister-in-law.

Splendid again, I should say.

When she and Gene were married, she was a bona-fide beauty, having been second runner-up in the Miss Texas Pageant. I'm sure that she and her very middle-class East Texas family looked on the marriage as a very good one—Gene was an up-and-coming young entrepreneur and had not yet been publicly tied to anything shady. It was the kind of marriage that seems constitutionally guaranteed to every Miss Texas Runner-Up.

Things never lived up to her expectations. Gene made lots of money, but the shadiness started coming out. His affairs began while she was pregnant with their one and only child, Brian. Gene was rich, but Grace saw few benefits from it. He wore expensive suits and drove a Mercedes—for business reasons, of course. Grace drove a clunker and ran into trouble if she splurged on a new pair of sneakers to wear around the house.

Before long she became what can only be described as mousy. The exceptions were when Gene needed to show her off as part of some deal he was cooking. Then he sprang for the works at a beauty shop and sent her to Sakowitz for a new outfit.

Jane's description of the way Gene treated Grace was tidy, if not original—"Cheap-shit."

"Why does she put up with it?" I asked, not more than a hundred times.

"Because women always have."

"You wouldn't."

"I might," she said, astonishing me. "But just don't try it."

In the last three or four years before Gene was killed, though, he was rich enough that something like the trickle-down theory began to work, and he was more generous with Grace. But the mousiness seemed to be there to stay.

Wrong.

There was nothing at all mousy about this woman dressed

in a white silk blouse and white slacks with a Hermés scarf knotted at her waist, who sat across the sunroom coffee table from me. Her dark hair was smooth and lustrous, with just enough gray strands in it to make her look intriguing. Her body was tight and lithe. And her face seemed years younger than when I last saw her. She might almost have aged backward since the day Gene was shot.

"Things have changed for you," I said.

She smiled, and I could see more than a hint of that Miss Texas Runner-Up. "They have, haven't they? It's astonishing what living well can do for one."

"It agrees with you. It definitely agrees with you."

"Hugh's good for me," she said, almost beginning to glow.

"It's obvious, Grace."

"He's a wonderful man, Mel. I didn't know there were men like him. He's brilliant, you know. But he's so kind and generous. And thoughtful." She blushed. "He brings me presents."

I had never seen Hugh in person, and he didn't go out of his way to be noticed, but occasionally his picture would be in the paper when the Houston Historical Preservation Commission, of which he was a director, did something of note. And he turned up on TV sometimes, the last time being when the new George R. Brown Convention Center was dedicated. He was tall and slender and patrician, but there was a look in his eyes and around his mouth that convinced me that he'd probably be a great guy to sit around and drink beer with, even though he was Very Rich.

At the convention center dedication, I was sure that he was having a lot of trouble with his eyes and his mouth because, although he had some nice things to say to the TV cameras about the tremendous economic benefits of the center, I had the feeling that he shared my opinion that it looked like nothing in the world so much as a robot's birthday cake. Someday, maybe, I'd run into him at some function, and I'd ask him.

Grace pushed a crystal ashtray toward me and watched me light a cigarette. Then she said, "I still talk with Jane occasionally."

I made a noncommittal sound.

"You were such a fool to let her get away from you," she said, not unkindly.

Not unkindly or not, I didn't need this. Not today. "About the same kind of fool you were to put up with Gene."

She made a wry face. "What can I say?"

"He was killed three years ago. It doesn't seem possible, does it?"

"Is that what this is all about, Mel? Are you going around observing the anniversary of Gene's death?"

I looked up at the wet gray sky. "Not intentionally, I assure you."

She looked at her watch. "We'll be having tea in a moment. Unless you'd like something stronger."

"Tea's fine."

Primly she crossed her ankles and put her hands together in her lap. "Just why are you here, Mel?"

I didn't have to answer just then; it was tea-time. It was brought by yet another servant, a slight fiftyish woman who might have been either French or Filipino and gave an air of being both pleasant and ferociously efficient. She loved her starched charcoal-gray uniform. And obviously, she had been taught "tea" before she could walk.

There were milk, lemon, sugar lumps, a plate of intricately decorated little cakes, and scones, along with pats of deeply yellow butter carefully impressed with ornate *R*'s. The teapot bore a vague resemblance to the America's Cup and was probably even older and more historic.

My usual exposure to tea was late at night when I wanted something less full of caffeine than coffee, and ran the tap water hot and used instant. I tried to remember how my mother had taught me to handle real tea in order not to embarrass myself too much.

Then I remembered that it was Grace before whom I was worried about embarrassing myself. True irony. This little snack would have eaten up about a week's worth of the food budget Gene allowed her—unless he was expecting "clients." The times, they change.

I sat back with cup and saucer.

Grace said promptingly, "You were about to tell me what you're up to."

I did. "Have you heard about Roy Purdy yet?"

She took it entirely too calmly. "Roy Purdy?" she said, raising an eyebrow. "What is there to hear about Roy Purdy?"

"He's been cleared. He didn't kill Gene," I said, and carefully watched her reaction.

Still too much calm. "That's absurd. How could he be cleared?"

I told her, although I was certain that she already knew.

"This isn't some story you've made up, is it, Mel?"

"Of course not."

She looked up at the gray sky. "Well, if he didn't do it, he shouldn't be in prison."

"Get off it, Grace."

She looked at me as if I had just suggested she leave all this and move in next door to Sam and Bella Hauser.

I said, "You've already heard all about it, haven't you?"

She didn't try to drag a dead horse forever. "All right. Yes. I've already heard all about it."

"How did you hear?"

"Is that something you really need to know?"

"I don't know."

She laughed. "If you're going to play detective, you're going to have to do better than that."

"This is my first and last case. I need a little help from my friends. How'd you hear about it?"

"Oh, all right. Jane called."

"Is that the whole truth? Did somebody else call and tell you about it. And Jane called, period?"

"Don't be tiresome, Mel. If I were you, my next question would be 'If Roy didn't shoot Gene, who did?' And my answer would be 'My God! How would I know that?'"

"Thanks a lot," I said.

"Why in the world are you even worrying about it?"

I had to chuckle at myself. "I kept asking myself that. Then it got answered for me. Roy Purdy's been locked up for a murder he didn't commit—he was framed. If I were him, I'd come stomping out of Huntsville and tear hell out of whoever it was who framed me."

Grace frowned. "There is that, isn't there?"

"Don't jack me around, Grace. You've already thought of that."

She gave me a sardonic look. "My. We are getting good at this, aren't we?"

"If he can't figure it out exactly, he might just be angry enough that he'd go after all the likely candidates. That'd include you."

She gave me an amused look. "And you, also, of course." Then she looked around, and it was obvious that she was taking in the walled acres surrounding her and the TV at the gate and the servants and the dogs. "In the last couple of years I've learned to be secure for the first time in my life. I don't think I'm going to be worrying too much about that."

"But then again," I said, "he might have done some thinking while he was in prison and figured out he'd be stupid to do something that would get him sent back. He might just go to the cops and let them take care of it for him."

"Don't try to scare me, Mel. First of all, there's nothing to scare me about. Second of all, even if he did go to the police and convince them I did it, I'm not worried. Women like me don't get convicted of things very often. Unless they're really awful things. For one thing, besides being able to provide an awfully good defense, I'd have a whole parade of witnesses who'd get up and swear that, if I did it, I ought to get a medal." She tilted an eyebrow at me. "One of the first would be my very own former brother-in-law. Right?"

"Right."

"I hated him as much as you did, Mel."

I looked at the rain-damp ficuses. "If anybody could, you could, Grace."

"Whether I killed him or not, I'm not going to worry about it. I worried about your brother for twelve years. That was more than enough."

I couldn't argue with any of that.

But one thing did start bothering me. I was bothered when Elaine Crenshaw had seemed to be avoiding saying that Roy "killed your brother," using, instead, the phrase, "Roy went to prison." Now I was getting the feeling that Grace was doing the same kind of thing.

I said, "How come you keep beating around the bush? How come you won't just come out and say you didn't kill him?"

She shrugged. "Fine. I'm not worried. Why should I be? I didn't kill Gene. Furthermore, I don't know who did."

She changed the subject by looking at my cup and asking, "More?" But her tone told me that it was getting time for me to be going back to the real world.

I shook my head and set my cup and saucer on the coffee table.

We both started into the business of getting up and getting me out of there.

But I stopped and sat back. A thought had struck me. It shouldn't have taken this long because I'm a writer and even science fiction writers know about things like foreshadowing.

But however long it had taken, I had finally realized that Grace had said a couple of things earlier that I should have paid attention to.

She raised an eyebrow because I had interrupted the standard leaving ritual.

I said, "Something you said—that I was going around observing the anniversary of Gene's death. And then you said that I'm playing detective."

She shrugged. Just a bit elaborately.

"You've talked to Elaine Crenshaw. Maybe you talked to Jane, too. But you've definitely talked to Elaine."

She wasn't exactly tickled to have been caught. But her look told me that she considered it no big thing. Sarcastically, she said, "Mike Hammer lives." A moment later she added, "Yes. I chatted with her earlier. I chat with a lot of people. Just what business is it of yours?"

"That's how you heard about Roy."

"I think she mentioned it."

"'Mentioned it?' I'll bet she more than just 'mentioned it.'"

"Don't push, Mel. If it's any business of yours—and it isn't—she was shocked by the news about Roy. Very shocked."

"I'm kind of shocked, too. I didn't know you were chummy with Gene's ex-girlfriends."

I thought she'd be angry; instead, she laughed. "Oh, good God, Mel! Grow up. You don't think at that late stage I was worried about one girlfriend, more or less. Besides, Elaine was my friend before Gene had anything to do with her. And she felt so badly about it after she found out what a skunk he was and broke off with him that I couldn't possibly have been angry with her." She added, "We're both much too busy now to see much of each other. But when something like this comes up, particularly after you went barging and bumbling into her house without even telling her why you were there, it was only natural that she call me."

She stood up. It was definitely time for me to go.

She guided me back to the entrance and came outside and we paused, shielded from the rain by the broad overreach of the roof.

"I wish we could have been friends, Grace," I said.

"I do, too, Mel. I mean that. But we can't. You're nothing like Gene, but you're his brother, and that's too much."

"And you were his wife."

We looked at each other for a moment.

Then she said, "Brian is growing up so fast. He's gotten addicted to science fiction, and he loves your books. He's always liked it that his uncle remembers him with a check on his birthday and at Christmas. But he'd be thrilled if you sent him one of your books. I think he might like to get to know you."

I was oddly moved by the idea. Because of my dislike and avoidance of his father, "my nephew Brian" had never been anything much to me before but an abstraction. But Gene was dead, and Brian was a person all his own. "I might like that, too," I said.

"He's playing football at Jesuit on Friday nights this fall." She smiled fondly. "At least, they're letting him and some of the other eighth-graders put on uniforms and sit with the older boys. He'd be thrilled if you took in a game. Hugh's not very sports-minded."

"I might do that, Grace."

"He'd love to talk science fiction with you," she said. Her voice changed so that, for a moment, I thought she was going to warn me about the dogs again. "But I don't think he'd be at all interested in your detective sideline."

"I get the point, Grace," I said, moving on out into the lightly falling rain.

"I thought you would."

My surreal reflection in Jane's stainless steel was distorted even further by the raindrops that were dotting its surface and sliding down it. I said, "Someone told me recently that Gene said you and I were having an affair."

"Really."

"Did you know he was saying that?"

"He said whatever suited him at the moment. You know that."

I had another first-ever question for her. "Why did you stay with him for so long?"

Her reflection slid onto the stainless steel now. I turned and saw that she stood near me. Raindrops glittered in her hair.

She said, "For a long time, I thought he'd change."

"And then?"

"And then I knew that, eventually, someone would kill him and it would all be mine."

CHAPTER 7

The gate at Jane's studio was locked, and I rang the bell.

There was just a speaker here on middle-class West Alabama, not a TV screen. "Who is it?" it said, with her voice.

"Me."

The lock clicked. I pushed the gate open and went in.

In the early eighties Jane's work was starting to sell nicely, and I was starting to sell books, as well as stories, and filling stations all over town were going broke and closing. She bought this one on West Alabama, had a brick wall built around it, and it was her studio.

It was ideal for her. There was all kinds of heavy electrical wiring for her welding and cutting equipment, and hoists and the hydraulic lift that she used occasionally when she was working on something unusually heavy or large. When it was hot, she could close the big doors and turn on air conditioning. When it was cool, she could open the doors and work more or less in the open air.

The driveway areas were spotted with various pieces of

various sizes that she was "aging," which translates to mean that they were sitting out to get rusty.

She was working in the middle bay, welding a foot-square piece of steel plate onto a three-feet high heavy steel object that looked as if it might turn out to be something like a bird about to take wing.

She wielded the welding torch with one hand while the other held the piece of steel plate in place with the aid of a clamplike tool she had fashioned out of the same kind of steel rods that she used in her sculptures.

I walked around in front of her so she could see me through the practically opaque glass in her welding mask, and she waved the torch at me in acknowledgment and went on finishing what she was doing. She was wearing sneakers and blue jeans and a man's T-shirt. Her hair was pulled back in a loose ponytail.

I browsed around, looking at things that were sitting in the other two bays. She hadn't done much stainless steel for a while, working instead these days in raw steel that she bought in rods and bars and heavy inch-thick plates.

In one of the bays I saw a piece that I wanted. It was about four feet high and from the side looked a little like those statues on Easter Island. From the front it was the Picassoesque head of a woman.

The torch stopped whooshing, and I hurried back to the middle bay to watch her take off the welding mask. It always did something primitive to me to see her arch her back and pull away that black covering from over her face and breasts and then take off the rubber band and shake her hair free.

"Hi," she said.

"Hi."

"Why don't you get us a beer?"

The part of the station where they used to keep the cash register and credit card machines she had converted into a workroom, where she did her sketching and drafting. There was a refrigerator there. I got a couple of cans of beer and went back to the middle bay to find her studying the new piece.

"Thanks," she said. "Do you like it?"

"I think so. But I still like the stainless steel stuff best."

She looked thoughtfully up into the hoists. "Maybe I'll do some more before long. But the rough stuff's selling better now."

She hung the mask on the wall and then went around the bay, picking up this tool and that, replacing them on their pegs. There were dark iron forceps and clamps and tongs of various sizes and configurations that she used to hold pieces of hot steel while she worked on them, or used to clamp pieces together while she welded.

Most of her tools she made herself. Sometimes, in sculpting a particular piece, she would actually have to spend more time designing and making specific tools to work it than on the piece itself. A local gallery a few years ago had displayed an array of her tools as works of art in themselves. They sold well. And if the Contemporary Arts Museum solved its management problems and settled itself down again someday soon, there was talk of mounting an exhibit of her tools. A full-service lady, my Jane.

Sorry. Strike the "my."

Her T-shirt was damp from the light rain or perspiration or both, and her breasts worked wonderfully as she moved.

"I wish you'd told me it was David you're marrying," I said. "Even though I told you I didn't want to know."

She hung up a heavy clamp that could have subdued stallions and brushed her hands together and sat back against a wooden stool, cooling her hands against her beer can. "I shouldn't have told you at all," she said. "Not yet."

"Aren't you sure?"

"Oh, Mel, yes . . . I don't know."

Time was when that tone meant she needed me to come to her and hold her. Time was.

I sat on a stool and tasted the beer. "You had to tell me."

She smiled sadly. "I'm getting older. I want babies. I wanted yours. But we just never got around to it. There never was the time."

"It was probably a good thing," I said. "Babies. And then a busted marriage."

"Damn," she said. "Damn!"

"Do you love David? You're not just marrying him to have babies, are you?"

She looked out at the rain and laughed. Not too happily. "Are we having this conversation?"

"Sure."

She laughed better now. "Yes, we are, aren't we?" She moved her shoulders and reached up to push her hair back.

I knew exactly how her breasts would feel under my hands at this moment.

"We should have started right in at the beginning having babies," I said. "We shouldn't have worried about not having as much money out of the estate as we thought we would, and we should have taken that trip to Australia anyway and started a baby there. Maybe we would have just stayed there. But wherever we ended up, that would have made us work harder at staying married."

She rubbed the beer can over her cheeks, liking the cold. Softly she said, "You are such an idealist."

"We worked past a lot of things, Jane. We worked past Gene trying to break us up. And that money thing. We even worked past the divorce for a long time, you know. We worked past it until now."

She studied her hands and let her hair fall over her forehead. I think it was to hide from me the fact that she was very close to crying.

I said, "Maybe that was why we broke up. I never knew

why we broke up. But maybe I do now. Maybe it was because we didn't have anything to work past any more. Maybe that's what was wrong."

"I wish it were all that simple," she said to her hands.

"I'm in the eleventh grade again," I said. "I heard this morning that they got some new science fiction books in. And they got two Clifford D. Simaks I've never even heard of, and a new Robert Silverberg. And I've got them all three in my hands ready to check out because I traded my letter sweater to J. C. Tinkler for one of the Simaks he was about to check out, and I traded my parking sticker to Hunt Reese for the Silverberg.

"And I'm waiting in line to check them out, and the new girl they were talking about in homeroom this morning walks in. And looks around and walks out."

I was getting kind of choked up myself, damn it! And I walked over to the big doorway and looked out at the half-hearted rain. She had pulled in her car through the big gate and parked it under one of the canopies that Texaco had thoughtfully left for her. But she hadn't driven far enough forward, and the rear end stuck out and the metallic blue finish glittered under a million beads of rainwater.

In a moment I continued. "I dropped those books and ran after you. I couldn't work up the guts to talk to you for three weeks, but I followed you all the way up to the third floor. And then I walked by Mr. Harsh's door to peek in at you about ten times until the hall monitor ran me off.

"I went back down to the library, and those books were gone. I didn't get hold of *Way Station* for six months more, because of you. And it's the one book in the world I'd die to write, but I still don't mind that I had to wait to read it. Because I waited for it because of you.

"I don't want you to marry David Perryman, Jane. I don't want you to be married to anybody but me. Ever. I've wanted babies, too. You don't know how goddamned much I want them. If they're yours."

I stared at the rain. I couldn't believe I was saying this. Wrong! I couldn't believe I hadn't said it long ago. I couldn't believe I had let things get to the point that I'd have to say these things. It all hurt so goddamned much.

But let it hurt.

It couldn't hurt nearly as much as losing her altogether.

"Oh, Mel," she said.

"Jane, I . . ."

"Don't turn around for a minute. Don't say anything else. I love you for it, but it's too late."

I heard her footsteps cross the oil-stained floor, and heard the bathroom door go shut.

I walked on out into the drizzling rain. It was easier than admitting to myself that I was crying.

In a little while I went up front, under the canopy that used to keep the rain off the people who were buying the expensive Ethyl gas, and wiped my face and waited.

Jane came out in a few minutes, her face pale.

I said, "I won't hassle you any more about it. But David had better take goddamned good care of you."

"Don't make me cry any more, Mel."

We smoked cigarettes and looked at the rain for a couple of minutes. Then I said, "Roy Purdy's getting out tomorrow. I'm worried about what he might do."

"Do?"

"He might be really screwed-up. He might think just about anybody framed him. He might not know exactly, and just go after all the candidates."

"I've thought of that."

"Do you still have that gun?" I said.

"Yes."

"Put it in your purse and carry it with you. Be careful. Don't go out when it's full moon."

"Oh, God!" She laughed. Too hard.

"I mean it, Jane. Don't take any chances until we find out what he's going to do."

"All right."

"If he did anything to you, I'd have to kill him."

Her face was paler than I had ever seen her. There were dark hollows under her eyes.

I wanted to go to her and hold her.

I didn't.

"Just please take care of yourself," I said.

Then I left.

I thought I had left the blinds open when I went charging off to try out my detective skills on Sallie Lacie. I like real light, even when it's drizzling rain and not worth much. But apparently I hadn't.

I unlocked the door and walked into my dark living room and reached for the light switch.

It clicked when my hand was still a foot away.

"Show the gentleman to the sofa, Lupe," a man said.

Lupe did. I took one look at him and saw that, if he were Japanese, he'd be a sumo first-round draft pick, and I let him show me to my sofa.

"What the hell were you doing at my house, bothering my wife?" the man said. He was pushing forty and probably stood over six feet, but it was hard to judge because he looked almost skeletal in his dark business suit. His face was tanning-salon-dark, and I'm pretty sure he was wearing what was probably a pretty good-quality hairpiece. He looked like a wimp. But he had Lupe with him.

I didn't need to be a card-carrying detective to figure out who he was. "Crenshaw," I said. I glanced over at the security box on the wall in the entryway. Its green light was glowing cheerily, saying that everything was okay. "How the hell did you get in here?"

Crenshaw smirked, something his skin-and-skull face made it easy for him to do. "My company's the authorized distributor for those alarms."

I looked around at Lupe; he was smirking, too, but there was a lot more meat in it.

Crenshaw got serious. "I don't like people that come around bothering my wife."

He was playing with my stainless steel ostrich egg. Except that he wasn't strong enough to really play with it. I hoped he'd drop it on his foot.

"I don't like people that break into my house," I said.

Crenshaw tossed the egg to Lupe, who was standing behind me. For a moment—as I'm sure he intended—I thought he wouldn't be able to toss something that heavy that far, and I was in the way.

But it cleared my head by a couple of inches, and Lupe caught it behind me with a sound like a steak slapping into a skillet.

"What the hell was your idea in disturbing her, Morris?"

Lupe moved up to the back of the sofa and leaned his thighs against it and stood there playing with that solid steel egg as if it were a Ping-Pong ball.

I weaseled, of course. "I wasn't disturbing her. I was trying to warn her."

"Warn her?"

"About Roy Purdy."

"What the hell business of yours is it about her ex-husband?"

"There's some people he might go after when he gets out. She's one of them."

Crenshaw studied me for a moment. Then he made up his mind. "Okay, Lupe. Go sit down somewhere."

Lupe did. But first he had to play. He tossed the egg to my lap.

I caught it just in time.

And I guess more and more of the goddamned detective crap was creeping up on me all the time because I—Quick!—tossed it right back at him, with both hands.

He caught it, but not before it sank about eight inches into his belly. Then he stood there, trying to breathe, looking murder at me.

"That's enough," Crenshaw said. "Put it down."

Lupe did. On the floor. Then he went over and sat down on the camel bench by the fireplace.

"That was stupid," Crenshaw said, sitting down across the coffee table from me.

"I get that way sometimes."

"Tell me about warning Mrs. Crenshaw."

"What would you do if you just got out of prison where you'd been because somebody framed you?"

He waited for me to tell him.

"You'd go after somebody," I said. "Maybe you'd have to go after several just to make sure you got the right one."

He nodded; he wasn't stupid.

He really wasn't stupid. "Funny, you didn't manage to communicate this message of warning to my wife. She had the distinct impression that you were trying to shock some kind of statement out of her."

I was at a real disadvantage, so I tried boyish charm. "I went off kind of half-cocked," I said.

Crenshaw wasn't amused.

I hurried on. "I'm curious about who really killed my brother—sure. But the important thing is that Roy Purdy is probably going to be real pissed-off, and a hell of a lot more curious about it than I am. And less subtle about how he tries to find out. Or everything I've heard about the accommodations at Huntsville is wrong."

I lighted a cigarette, and Crenshaw suddenly looked frosty again. But it was my house, and I'd smoke in it if I damned well wanted to. Unless Lupe objected, of course.

Crenshaw said, "Granted. To an angry, vengeful man, my wife might seem to be a suspect. But there are others, aren't there?"

"That's right."

"According to Elaine, they include a man named David Perryman. And your brother's widow, of course. And your former wife. The reason for that one escapes me, Mr. Morris. Why would your former wife be a suspect in your brother's death?"

I didn't want to be talking about this. Not twenty minutes after leaving Jane at her studio.

But there was Lupe.

I cleared my throat and said, "He tried to rape her. A couple of days before he was killed."

Crenshaw leaned back and made a lemon-sucking face. "I see. And that makes you a suspect in his murder, also, of course."

Suddenly I wondered who the hell was supposed to be playing detective, anyway, and started to say something about it. But once more, there was Lupe. I said, "It would. But I was alibied. They checked it out."

"You were alibied, but my wife and the widow and your former wife and this Mr. Perryman weren't?"

"I don't think the police even went that far. They checked on Roy Purdy first because he was the partner Gene bankrupted, and they checked me because I was the brother and there'd always been bad blood between us. They got as far as verifying my alibi, and then they found the gun with Purdy's fingerprints on it. That took care of Roy, so they didn't need to go any farther." I explained the fingerprints-on-the-gun situation.

Crenshaw said, "But as far as you know, these other people may have alibis that are every bit as solid as yours."

I pointed at the telephone. "Call up Elaine's hairdresser

and ask if she was there under the dryer three years ago on 27 October at ten A.M. while Gene was getting killed."

Things suddenly were very quiet. With a sinking in my stomach, I realized that we were about at nut-cutting time.

Crenshaw's skull-like face was frozen, his eyes hooded, while he sat there deep in thought. I told myself that he was doing nothing more ominous than trying to recall exactly the movement of commode lid futures on the stock exchange today. But I didn't believe it for a second.

I glanced at Lupe. He was thinking, too.

Damn! My timing had been bad when I was talking with Elaine. It hadn't improved since then.

Thought-time was suddenly over for Crenshaw. He unhooded his eyes and turned his head and looked at me.

I told myself that there was one thing about sumos. They were big and they were tough. But they were slow, too. Weren't they?

A little movement of air tickled the hairs on the back of my neck.

It was Lupe. Standing directly behind me. He wasn't that slow.

I braced. Got ready to dive forward over the coffee table.

Crenshaw stood up.

I got really ready. Behind me, there was a sound like meat rubbing against meat—Lupe was ready, too.

Then Crenshaw was giving me a thin-lipped smile and motioning Lupe toward the front door.

I stared, feeling the muscles in my thighs start to twitch with the aftermath of too much strain.

Crenshaw smiled some more. "I think we can handle this from here, Mr. Morris. We'll take our own precautions about Mr. Purdy. And anything else that might come up. Pardon our intrusion."

He moved to the front door where Lupe waited with his hand on the knob.

What in bloody hell had happened, I wondered. What had he figured out that had suddenly turned everything off?

Maybe I'd just pick up the telephone and call Elaine and ask her, after a while, I told myself.

Crenshaw might have been reading my mind. "If anything else occurs to you, call me. Not my wife."

Lupe smiled at me.

"Yes, sir," I said.

I picked up the egg and tried to toss it around like Lupe had. No way. Wiping the fingerprints off it, I set it back into the depression in the wood block that held it in place on the coffee table.

There was a message on the answering machine from Zoe. I called and got her answering machine and left a message for her.

Then I went in to the computer and called up my list again. Wasn't that what detectives were supposed to do at the end of a long, hard day? Sit down and figure out which of the suspects were most suspect.

CANDIDATES LIST

Mel Morris—Alibied
Roy Purdy—Alibied about three years late

Those two, I left as they were. And the next three.

Grace Morris—Gene's widow/ now Mrs. Hugh Rand
David Perryman—Son of Kent Perryman
Elaine Purdy—Mrs. Roy Purdy then/ divorced and Mrs. Tom
    Crenshaw now/ Gene's last girlfriend

Finally, now, I needed to make some changes. A little progress, at least.

Sallie Lacie—Didn't do it. Ill.
Sam Hauser—Didn't do it. Stroke.

I tried to grasp at a straw or two. Sam Hauser was ruined by a stroke. No way could he have walked in to shoot Gene.

But there was Bella. She was a tough old broad. After their resort scam folded and became public, there was some talk that she had really been the brains behind it.

Gene's involvement? He came in after these two high-profile pillars of the community had already used their names and reputations to perpetrate their scam, and just used their own greed and the Houston Bust against them—monumentally and most profitably, I'm sure—but this time, at least, it wasn't a scam that he initiated. Sam and Bella blamed him for everything, of course, but legally, as usual, he was in good shape. He did definitely fleece them. But this time he was fleecing hyenas instead of sheep.

Maybe Bella killed him. With as much hatred as I saw in those ruined eyes of hers, she could well have killed him.

I started to type her onto my list.

And stopped.

I remembered the hatred in those eyes of hers. But I also remembered how she had kept wringing her hands in her lap—they were so twisted and clubbed with arthritis that they looked like naked baby birds. No way could she have handled a gun with those hands, no matter how tough she was or how hard she hated.

That left just the name I had added last. There was no change there, either.

Damn it!

Jane Morris—Once and now Jane Saunders/ the Prettiest Girl
   in the Eleventh Grade

   I'd pared it down a little. David Perryman. Grace. Elaine.
Me.
   And Jane.
   Damn!

CHAPTER 8

"This is my daughter, Celeste," Gould said, smiling proudly.

I said, "Hi, Celeste."

She was about fourteen and anorexic. The only way that she and Gould resembled each other was that they had matching braces. "H'lo," she said, around about four pounds of gum. Looking accusingly at her father, she added, "I don't see any books."

Instead of backhanding her for her rudeness, he pointed toward the closed office door. "Honey, they're in there."

"Go ahead," I said. "The light's on the right. Look around while I talk to your dad for a minute."

She went toward the door as if she expected Freddie and his iron fingernails to be behind it. But she finally opened it and turned on the light and went inside.

"She just freaked out when I told her she could come over and see your place," Gould whispered.

"I could tell," I was thinking. But I said, "Glad to do it." Then I looked at his attaché case. "Did you bring it?"

"Sure." He lifted the attaché case and set it on the mail

table and opened it. Then he whispered again. "Anybody finds out you've got this thing, I'm gonna have to say you stole it off my desk today."

"I understand. No problem."

There were two stuffed-full legal-sized manila folders in the attaché case. Gould lifted one out, leafed through it, gave me a momentarily confused look, and put it back. Bringing out the other one, he glanced in it. "Yeah. Here you go." He handed it to me. "These things get copied but, damn, they get pissed if they get out of the department."

"I'll guard it with my life."

He closed the attaché case and set it on the floor by the mail table. I stuck the file he gave me in the drawer.

Then we went into my office.

Started, anyway. Gould tugged at my sleeve when we were about halfway there. "Listen, could you give her one of your books? And sign it?" He stuck his hand in his pocket. "I'll pay you for it. But it'd tickle her to death to think you just up and gave her one of your books because you wanted to."

I suddenly realized that I liked this silly little shit. His daughter ought to get a swift kick, or two. But he was a nice guy. "Put your damned money away," I said.

Celeste stood with her feet crossed and her hands behind her back, chewing her gum and looking at the things on the wall as if she'd just realized that her training bra was too loose. How the devil did she handle the gum and those braces in the same mouth, I wondered. Obviously, she had some kind of talent.

Gould said, "Isn't this something, honey?"

She squinted over at me. "You don't look like an author."

Gould shot me an embarrassed, apologizing look. "Now, honey, how are authors supposed to look, anyway?"

She shrugged.

I figured the next thing out of her mouth was going to be "Do you know Isaac Asimov?"

I was wrong. It was her gum, while she gave a disappointed look at the original cover artwork for *Flag Planet*. Then she sucked it back into her mouth with no discernible braces problem at all, and said, "Do you know Isaac Asimov?"

"No. I've never met him."

She gave her father an "I told you so" look. Then she pointed. "What's that thing?"

"Nebula Award," I said.

"Hey!" Gould said.

"What's that?" Celeste asked.

"Just a little token of recognition by my peers."

"It's like the Academy Award, but for science fiction," Gould whispered to her.

"Hmmm," she said.

I really liked him now. The quality of his kid wasn't exactly impressing me, but he got A+ in flattery.

Celeste looked at my prized *Omni* montage. "That's just a bunch of stuff pasted together."

Gould was getting embarrassed. "Listen, honey. Here's Mr. Morris's books in this shelf." Pushing at her shoulder, he terminated her art critic career.

I said, "How about a Coke, Celeste?"

"Don't you have any Diet Dr Pepper?"

"Afraid I don't. It's Diet Coke, though."

"Ugh!"

"That'll be fine," Gould said. "She'll love it."

"How about you, Lieutenant? Would you have a beer with me?"

Celeste gave him a total put-down look.

"Yeah," he said defiantly. "That sounds terrific. I'm off duty. A beer."

"Just look around anywhere," I said, and left them there.

On the way to the kitchen, I took a detour and stopped by the mail table. Taking the folder out of the drawer, I dropped to one knee and traded it for the one Gould had put back in his attaché case.

Then I brought a glass of ice for the Coke, and glasses for the beer on a tray into the office.

"Don't you have any straws?" Celeste said.

"Pour it in the glass and drink it," Gould told her.

"What are you reading now?" I asked.

Her answer almost knocked me down. "One of yours— *The Golden Spire.*"

"Do you like it?"

Big shrug. "I don't see why they ever landed on that planet in the first place. But maybe it'll get better."

Gould started to try to ease over her gaffe, but I waved him off. "If they hadn't, there wouldn't have been much of a story."

"Couldn't you have written about why they didn't land?"

"I guess I could have," I said, just about surprised out of my socks. I hadn't intended this to get to the sitting-down-and-wasting-a-lot-of-time stage, but now I motioned Gould onto the loveseat and sat down in my desk chair, not disturbing Celeste in her slouch in front of the book-shelves.

I said, "Have you read anything else of mine?"

Shrug. "I guess."

"What?"

"Well. *Varig's World.* And *Trial Sleep.* And *Shuttlemaster.* Like that."

"What'd you think?"

"Well, when they do that matter-transmission, like when they go in that machine on one world and come out of a machine on another world, like in *Trial Sleep*, are they really the same people? Or do they just think they are?"

I couldn't believe it. This kid was talking as if she was going to grow up to be John W. Campbell.

I got into it. Really got into it. I had figured on a half hour of excruciating boredom. It turned into three hours of some of the most enjoyable talk I'd had in months.

The kid was naive, of course. And she had a few years to go before she could really be an authority, but she was actually thinking!

The only problem was when she asked me what I was working on now. It's kind of hard to explain to your brand-new Number One Fan that, suddenly, you can't get past "CHAPTER TWENTY-THREE," so I lied and said, "Nothing." And hoped that it really was a lie.

I ended up sending her home with an armload of books, some of them mine and signed, but some of them other people's too. She got to me enough that I even gave her my copy of Simak's *Way Station*—which was not as much of a supreme sacrifice as it may sound since I had the copy of it I swiped from the high school library.

After they left, I settled down with my bootleg copy of the police file on Gene's murder.

I had some idea of what I was getting into, but there was stuff in the investigation file that I would just as soon I hadn't seen.

Pictures of Gene's body, for example.

They were just Xeroxes of the real photos, but they were still grim.

I leafed through to the autopsy report and very carefully avoided the sketches and photo copies that came with it, but muddled through the description of the wounds that detailed the fact that one bullet took him just about at the middle of the chin, another in the upper left chest, and the other two very close together in the sternum.

That's heavy death.

On Tuesday morning, the day after the killing, according to the reports, the convenience store clerk had seen the story about the killing on TV and thought over what he might have seen and called the cops. They found the gun in the Dumpster. Before noon the next day—Wednesday—they had a positive ID on the prints on the gun and Roy Purdy was in jail.

During the interim, though, they pulled together a hell of a lot of information about a hell of a lot of people. They interviewed neighbors of the people most closely involved with Gene, and all the people who had worked at Morris, Purdy Properties, Ltd., and the possible suspects themselves. And boiled it down like this:

Morris, Mel—Victim's brother; lots of bad blood for years; Prior record: juvenile—probation—records sealed, but when asked, subject freely said it was possession of controlled substance at age 15; car theft—dismissed; DWI—probation; Subject threatened victim on several occasions, latest being two days before perpetration.

Morris, Grace—Victim's wife; inherits big money; unhappy marriage; no Priors.

Morris, Jane—Victim's sister-in-law; claims attempted rape by victim two days before perpetration—no medical report—no police report; no Priors.

Purdy, Roy—Victim's business partner, blames victim for bankruptcy—several fights, threats, latest one on day before perpetration; wife had affair with victim—Purdy knew it; no Prior record, but mention in DV Police Reports 8/19/84, 12/21/85, 2/14/86, 4/27/86.

Purdy, Elaine—Victim's business partner's wife; had affair with victim, apparently terminated by victim early summer '86—she wasn't happy about it—employees heard her threaten victim on at least two occasions in person at office, latest 4 days before perpetration: no Prior record.

Perryman, David—Victim and Perryman both worked same time for Perryman's father, Kent Perryman, who suicided '76 over allegations made by victim to State Bar, which ruined elder Perryman's law practice; younger Perryman blamed victim for father's death; latest verified contact 4 days before perpetration in parking lot of Harris County Courthouse—Perryman had just lost suit against victim brought by Sam and Bella Hauser—confrontation broken up by security guards who say victim taunted Perryman—didn't get to fists, but Perryman very angry, made threats—no police record/involvement.

Lacie, Sallie—Affair with victim approximately Dec 85 to Mar 86; native Louisiana; in town since Jun 85; divorced; no Priors; 22 Mar 86 patrol cars responded to calls from 5152 and 5158 Monte Cassino reporting gunshots at 5154—Lacie's townhouse—shots evident in entryway and front door, but no evidence of personal injury—no complainant came forth—Lacie told investigating officers she heard a noise and she shot—no charges—no further action; at time, according to police report, neighbors described man they believed she shot at but no positive ID and Lacie stuck by claim of prowler; checked today with neighbors—two of them ID victim's photo as man who they saw frequently at Lacie's and believe same she shot at—this one did more than yell at him and make threats.

Hauser, Sam—Prominent ranch and political figure; indicted, convicted, probated in connection with Lake Bountiful time-share scam; Victim was involved with Hauser, but no evidence he was in scam and not charged; Hauser filed personal and corporate bankruptcy Feb 86 after trial; made repeated threats against victim; Pursued him in court until recently with no luck.

There was a list of the cars owned by everybody, prompted by the clerk's seeing a gray car. Grace Morris had a gray 1982 Pontiac. David Perryman had a beige 1984 Toronado "which might look grayish on a rainey [sic] day." Roy Purdy had a blue-gray 1986 Cadillac. Elaine Purdy had a gray 1986 Buick. Jane Morris had a silver-gray 1983 Oldsmobile. Mel Morris had a red 1986 Mustang convertible.

Then there were the alibis. Spotted here and there among the summaries, which were handwritten by various police officers, were terse, hard notes done in the same all-cap no-nonsense printing. Curious, I determined that they were made by Lieutenant—then Sergeant—Gould. It would seem that, although he might look cute and roly-poly, he didn't necessarily do his job that way.

> Mel Morris says he was on telephone with editor—Joel Younger, Sr. Editor, Hartman Press, Inc., NY. Called Younger. Verified time and length of call.
> OK

> Roy Purdy says he was at Medical Center Bank. Teller Rita Preble verifies.
> ARE YOU SURE?
> She says so.
> HOW DOES SHE KNOW WHAT TIME IT WAS? GET PROOF—NOT JUST

SOMEBODY'S VERIFICATION.
Somebody's verification was OK for Mel Morris's alibi.
SHE'S HERE. CHECK IT.
Yes, sir, Sgt. Gould!

Sam Hauser—stroke victim. In a wheelchair. No way he could go out and shoot somebody.
OK

David Perryman broke ankle 25 Oct 86, skiing in Colorado. Crutches. He's out.
CHECK WITH HIS DOCTOR
Doctor H. M. Casey verifies no way Perryman could navigate without his crutches.
OK—NEXT TIME, DO THAT FIRST

That last entry stopped me for a moment. Strike David off my list. And it occurred to me that I could have saved myself a lot of trouble about the other people if I had had this file before I ran off private-eyeing.

There was a break in the alibis summaries now, because some of the pages in the file were out of order.

The next thing in line explained those "DV Police Reports" that were mentioned in the Roy Purdy information.

"DV" stood for "Domestic Violence," I discovered, with some shock. Four times the neighbors had called the cops because Roy and Elaine were having big fights. On one occasion her jaw was dislocated and she was "transported" to a hospital. On two of the others things sounded damned gory, but not bad enough to require treatment. Elaine refused to press charges each time.

I sat back and thought about this. Elaine definitely had a motive to kill Gene—a couple of them—he'd cheated them out of their money and he'd stopped cheating with her. Maybe she figured that she had a motive to take care of her husband, too—he was a wife-beater. What better way to take care of them both than to use Roy's gun to kill Gene?

I wondered what Crenshaw would have Lupe say to me about it if I mentioned this to him. I decided not to.

I kept on leafing through the papers.

There were copies of those "Priors" of mine, of course. Except there wasn't any paperwork on my juvenile dope charge because the records had been sealed. With or without paperwork, though, that one still pissed me off when I thought about it. I had taken it entirely on myself because I was only fifteen, and spending a night in Juvenile Hall and getting hassled and put on probation was easier than trying to make anybody believe what had actually happened—that it was Gene's grass I got caught with—particularly when he was the one who turned me in.

The report on the car theft charge, however, gave me a little feeling of personal triumph because it was one of the few times when Gene messed up and didn't really put it to me. The report noted that there was strong cause to believe not only that I was innocent, but that the car had actually been stolen by my brother and driven by him to my apartment in Austin to lay blame on me. There wasn't quite enough evidence to proceed against him, though.

The drunk-driving charge? Well, what can you say? It was a night when they were going for a new DWI record, and the sticker on my back window that said I belonged to that local organization that makes a big deal of unselfishly giving money to the widows and orphans of police officers was expired.

Slogging on through the file, I began to wonder when the cops had time to do anything else but this kind of paperwork stuff—not exactly an original idea.

In the back of my mind I was also wondering just why I

had the distinct feeling that there was something in this file that Gould hadn't wanted to turn over to me. If not, why check the two files as he did, and then put back the one he had first started to give me? What was it? And where was the rest of the alibi stuff?

I was thinking about that when the telephone rang.

It was Zoe.

"Sorry it's so late," she said. "I was going to just leave a message on your machine."

"Maybe I should beep or something."

She chuckled. "I ran onto something else that you might be interested in. Thought I might give you a call, even if it is late."

"I'm glad you did. What did you find?"

"Elaine Maris's engagement announcement. In June of 1975."

"Okay," I said, somewhat absently, as I continued to rummage through the file.

"She was going to marry Thomas John Crenshaw."

That got my attention. "Back then? You're kidding!"

"No, I'm not. But then, in December 1975, her wedding announcement was in the paper." She paused for big drama. "Guess who the happy groom actually turned out to be?"

"Okay. Who?"

"William Roy Purdy. And then a week later Mary Ann Sprague announced her engagement—to our friend, Thomas John Crenshaw."

"I'll be damned!"

"I thought you might find it interesting."

At the moment I was finding something else more interesting. It was the next page of alibis. I scanned down it. It noted that Sallie Lacie was ill from major surgery and follow-up treatment and was off the cops' list.

But what really grabbed me was the rest of the page.

Grace, Elaine, and Jane, in that order, were each cleared. With the notation, "Newspaper Clipping." And Gould had marked "OK" under each one.

"Newspaper clipping?" What the hell did that mean?

"Mel?" Zoe said.

"Yeah."

She sounded a bit miffed. "I hope I'm not keeping you up."

"Sorry. I just got sidetracked for a moment."

"Jane's cleared!" I was thinking. I wouldn't worry, at this moment, about the fact that a hell of a lot of other people were, too.

"What this means, of course," Zoe was saying, "is that Elaine was going to marry Tom Crenshaw. But Roy Purdy came into the picture somehow, and she married him instead. And Tom married someone else. But after Roy was sent to prison for killing your brother, she and Tom bounced back together. Sounds very sweet, doesn't it? 'Childhood Sweethearts Reunite.'"

"Yeah," I said, paying attention, but still rummaging.

"I remembered something else, Mel. When I saw the announcements with Elaine's maiden name—Maris."

"Mm-hmm."

"Her father was Dudley Maris."

"Okay."

"Doesn't that name ring bells with you? You are a native, after all."

I was also suddenly finding that "Newspaper Clipping."

"Uh, bells?" I said, staring. "No."

"Great Texas Insurance. Surely you remember that."

I forced myself back to her. "Great Texas Insurance. Maybe that does do some bells. But I don't know why."

She sighed. "Everyone's so young. All right. In 1963 Great Texas Insurance folded. It was a huge scandal. And Elaine Maris's father, Dudley Maris, was the major stockholder and the CEO. He wasn't prosecuted, but they were broke, Mel. Stone broke. I remember Elaine's mother, Dorothy. She used to have the most wonderful parties. And then one day I saw her running the cash register at an Eckerd's Drugstore. That's how broke they were. I could never go back into that Eckerd's again, I felt so badly for her."

The newspaper clipping was getting to me. I said, "Yeah. Okay." And then, "Zoe, who's Peggy Cheatham?"

My sweet friend, Zoe, suddenly sounded as if I had asked her if she wore a jock strap. "Who?"

"Peggy Cheatham."

"Why in the world would you ask me who Peggy Cheatham is?"

"Her name's on this clipping."

Icily—"She tries to write a column for the other paper. What clipping?"

I described it to her. It was dated Wednesday, October 29, 1986.

The caption under the photograph was, "Three Girls About Town Arriving For An Elegant Monday Brunch at Dino's." The "Three Girls" were Jane, Elaine, and Grace.

"'Three Girls About Town'?" Zoe said scathingly. "That certainly sounds like Peggy Cheatham." She decided not to punish me any more and turned nice again. "Why in the world do you sound so concerned? Peggy's always doing things like that—lots of photographs. They keep her from having to write more than she can manage."

Suddenly she drew in her breath so sharply that I could hear it. "Wednesday, October 29, 1986? And it says they were there on Monday? Then that photograph was taken on the day your brother was killed. No wonder you're concerned."

"Yeah, I guess," I said, studying the photograph some

more. It was a photocopy of a newspaper photo, of course, so it wasn't exactly crystalline, but they looked very chic and happy.

Something minor but shocking occurred to me. "Listen. Why would they run this article, anyway? They just got through with the big story about Gene's murder. And the day this ran, they must have been running the story about Roy being arrested, too."

"Oh, please, Mel," Zoe said. "Surely you don't think that Peggy Cheatham"—sniff—"and I are accorded as much importance as what they call 'Hard News.' How did you think it worked? That maybe I go running down to production and yell, 'Hold the presses! Lynn didn't attend Lilah's party, after all.'" She dropped the sarcasm and started sounding a bit mournful, as if that was something she had always wanted to do. "Things like my column and the things Peggy puts out are all printed ahead of time. The whole section is."

"Okay," I said, feeling somewhat stupid for not having realized that. But something else was explained—why I hadn't noticed the photo and column in the paper and why Jane hadn't proudly pointed it out to me—we were mostly interested in the front page at the time.

I looked at the photograph. It was from a time when Jane and I were still together, and I had a little stab of pain over that.

Jane was in the middle, between Elaine and Grace. She was wearing the dress I gave her to celebrate her getting the Wortham Theater Center commission. It was black-and-white silk. The first time she wore it we were going to go out to celebrate. But we celebrated at home, instead. Those were still the good days.

Abruptly I pulled myself out of that.

The column itself. There was only the barest mention in the body of it about Jane and Grace and Elaine. Most of it was

froth about Dino's being in a frenzy because the revered
maître d', Joseph Malducci, was retiring and moving back to
Italy and this was his going-away party.

I mentioned that to Zoe.

She sounded really mournful as she said, "Oh, of course.
I remember that. It was so sad. He went home to Rome to
retire and dropped dead of a heart attack not a week later. And
he was such a nice man."

I studied the smudged photograph copy some more. Jane
was holding what appeared to be a long-stemmed rose. Elaine
probably was, too. The important thing, though, was the
clock. It was an ornate wall clock, so close behind Grace's head
that she might have been wearing it as a hat. The time it
showed was nine-forty-five.

"Arriving For An Elegant Monday Brunch," the caption
said. That was the "Newspaper Clipping" alibi. They were
arriving for brunch at Dino's, in the Galleria, at 9:45 on the
day Gene was killed—at 10 A.M.

I had a sudden flash in my head of my list as it would look
now:

CANDIDATES LIST

Mel Morris—alibied
Roy Purdy—Alibied about three years late
Grace Morris—Alibied—brunch at Dino's
David Perryman—Unable—broken ankle
Elaine Purdy—Alibied—brunch at Dino's
Sallie Lacie—Unable—ill
Sam Hauser—Unable—stroke
Jane Morris—Alibied—brunch at Dino's

That kind of took care of the field, didn't it? It was a
candidates list without a candidate left.

Except that one of them was hanging up there at the top
without a capital *A*.

"Mel? You're gone again," Zoe said. "What in the world's bothering you?"

"I think I'm just tired, Zoe. I think that's all."

"I called you too late. I'm sorry."

"No. I appreciate your calling. You've been a big help. I mean it."

"You're sure everything's all right?"

"I'm sure."

We hung up and, to myself, I changed that to "Maybe," and went on looking through the file.

The detail was unending, it seemed. Copies of reports on the interviews with Sallie Lacie's neighbors, with the convenience store clerk, a transcript of the interrogation of Roy Purdy, etc. Etc.

I could be all night wading through this mess.

I went into the kitchen and got another beer and came back and sat down and stared at the mass of paper.

Why the hell did Gould switch the folders as he did? What difference did it make which one I got?

Obvious. There was something in the file he didn't want me to see. So he had pulled it out of one copy and . . .

I pounced on the file, went to the back of it.

And there they were—two folded sheets of paper.

He had done the most natural thing in the world. He had pulled these out of one folder and folded them and stuck them in the back of the one he intended to keep.

For a moment I was tickled because I had figured it out.

Then I unfolded the sheets of paper.

The first one was a copy of a body-shop repair ticket. For a 1983 Oldsmobile—Jane's. The repair job was to replace the front bumper and straighten and repair the left front fender. The person leaving the car and authorizing the repairs was

"Mel Morris." The time-in stamp was clearly visible. It showed, "27 OCT 86 11:58 AM"

Damn!

Then I told myself to take it easy. So I had Jane's silver-gray Olds on the morning Gene was killed. So what? That didn't necessarily mean anything.

Did it?

"Hell, no!" I told myself.

And went to the second sheet.

No "Hell, no!" now. This was gooseflesh time.

It was a copy of a telex. From the New York City Police Department to the Houston Police. On 29 October 1986, at the request of the Houston cops—Sgt. R. P. Gould, to be specific—a New York City police officer had visited the Hartman Press offices and met with Senior Editor Joel Younger to get written verification of the information Younger had given a Houston homicide cop by telephone on the morning of 28 October.

The New York City police officer hadn't been able to get that verification. After more thought, and checking with his secretary, Younger recalled that, in the middle of his long telephone conversation with one Mel Morris in Houston, Texas, the secretary had informed him that there was an urgent call for him from one of the company V.P.s who was in London.

Younger put Morris on hold. Then his secretary went on the line to advise Morris that the London call would take at least fifteen minutes. She said that Younger would call him back when it was finished. But instead of hanging up, Morris stated that he knew how busy Younger was and wouldn't take the chance of something else coming up and keeping him from calling back. Morris said that he would just "sit here on hold" until Younger got back to him and they could get their business completed.

According to Younger's secretary's log, he talked with
London from 8:49 A.M. to 9:12 A.M., and Morris held for that
time.

At the bottom of the telex copy was some more of
Gould's harsh, terse printing:

KILLING AT 10:01 A.M. HOUSTON TIME
9:01 NEW YORK TIME. MORRIS ON HOLD
AND UNACCOUNTED—FOR FROM 9:49
TO 10:12—23 MINUTES. MURDER SCENE
4–6 MINUTES FROM MORRIS'S RESI-
DENCE.

Below that, there was another, somewhat later note:

DOESN'T MEAN ANYTHING—WE'VE GOT
PURDY NOW

The gooseflesh was eating me alive.
"Shit!" I said aloud.
That list of mine would look like this now:

CANDIDATES LIST

Mel Morris—NO ALIBI
Roy Purdy—Alibied about three years late
Grace Morris—Alibied—brunch at Dino's
David Perryman—Unable—broken ankle
Elaine Purdy—Alibied—brunch at Dino's
Sallie Lacie—Unable—ill
Sam Hauser—Unable—stroke
Jane Morris—Alibied—brunch at Dino's

Lieutenant Gould undoubtedly had a Candidates List of
his own. It would look just like this one.

* * *

It was almost eleven o'clock. But I drove by Jane's.

There was a shiny brown BMW in her guest parking spot.

I looked at it for a while.

Then I drove away.

Then I drove away.

CHAPTER 9

Galveston.

Fifty-odd miles south of Houston on the only stretch of highway I know of anywhere which has been continuously under construction since World War II. Site of the greatest natural disaster in U.S. history—the 1900 hurricane that killed more than six thousand people. Site of the greatest concentration of buildings with cast-iron facades outside of old New York. It's an old town, as towns go in this part of the country, and once it was going to be the major port and the major city, but Houston stole all that away. Now it's just a little tourist town on an island. A mix of genteel shabbiness and glitz in the daytime that looks smearily attractive on a rainy night.

But the neighborhood is nice because the Gulf of Mexico is there.

I parked near the seawall and pulled on a windbreaker and stuck a pint bottle of Wild Turkey—or whatever it is that passes for pint-size these days—in my pocket and walked out onto the longest jetty.

There was wind off the water—I guess there were

thunderstorms somewhere out in the Gulf on the edge of whatever weather system was stalled over southeast Texas—and it must have been high tide because there was lots of spray thrown up by waves hitting the jagged chunks of junk concrete that had been dumped to build the jetty. The wind carried it at me like little droplets of rain coming from the wrong direction—straight-on, instead of down.

It was after midnight now, and the place was deserted except for an ancient black woman sitting about thirty feet back from the end of the jetty all huddled up in an aluminum-framed deck chair. In the dim light cast by the pole lamps set every thirty feet or so along the jetty, her crackly yellow rain slicker glowed as if it were made of gold as old as she was. She was fishing off the side.

"Any luck?" I said.

She chuckled. "Lots of luck." Waving a bird's-claw hand at the red plastic bucket sitting beside her, she showed me that it was more than a quarter full of squirming fish of some kind.

Something must have twitched at her line because she whipped the hand back to her fishing rod and waited with frozen intensity.

I looked back toward the town. In the darkness at the base of the seawall, there was a ragged gray line of froth sent up by breaking waves. Above the top of the seawall glittered the lights of the hotels and motels and restaurants, which were almost deserted now because October was not high or even medium tourist season, but the lights were always there in the hope that one might come along.

I had been here before. Fifty-odd miles isn't too far to drive if your big brother has been a shit or you've had a fight with the girl you'll always love or your marriage to the girl you'll always love has gone to hell. Or if the girl you'll always love has decided to remarry and your big brother has come clawing up out of his grave to torment you again. Not when you can drive it and then climb down the seawall and walk out onto the jetty and sit down and let the ocean sounds throb and moan at you.

"He was just playin' with me," the old woman said, relaxed again.

I pulled the bottle out of my pocket and twisted off the seal and the top and handed it to her. She took a hit and then another. "Whew! That's the right stuff!" she said. And took yet another drink.

Then she handed it back to me. "You better take this. That stuff's too good to let a stranger have hold of it for too long."

Suddenly she squealed and started threshing at the air with her fishing rod. "Got 'im this time!"

I watched her reel the fish in until it was out of the water and flashing silver as she dragged it up over the concrete chunks.

Then I went on to the end of the jetty and climbed down until I could sit down a couple of feet above the reach of most of the waves, completely out of sight of Galveston and the old woman and everything but the sea.

The air was probably 75 degrees or so, and the water may have been a little warmer. But the wind and the damp made it all feel very cold.

I warmed myself up with some of the booze. "Whew! That's the right stuff!" I told the Gulf of Mexico.

And I sat there and got soaked and chilled and shivering, and took a therapeutic hit at the bottle from time to time, and lost myself in the throbbing and pounding and hissing of the waves, and thought about Gene.

He was evil.

There's that stuff you read about babies. How they've got it made inside the womb. Then they're expelled into a completely different world, and it's a hell of a shock to them.

And here's where the stuff you read leaves off and I begin.

Probably they hate it at first.

But pretty quickly they figure out that it's not so bad, after all. In fact, they've got it made. They're king of the world. They squall and somebody jumps. They shit and somebody jumps. The whole world exists for them. Period.

Somewhere along the way, though, they get off that idea. They find out that, in fact, the world doesn't exist for them at all; the truth is that they're a very small cog in it, and the best thing they can do is learn how to fit in with all the other little cogs and help make the big machine keep on creaking along.

Most of them make the transition okay.

But I wonder if, once in a while, one of them doesn't.

Like Gene.

Mom and Dad were nice, ordinary, loving, standard people, with ordinary faults. Mom wasn't much of a cook, and she tried too hard to be one. Dad was mechanically a dolt. Mom thought masturbation was the chief evil of the world. Dad thought voting Republican was.

But somehow they must have messed up in getting the idea across to Baby Gene that he wasn't really the king of the world, after all.

Probably they tried. Not consciously, of course. But parents have their ways of getting it across to the kids about who really runs things. Mom and Dad must have slipped up somewhere, though.

Even so, it should have become abundantly clear to Gene that his reign was over when he was about five and I came along.

But it didn't.

I've read somewhere about studies they've done of baby animals. There are "windows" during which certain things can be taught them by their mothers. I don't remember the figures exactly, but, for example, say that it's between fourteen days old and seventeen days old that kittens can be taught by the mother cat to use a sandbox. If she gets her timing right, everything's okay with no problem, but if she misses that time for some reason, they'll never get the idea.

Maybe Mom and Dad missed the "window" during which Gene could have been taught he wasn't king, and that meant he'd never get the idea at all.

I came along, and he instantly hated me because what is it that a king hates most of all? Another king in the same place.

I don't remember any of the early stuff, of course. But I do remember Mom and Dad telling cute stories to their friends about Gene's having been jealous of his little brother, "but he really loved him."

Bullshit!

When I was twelve, I tried to kill him.

It was that bad. I kept telling myself that, in less than a year, he'd be going off to college and be gone most of the time. But he seemed to have realized that, also, and it was as if he was trying to get in a whole five years' worth on me before he went.

I was scared all the time. There are lots of things that big kids can do to little kids that don't show. Most of them Gene seemed to know about or be able to improvise. I was getting crazy.

Besides that, Grandma had finally caught me stealing out of her purse. I tried to tell her—and Mom and Dad—that Gene made me do it. But he just widened out those scary, empty eyes and looked wounded and said, "You mean the kid is actually saying I'd want him to steal money from an old lady?"

For once I stuck to my story. But he stuck to his wounded innocence, too. Mom and Dad and Grandma acted as if they were trying to believe me, but after that, if I was anywhere in the neighborhood, Grandma wouldn't even go to the bathroom without tucking her purse under her arm and taking it with her.

Gene had this look to him that, even though I'd grown up

with it—or maybe because I had—never stopped giving me gooseflesh. Mostly it was those eyes of his that were so palely gray that they just didn't even seem to be there. In the funny papers, on Little Orphan Annie and Sandy, that's kind of cute. But a person with blank holes where his eyes ought to be is scary as hell. And every time he looked at me, I wanted to shiver.

We went on vacation almost every summer to Colorado, and times like that should have been great, but it just gave Gene more time to work on me.

While we were there, that summer when I was twelve, I decided to kill him.

He was going to some kind of teen party down in the town that night. I crawled under the rented car and unscrewed a brake line because I knew from TV that cutting them was stupid. Pretty soon he left, and I sat there in the cabin trying to get interested in a new science fiction serial in *Galaxy* magazine as the car drove out. And I realized that how scared I had been of Gene was nothing compared with the scared I was now.

I tried to hold my breath.

I tried to figure out how to tell Mom and Dad about it, so they could do something. But they were off walking on the mountain somewhere because, on these vacations, they liked to spend a lot of time by themselves.

I wished that I could be the one to die.

A couple of miles down the twisting road, the car crashed.

The noise seemed to shake the whole mountain.

Mom and Dad never got tired of telling how scared I was and how I ran the whole way down to the crashed car, trying to save my big brother. They were right and wrong, and I always wished they'd shut up about it.

The car was a mess. But Gene just had a broken arm and a cut on his forehead that left a permanent scar.

After I had time to get over feeling guilty and relieved that he wasn't really killed, I decided to make the best of it. I told Gene I did it. And that he'd better start leaving me alone, or next time it wouldn't just be a warning. He acted as if he didn't believe me. But he did. He left me alone for a long time after that.

It was better from then until he went away to college.

But his times at home gradually got bad again after that.

At least, though, Mom and Dad and even Grandma started wising up. I was a pretty good kid most of the time, it turned out. Except when Gene was home. And finally they stopped automatically thinking I was the bad guy.

He hated that, of course.

When I started going out with girls, he really started messing around with my life again. It's amazing what impact a good-looking big brother, home from college for the weekend, can have on some fourteen-year-old girl you're trying to impress.

I wasn't so bad myself. I didn't get fat, I got practically no zits. And I was playing football. But about ten minutes of your big brother with "those cute eyes" sitting around telling cute stories about how much you wet the bed and what an awful time they had stopping you from picking your nose, and most fourteen-year-old girls start getting queasy.

He was gone most of the time, though.

But not enough of the time. When I was fifteen and he was home for the summer, he got pissed-off at me because I wouldn't give him some tickets I had to a rock concert, and he hid some grass in my scooter. Then he had a "fit of conscience," which I guess was a warm-up for when he'd go to the State Bar and ruin Kent Perryman, and showed up at the Summit, where they were having the concert, and pointed out my scooter to the security guards, saying nobly that he was just doing it to try to get his kid brother off drugs.

I spent a really brilliant night in Juvenile Hall and got

probation, without bothering to try to get anybody to believe what really happened.

Mom and Dad, though, were beginning to see that something funny was going on between Gene and me and didn't give me half the hell that I thought they would, mostly because Gene hadn't been able to cover up the fact that he turned me in, and they thought it was very funny that he had known the stuff was there—and I did a great silent, suffering martyr job, of course. Even Grandma was supportive enough the next time I went to her house to mow her lawn that she left me alone in the same room with her purse for a couple of minutes while she went to get cookies out of the oven.

This drug situation was one of the few times in his life when Gene made a serious miscalculation about a victim—he hadn't been paying attention to the fact that I was growing up fast, and I took care of him myself. Those empty eyes of his got very wide when I caught him in the garage and he suddenly realized that I was already as big as he was—and a whole lot angrier. I beat the crap out of him and enjoyed every second of it. I enjoyed it even more when he went dragging into the house and Mom said, "Gene! What happened to your face?"

He said, "Mel jumped me in the garage. From behind." Dad walked into the kitchen, and he said it again.

Mom and Dad exchanged a look, and Dad said, "If it was from behind, why's your nose bleeding?"

Mom handed him a roll of paper towels and said, "Don't drip blood all over my house."

Dad said, "Boys will be boys," and went back in to watch the rest of the Astros game.

Gene pretty much let me, personally, alone after that. But he still loved making me look like a fool in front of the girls I was dating. For a while I was very philosophical about it. If I couldn't hang on to a girl through an encounter with my brother, I didn't want to hang onto her anyway. At least once, when a girl hinted that she wouldn't exactly barf if I asked her to go steady, I told her to wait until after the next time my brother was in town. Then we'd talk about it.

And suddenly I was sixteen, and there was Jane.

Gene was home for Thanksgiving, and Jane was coming over, after her family did the turkey, to watch the big game with us. I was terrified. There was no way I could be philosophical about her. I started thinking about brake lines again.

But she was absolutely wonderful. She put down my big, impressive, pre-law brother like he was Alpo.

I was in heaven. Talk about going steady!

But things were a little different now. Before this the girls were just kids to Gene. Now it had gotten to the point that he could almost legitimately try to be my rival. It wasn't a twenty-year-old man playing word games with a fifteen-year-old little girl. It was a twenty-one-year-old seeing that sixteen-year-old Jane was close enough to being a woman that it didn't make much difference.

When he was home, he started calling her and asking her out behind my back. He showed up at a couple of dances at which he should have been embarrassed to be seen, and played cutting-in games.

She did some more Alpo. It was wonderful!

Then we had a party at my house. It was spring vacation for Gene—something Jane and I overlooked when we planned things—and he was there. Sometime in the evening he caught her alone on the terrace and put the moves on her. Very seriously. Today we'd probably call it attempted rape.

Back then it was just the tough moves.

I walked out there with some more punch just as she was pushing him off and, once again, I beat the shit out of him, with him claiming all the time that Jane had come onto him.

His big problem was that Mom and Dad had happened to see just about the whole thing from their bedroom window.

He was Kibbles 'n' Bits now, the son-of-a-bitch.

For the first time in my life, I was proven totally innocent in a conflict with Gene. Mom and Dad finally had the proof of their own eyes that I was a good guy.

The following couple of weeks were probably the best in my life.

Then they were killed when the gas leaked and blew up the house.

Gene pretty much stopped direct conflict with me after that. Instead he got himself in position to strip a bunch of their estate. The only big direct thing he did after they were killed was to steal a Corvette and park it in the middle of the night in the garage under the apartment Jane and I had during our first year at Texas. Then he got the law school buddy who owned it to call the cops and report it stolen and say that he'd seen me messing around it.

There was a little hassle over it, but the buddy—who's a state senator now and a big wheel on the Legislative Ethics Committee—didn't remember all his lines just right, and nobody took it seriously, and it was dismissed.

That was the last time I beat Gene up. And I didn't even bother to do a good job of it. He didn't deserve it.

My dogmeat brother.

"My frozen ass!" I said to Galveston Bay.

I needed to get away from there and get warm again. But there was still some Wild Turkey left, and I warmed myself up a little with that.

And besides, that's not quite the end of my story about Gene.

He never stopped coming on to Jane.

She put him down every way a woman can put down a man, and he kept on.

I had no intention of inviting him to our wedding, but Grandma couldn't stand not having all the "family" there, so I gave in. He was already married to Grace, but he came on to Jane at the reception.

He never stopped.

On the Friday afternoon before he was killed, he made his biggest try ever. He went by her studio and talked his way in by telling her that he wanted to buy a piece of her work for the Morris, Purdy office—which we'd heard was going under, but didn't know for certain yet—and he "and his secretary" had stopped by to look.

Jane opened the gate and, when he came around to the bay where she was working, she found out the secretary wasn't with him. He told her how he'd always known she wanted him, and finally he couldn't stand her putting him off any more, whether she was married to his brother or not.

Then he went after her.

She's not exactly a wimp, my Jane, and she fought like hell, and she had all her equipment around her to help. In fact, she would probably have meatballed the son-of-a-bitch with her cutting torch if he hadn't finally got away from her and run out of the front gate.

I was on a fitness kick about then, riding a bike every afternoon, and dropping by Jane's studio so I could stuff it in the trunk of her car and moan while she drove us home.

I saw Gene barreling out of there and went in and found out what had happened.

I was pissed.

I jumped into Jane's car and damned near wrecked it getting to Gene's office and pulled him halfway over his desk by his tie and said as many rough and emasculating and threatening things as I could manage. And slapped his god-damned face a time or two for humiliation and then shoved the employees aside and got the hell out of there.

Then a couple of days later somebody killed him, and it couldn't have happened to a nicer guy.

And a couple of months later Jane and I started figuring out that our marriage was falling apart.

It was. And it did.

The Wild Turkey was gone. I was freezing.

I climbed back up onto the top of the jetty and discovered that the old lady was gone, too. But the lights of the town were just as bright and glittery and meaningless as ever.

At the car I managed on about the fifteenth shivering try to get the key into the trunk lock, and found a towel and a pair of gym shorts and took another thirty tries to get the door open. I got rid of my waterproof windbreaker and my soaked shirt and shoes and socks while I stood in the street, and then got in and started the motor and wondered how many hours it would take to get heat. I squirmed around and got rid of my wet jeans and pulled the shorts on, just to make the cops happy, in case, and dried off as well as I could with the towel that smelled like buzzard sweat, and started home.

About the time the heater started living up to its name and I started not shaking and was trying to figure out how to stop someplace and get some dry cigarettes without getting arrested, I brought the story of my big brother, Gene, and me completely up-to-date.

He needed killing like few people do.

I used to think I had an alibi.

I drove by Jane's again.

That goddamned BMW was still there.

I went home.

The telephone.

Lieutenant Gould.

"Gee, Mr. Morris, did I wake you up?"

"I don't know." Yes. The clock said 9:11. And there was a lot of light. I hadn't seen this much light in days.

"Hey, sorry. I'll call you back later."

"It's okay. I'm up. I was needing to get up."

"You sure?"

"Yeah."

"Well, I didn't mean to wake you up, Mr. Morris. But my kid just practically completely freaked out over how nice you were to her last night. I wanted to thank you."

"She's a good kid. She thinks." It was 9:11, about to flip over to 9:12. Why the hell hadn't I set the alarm, I wondered. I got up and went to the windows and stared. Blue sky. Blue sky everywhere.

"Listen, you have a chance to read over that file yet?" Gould asked.

"Yeah."

"Something, isn't it?"

"Yeah."

"Bet you never saw anything like that before. Bet you think we cops don't do anything but fill out reports."

"There was a lot of it, Lieutenant."

"Any ideas?"

"I don't know. There was a hell of a lot of material there."

"No shit! And that was a short one. Just a couple of days, and we had the gun with Roy Purdy's fingerprints on it, and we didn't need to keep digging—we thought. You ought to see a real file that covers weeks. Months, sometimes. They're in boxes, not folders."

"I'll bet."

"No ideas, huh?"

"I don't know. Probably not. It looks like you covered everything."

"Covered everything? Listen, if we'd covered everything, Roy Purdy wouldn't've got framed."

"I guess not."

"Well, you keep thinking about it, Mr. Morris. Anything hits you, you give me a call."

"I thought you weren't interested. Cold trails and all that. I thought it was just ancient history to you, Lieutenant."

"Sure. It was. Still is, matter-of-fact, 'cause we're not

going out and busting our ass, or anything. But you were so interested I got curious. You know how it is."

"I guess so."

"You be sure and keep in touch. And thanks again for being so nice to my kid."

"My pleasure, Lieutenant."

I stared at the clear, blue sky. It wasn't raining. It looked as if clouds hadn't even been invented yet. It looked like a damned nice day for a drive.

Gould cheerily said, "Keep in touch, Mr. Morris."

"Sure thing."

CHAPTER 10

I should have been at home writing Great American Science Fiction.

Instead, I sat in the car with the top down and waited. And did some wondering about just what the hell I was doing here. But I had planned this. And going ahead with it was easier than just sitting around and stewing over things. Instead, I'd be on the move and stewing over things.

Why the hell did Gould call me this morning? To be a nice, grateful daddy? Maybe. But maybe just to keep me nervous.

That son-of-a-bitch Joel Younger! I left Hartman Press for a different publishing company on a hunch. I wasn't sure at the time that I wasn't making a big mistake, but I was damned glad now that I did it.

Instantly I felt bad. Joel wasn't a son-of-a-bitch. He was a damned nice guy, even if he did seem to think that it was galley proofs that Moses brought down from the mountain. The only real bitch I had with him was that his secretary was too efficient and he told too much of the truth.

I felt down on the left side of my seat again. For the

fiftieth time I verified that my .38 was positioned perfectly so
that it was both out of sight and instantly available.

What was I doing here? Who the hell knew?

What would Lt. Gould think about this? Who the hell
knew that, either? But I was probably going to find out.

Would he say, "Listen, Mr. Morris, my kid just practically
freaked out when I told her you went up to the prison to pick
up Roy Purdy."?

"You think too damned much," I told myself. And
wondered why I didn't put this damned thinking and energy
into finishing the new book.

For the fiftieth time, at least, I tried to think of somebody
else who ought to be on that "Candidates List." For the fiftieth
time every one I thought of was pushing detection right across
the line into science fiction.

There was another car waiting in this little strip of
parking lot. A very used '76 or '77 Oldsmobile Cutlass. All the
shine had worn off long ago, but the color was still that funny
shade that one minute you see as light blue, the next as light
green. Two women waited in the Olds. One of them was old
and as faded and worn-looking as the car; the other was young
and lithe, but her eyes were going the way of the older
woman's and there were already worry lines around her
mouth.

An inmate's mother and sister, I guessed. And then
amended it to mother and wife. A sister's eyes might have
gone like that, but the worry she felt wasn't the kind to etch in
so deeply around the mouth.

We didn't wave or smile. But we were aware of each
others' presence here and appreciated the company. I thought
of offering them some of the coffee I brought along in a
thermos, but didn't. Somehow any attempt at contact would
have broken the tenuous bond among us.

For the hundredth time I looked through the chain-link

fencing to see if anything was happening. For the hundredth time nothing was.

This was a release gate. Or maybe the release gate.

Nothing looked very much like a prison to me. I had always pictured prisons as being squat stone fortresses set away from everything in a place of bleakness and desolation. This was just a red brick building that might have been an elementary school, behind a chain-link fence that might have been put up to keep the kids from chasing softballs into traffic.

And it was practically downtown. A Blue Bell Ice Cream Company truck passed by and backed up for a delivery at the convenience store down the block on the other side. Above the treetops I could see the golden arches of a McDonald's sign.

There was movement in the Oldsmobile. The older woman clutched at the steering wheel and peered forward through the windshield. The younger one was grinding her shoulders into the seat back, and working on those lines around her mouth some more.

A door near the gate in the fence was being opened. A man emerged. His hard, wary face and his uniform were the first things that really looked "prison" to me.

He gestured with weary impatience, and a second man stepped out and looked around, squinting against the sunlight. He was carrying a brown paper grocery bag and wearing a jeans jacket and jeans that had that bright, unwashed, brand-new look to them.

I was sure that I'd have some more wait; this couldn't be Roy Purdy. This was just an aging, graying, tired-looking man dressed in cheap blue jeans that didn't fit him and never would. There was no werewolf or young Rory Calhoun about him at all.

I looked over at the Oldsmobile, thinking this must be

the man for whom they were waiting. But no. The tension was gone from the two women, along with any interest.

The guard unlocked the gate. The man looked at it for a moment as if he were afraid that it might be pulled shut if he moved toward it. The guard looked bored. Finally the man clutched the paper bag closer and stepped through, flinching in his whole body as the guard clanged the gate closed behind him.

He looked around confusedly and then started walking down the sidewalk, holding that paper bag in his arms as if it were a baby.

He couldn't be Roy Purdy. He reached the corner and stood there for a moment, clutching the paper bag. Finally, he looked around him, still squinting painfully against the bright sunlight, until he spotted the bus stop in the next block.

I started the car and pulled out into the street. The two women in the Oldsmobile looked at me as I passed them, then looked back toward that red brick building as if I had never existed.

I pulled up to the curb and stopped. "Hello, Roy," I said.

He stopped, too, and turned on the sidewalk to face me. He looked like Roy Purdy's father. "Afternoon, sir," he said, ducking his head as if he were afraid I was going to send him back inside.

"How are you doing?"

"Fine, sir." He brought his eyes up in degrees, as if he had long ago discovered that eye contact was something that drew far too much attention, in a place where you wanted no attention at all. But finally he started to look at me. "Do I know you?"

"Mel Morris," I said.

He nodded to himself. And looked away.

"I came out to give you a ride back to Houston, Roy."

"There'll be a bus along."

I leaned across and pushed the door open. "Get in."

He did.

He looked as if he'd aged twenty years since I saw him at his trial. There were pits beneath his eyes and below his cheekbones. His hands looked too big and bony.

"You can put your things back of the seat. There's coffee in the thermos there."

He squinted up at the sky.

"You want me to put the top up?" I said. "Too much air for you?"

"No."

"I'd feel better if you'd fasten your seat belt, Roy. I don't want to get a ticket."

He lifted the bag, but instead of shoving it down behind the seat, he squeezed it between his right leg and the door. Then he worked at the seat belt until he got it fastened—it was something he hadn't had a lot of recent practice with.

"Coffee," I said, reminding him.

He nodded and picked up the thermos and poured coffee into one of the Styrofoam cups nested inside the cap. I held my cup his way. "I'll take some more, too."

He poured it and then put the thermos back and sat holding his cup, staring ahead through the windshield.

I didn't bother him for a while, just concentrated on finding my way out of town and back onto the highway home to Houston.

He just rode along. While we were in town, he looked around at the cars and the trucks and the buildings and the trees. On the highway he looked around even more, but with a kind of timidity, as if he was having to get used to being able to see for such distances. I wondered if it would have been easier for him if it had still been cloudy and rainy.

When we were ten miles out, he finally spoke. "Why're you doing this?"

"You've had a bad time. I thought I'd try to make up for it a little."

"It was God's will."

"Cigarette?" I said, realizing it was inappropriate as hell. Maybe saying it just because of that.

He shook his head and waited until I had one going. Then he turned toward me. "Have you accepted Jesus Christ as your personal Savior?"

I've never been fond of talking with or dealing with people who act as if God is in the habit of dropping by and using their swimming pool. But I don't kick jokes back at them. "I don't quite see it that way," I said.

"The sword of the Lord will come in the night and strike down the unbelievers."

"It's His sword, Roy. Not yours. Don't try to wield it for Him."

"Don't joke with me," he said, meaning it as no threat at all, but simply asking it as a favor.

"I'm not."

"What do you want with me?"

"I'm not sure. Part of it was that I didn't want you to have to come out of that place where you shouldn't have been and not find anybody waiting for you."

"I've got the Lord now."

"You've got a ride, too, and somebody who feels bad that you got a raw deal."

"I'll thank the Lord for that."

"Another part was that I'd like to know who you think really killed my brother."

"I don't know," he said.

"Thou shalt not bear false witness."

That almost got a reaction out of him. "What does that mean?"

"It means if you want to play Scripture, fine, I'll play it right along with you. You're bearing false witness if there's somebody you think killed my brother but you tell me you don't know who it is. You can square it with your Lord by just telling me you won't tell me."

"I'm not that Roy Purdy any more."

"Don't hide behind shit like that," I said. "The child is the father of the father. You were just framed, you didn't have a lobotomy."

"I've put that behind me."

I hadn't planned on it, but we were passing Conroe and I braked and turned off the highway. We were still thirty-odd miles out of Houston, but you could already see the haze that hangs over it, even on the clearest day.

"Where are you going?" Roy asked.

"Follow yon star," I said. "And the truth shall set you free."

I stopped in Greedy Gertie's parking lot and started running up the top, not giving him any time to argue. Thinking about arguing, he stepped out and started to reach in for his paper bag. "Why'd you stop?"

"This is a great place. I drive out here for lunch sometimes when I'm really hungry," I said. "Look out for your head. And leave your bag. It'll be here when we get back."

I locked the car and went inside. In a moment he followed.

It was dim inside. It was long enough after lunchtime that most of the truckers and the tourists were gone, and I picked a table and we sat down. The jukebox was playing something by Waylon Jennings.

The waitress was somebody he could have sung about—overweight, over-age, overtired, dressed in cowboy boots and a square-dance dress, and smiling as if she was really glad to see us, anyway.

I made it easy on everybody and ordered for us both.

"Two longnecks. Two chicken-fried steaks with french fries."

When she walked away, I said, "Sorry, but I don't think they have loaves and fishes."

"You're making mock of me," Roy said.

I lighted a cigarette and set the pack and the lighter in the middle of the table. "Why is it you people always think you're being mocked when somebody talks back to you in your own language?"

The waitress brought the beers, and I gave her a dollar bill. "Play some more Waylon Jennings," I said.

Roy stared at his bottle.

"Strong drink is a deceiver," I said. "You don't have to drink it."

"What are you trying to do to me, Mr. Morris?"

"It's Mel. Like in Gibson. And I'm trying to shake you off your pulpit for a while and get you to talk to me."

"Why?"

"I told you in the car."

He picked up his Lone Star and took a long drink. The first time anything like a smile crossed his face was when he set the bottle down. "Not like what they stir up in the back end of the laundry room."

"The Lord works in mysterious ways His wonders to perform."

"You don't quit, do you?"

"Self-defense. I've been among the born-again before."

"I'm sincere in my beliefs."

"I didn't say you weren't. I'm just saying don't try to shove them down my throat, and don't hide behind them, either."

The chicken-fried steaks came then. They weren't quite big enough to cover a manhole, but then you wouldn't want to waste them like that, either.

"Something else they don't stir up in the back end of that laundry room," I said.

We ate. You don't make Gertie's chicken-fried steaks wait for things as relatively insignificant as religion or guilt.

I'd never been able to finish one of them and didn't now, but Roy seemed determined. I sat back and ordered some more beer.

The jukebox kicked in a new record. For a moment I nearly panicked because the start sounded like "Folsom Prison Blues." But it was okay. What it really was was "Mental Revenge." Much better choice.

At last Roy put down his knife and fork and said, "Thanks."

"Glad you liked it," I said. "You ready to go at it again?"

"Go at it?"

"The subject at hand—who do you think killed my brother?"

He took a drink of beer and looked at my cigarettes, considered, and decided he'd stay off them.

Then he said, "You did."

I'd been pretty much expecting that, ever since I invited him into the car and he told me the bus would be along. But it still had a jolt to it, and I had to extend myself some to cover my reaction.

"I've got an alibi," I said, figuring that since he couldn't know the real story, it would at least get things moving.

Wrong.

"I had one, too," he said.

I didn't bother trying to hide my reaction to that. I killed some time by taking a drink of beer and lighting a cigarette.

"Maybe you'd just as soon we went back to throwing Scripture at each other," Roy said. I shook my head. "No. Let's find out why you think that."

"You had lots of motive. You wouldn't have any trouble handling a big gun like my .45."

"That's something I hadn't thought too much about," I said. And I hadn't, even though it should have been obvious as hell. For a detective, my mind seemed to be moving awfully slowly.

He lifted his hand off the table with his fingers curled, except for the trigger finger, as if he were holding the .45. "That's a big gun for a woman."

I threw out a name, ignoring the facts in the file some more. "There's David Perryman."

Roy shook his head. "If he was going to do it, he'd have done it years ago. Besides, he's a lawyer. They don't kill people. They just get to be rich or judges. Or both."

I waved at the waitress for the check. "Let's get out of here and talk on the road."

"Don't think so," Roy said.

She brought the check and picked up my twenty-dollar bill and went away with it.

Then I said, "What do you mean, you don't think so?"

"I mean, I don't think I ought to get back in that car with you. I'll get the waitress to watch out of the door while I get my sack and you drive off. But you want any more talk, we'll do it in here where there's people around."

I sat back in my chair. "How come you ever got in the car with me in the first place, then?"

"Curiosity, maybe. Figuring if I kept trying to convert you, you wouldn't get too worried about me."

"You really think I came out here to pick you up and get rid of you?"

"No. But I'm not going to take any chances, either."

"Fine. Let's talk. I decided I'd come pick you up for one reason—out of curiosity about who really did kill Gene—because I was bored and didn't have anything better to do at the moment than play detective. And I thought you might have gotten it all figured out by now.

"Later that reason got kind of unimportant when I figured out that you might come out gunning for whoever you thought framed you, singular, or if you didn't have it narrowed down, for whoever might have framed you, plural. That became the real reason I picked you up. Maybe there's nothing to worry about. Maybe you've genuinely got religion. Of course, there's plenty of people that manage to shoot with one hand while they hang onto a Bible with the other."

"I have 'got religion,' as you put it. I'm not out for revenge."

"Fine. I still didn't kill my brother."

The waitress brought the change and I said, "We're not leaving yet, after all. How about keeping this, and using that to play some more Waylon?"

It was fine with her.

"Then who did kill him?" Roy said.

"You're the one who's been where about all he had to do was think about it. You pick."

The waitress was at the jukebox punching buttons, and "Precious Memories" started. I wondered if, somehow, she was working with me—or maybe against.

Roy said, "If it wasn't you, I'd say next in line would be Grace."

"Motive?"

"Money. That he cheated me and other people out of. And he was an adulterer."

"Okay. Next."

"Your wife."

"My ex-wife," I said.

"Your ex-wife, then."

"Fine," I said. "Who's next?"

He shrugged. "Well, that gets us down to that lawyer."

"No, it doesn't. There's your ex-wife, Roy."

He almost reacted. He almost gave me a flash of the werewolf. But it died away before it could really get started. "Elaine? No. She was angry about the money. But that wouldn't be reason enough for her to kill him."

I pushed. Almost as much to try to get him to react again as for information. "She was angry about Gene dumping her, too. Don't forget about that."

No reaction at all. "She was getting over him. She didn't care anything about him after he showed what kind of man he was by cheating me."

I pushed some more. Maybe it was the Mike Hammer Syndrome coming out in me. "She wasn't over Gene, and you know it. Something else you know—you were a wife-beater. She could get back at both of you by shooting him and framing you."

Now I got reaction. There were suddenly white spots showing on his jaws, they were clamped down so hard.

For a moment I was afraid of him. And then I started believing what he'd been saying about getting religion because he fought down the anger and, with remarkable calm, said, "I don't like to hear things like that. They don't mean anything any more."

"I don't like to hear people accuse me of murder, either."

"The truth shall make you free," he shot back, grinning at me across the table. It wasn't a very happy grin, but it was probably better than I deserved at the moment.

"I like that idea a lot," I said wryly. Then I turned serious again. "Who else is there that we haven't talked about?"

"Who else?"

"Who else could have killed Gene?"

"I don't know of anybody else."

"No more possible additions to the 'Candidates List' at all?"

He screwed up his face for a moment, considered it, and

shook his head. "Nobody likely that I've figured out. There sure never was anybody that could knock you out of contention."

I got rid of my cigarette. I didn't just put it out, I killed it. "This isn't getting us anywhere, Roy. I'm leaving."

"I'll take my things out of your car and I'll go on my way."

"Suit yourself."

There was a different song playing now. Waylon's deep, hard-grinding voice sounding unbelievably plaintive and sweet with "Waltz Across Texas." It seemed like a damned good idea to me.

Reaching inside my jacket, I brought out an envelope and pushed it across the table.

"What's that?" Roy asked.

"A thousand dollars. A loan or a donation or whatever you want it to be. I just don't want you walking around broke."

"I don't want your money."

"Fine. Send it to Jim and Tammy Faye."

Through the windows I saw a car pull up to the gas pumps. I stood up. "Some witnesses just drove up. You can come on out and get your stuff out of the car. I want to get out of here."

When I got outside, I saw that the car was the old green-or-blue Oldsmobile. It was stopped beside the self-serve pumps. The younger of the two women was at the back of the car with a man. The older woman sat in the backseat, turning around every few moments to look, as if to reassure herself that he was really with them.

The man was dressed in a blindingly white T-shirt, so new that it still had package folds in it, and a pair of jeans that fit only a little better than Roy's. At first glance he seemed very young. But that didn't square with the fact that the woman was having to help him with the intricacies of the self-serve pumps. How long had it been since pumping gas for yourself became part of everyday lore? Six or seven years at least.

The man looked around as the screen door of Gertie's splatted closed behind Roy. His face was young and old at the same time, but he couldn't have been more than thirty. He would have been just a kid when he went to prison. A young, good-looking kid. He would have had a very bad time.

He and Roy didn't acknowledge each other.

I unlocked the car and handed the paper bag to Roy.

He didn't move.

Their five dollars' worth of Regular was in the tank, and the young woman was showing the young man who wasn't young any more how to push the slide down so the nozzle would fit back into the side of the pump.

I said, "Your witnesses are about to drive off and leave you high and dry, Roy."

He didn't move. "I just want to be let alone. I don't care who killed him. Nobody does."

The old Oldsmobile started up and pulled away.

I said, "Don't you care that somebody framed you?"

He shook his head. "That's how I found the Lord."

The waitress walked to the front window and glanced out, idly checking to see whether the afternoon clouds had appeared. I waved at her, and then waved her to the doorway. She opened the hard door and pushed the screen door halfway open and looked out curiously.

I said, "Listen. Take a good look at us, will you?"

She gave me that tired, pleasant smile. "Sure."

"Would you recognize us again?"

"I suppose."

"Good. Write my tag number down." I nodded toward Roy. "If this guy turns up dead in the next day or two, call the cops."

She chuckled. "Sure."

I plucked the paper bag out of Roy's arms and stuffed it down behind the passenger seat. "Get in. I'm not leaving you out here in the boondocks."

"Why'd you do that?" he said, when we were back on the highway, headed into Houston.

"I don't know."

"We did about all the talking you had to do, didn't we?"

"Probably."

He squirmed around in the seat and dragged a beat-up Bible out of his bag and sat there reading it as if nothing else existed in the world.

But suddenly, miles later, when we were passing the exit to Intercontinental Airport, he startled me with, "Signs!"

He was staring ahead, his face more alive than I had thought possible. "Look at the signs! I forgot about them."

He was staring at the signs that exultantly lined both sides of the freeway.

Directly ahead, still ten miles or more away, the downtown skyline was coming into view, impressive in the haze. But what was really impressive to me—and evidently to Roy Purdy, also—was the signs. Millions of them, it seemed. Large and small. New cars. Used cars. Car parts. Ice cream. Beer. Cigarettes. Continental Airlines. Everything!

"Visual clutter," some people called them, but to me they had always been a symbol of the lifeblood of this roaring, rambunctious, often obnoxious, but ever-fascinating city.

I'd arrive at the airport, coming home from some impressive place, and be depressed at getting back to Houston with its unbearable seasonless weather, freeways designed by and for stagecoach drivers, world-class potholes, no monuments except for the Astrodome, creeks that were called "bayous," funny-looking buildings, politicians who were too inept even to be corrupt, etc., etc.

Then I'd get on the freeway and there'd be all the signs, like frozen fireworks, celebrating being alive and being tough, and staying that way, Boom, Bust, or what-the-hell.

And I'd stop being depressed and start thinking about what these energetic masses of bright and glittering signs really represented and made possible: the Alley Theatre; the Astrodome; the masses of green, green foliage of the magnolias and oaks and pines and oleanders and crape myrtles; the Galleria; Memorial Park; the huge and sprawling Medical Center; the chillingly beautiful Transco Tower; River Oaks; and on and on and on.

And I'd be so glad to be home that I'd promise myself that I wouldn't bitch about Houston any more—at least not for a while.

Suddenly I liked Roy Purdy.

He looked over at me then, embarrassment reddening his face.

"It's okay," I said. "I like the signs, too."

He was really embarrassed now. He dove back into his Bible and didn't speak again until we were practically downtown.

Then he gave me an address on Smith, which was near downtown.

As I was easing off the freeway, I said, "I have one more question for you."

"What's that?"

"What about Tom Crenshaw?"

He looked surprised. "For a suspect?"

"Yeah."

He surprised me then, by chuckling. "You're joking. Tom Crenshaw? You know what he does? He gets up every morning and, before he puts on his underwear, he checks the label to make sure it's the kind all the other guys in River Oaks are wearing. He won't start killing people until everybody else does, too."

He looked suddenly ashamed of himself then and ducked back into his Bible.

I found the address he had given me. In an area that had never been anything but gray and bleak and decaying, even when oil was forty dollars a barrel.

It was the Merciful Lord Mission.

"Why here?" I asked.

"They want me," he said.

Gould said, "I just practically shit when I found out you went up to the prison and picked up Roy Purdy."

"No, you didn't. You knew all along I was going to do that."

He reached out and patted the stainless steel egg and laughed. "Don't get much past you, do I?"

"I'm beginning to wonder about that, Lieutenant."

"Oh, yeah? How's that?"

"Let's just drop it. I'm through with the detective shit. I didn't have any business screwing around like that in the first place."

"Are you serious?"

"As Terre Haute, Indiana."

He sat down on the sofa and gave me a flash of his braces.

"I just write some science fiction," I said. "That's all."

He studied his distorted reflection in the egg for a while. Then he said, "Speaking of writing stuff, I've got a little project for you."

"Project? What project?"

He studied me for a moment. Then, very calmly, with no warning at all, he said, "Why don't you get busy and write me up a confession?"

I sat down. Funny how a comical, little red-faced fat man can say just exactly the right thing and knock the wind right out of you without even making a fist. "What the hell are you talking about?"

"You know exactly what I'm talking about."

"You think I killed Gene."

"Sure."

"Oh, shit," I said.

"Who else?"

"'Who else?' doesn't exactly go over big in the courtroom."

He chuckled. "You got that right. But a confession'd be something else again."

"That folded-up New York telex was in both of those file folders, wasn't it?"

"Sure. But it was kind of neat how I worked it, wasn't it? So you'd be sure to switch the one I wanted to give you for the one I didn't. And look for something special in it."

"So I'd know you knew my alibi was blown, but so I'd think you didn't know I knew it."

"Gets a little twisted-up trying to talk about it, but I think you said it the right way."

"So I'd do something stupid," I said.

"There was a chance."

"I don't think I did, did I?"

"Not that I've been able to figure out. Odds in the office were you'd try to get rid of Purdy somewhere out in the boondocks. Probably fix up some kind of 'he jumped me, and I had to shoot him' routine."

"Which way'd you bet?"

"Well, I had to change about halfway along. After I brought my kid over here and you were so nice to her. I ended up betting you'd feed him and lend him some bucks and then just drop him off at the Mission." He chuckled, patted the breast pocket of his plaid sports jacket. "Made a little over a hundred bucks on it."

I sat there and wondered why the hell I tried to write science fiction. I could live it without even trying. "Can you prove I killed my brother?" I asked.

"Oh, hell, no. I told you that already. Cold trails. Cold witnesses. All we could do would be to make you look bad, and the jury'd snicker at us for about five minutes and then take you out to lunch to celebrate."

"Unless I did a confession for you."

"It's my last chance."

I had to chuckle. I still liked the silly little son-of-a-bitch. Except I was beginning to see that he definitely wasn't so silly, after all. "Sorry," I said—meaning it, surprisingly enough. "First, no confession. Second, I didn't kill Gene. Third, no confession, even if I did."

He showed only a trace of disappointment. "Well, that's the breaks. Sometimes it works. You'd be surprised."

"Not this time."

He stood up. "Well, keep writing, Mr. Morris. My kid says she wishes you'd write a sequel to that book of yours— *Varig's World.*"

I laughed outright now. "Jesus, Lieutenant. So do I. So do I."

CHAPTER 11

"I saw your lights," Jane said.

The night air smelled thick and wet. There was thunder in the distance, and lightning scratched across the clouds behind her head. I said, "It's going to rain some more."

"At least this time there's thunder with it. You never minded the rain when there was some thunder to go along with it."

"Neither did you."

"May I come in?"

"It's pretty late."

"It's not that late, Mel."

"Sure. Come in."

She did.

"What are you doing here?" I said.

"I don't know."

"What about David?"

"Just please hold me."

I did.

Pretty soon she said, "I'm still going to marry David."

"I know." We kept on holding each other.

"Will you sleep with me tonight? Knowing that?"

"I may not be much good, knowing that."

"Just sleep with me, then. I'm going to cry sometime. After while or sometime. And I want to be sleeping with you."

"Yes," I said.

We undressed each other. Silently. No jokes. You don't joke the last time.

But we did joke a little when we were in bed.

"See? You're not going to have any trouble at all," she said.

She was right. I wondered if I should feel guilty about not having any trouble when I was sleeping with an engaged woman. But I'd worry about that later.

"I brought my own rubbers," she said. "And I even said it."

The thunderstorm arrived just in time. It was loud and rambunctious, with lots of wind and crackling booms and splats of hard-driven rain against the windows.

In contrast, Jane and I were very slow and easy with each other. We had made love in thunderstorms before.

"I'm not ready to cry yet," she said, after we had been finished long enough that we were starting to breathe normally again, and the storm was diminishing into distant rumbling. She went up on her elbow and lighted a cigarette and set it in my lips for a moment. "Don't be pissed-off when I cry. Please."

"I won't be. I may be doing some crying myself."

"Oh, Mel."

"Damn," I said. And then, "You take care of yourself, don't you, Jane? You check on things."

She smiled quizzically.

I couldn't smile or make a joke of it, thinking about Sallie. "Your breasts. You keep watch on things like that, don't you?"

"What in the world? Checkups? Well, yes."

"I mean keeping watch."

"You're trying to talk about self-examination."

"Okay. Yes. You do things like that, don't you? You wouldn't be stupid and ignore something you shouldn't."

"Oh, Mel. You can be so sweet."

"I don't want you to think I'm sweet. I want you to keep tabs on yourself."

"I will," she said.

"Please."

"Promise." She hugged me for a moment. "If this is advice-time, you'll keep on being careful, won't you?"

"Careful?"

"Safe," she said. "I worry about you. Don't let somebody get you so carried away that you think you won't bother with it this time."

"I'll keep safe."

She gave me the cigarette again for a moment. "Saran Wrap's ours. I wouldn't want to think of you using Saran Wrap with somebody else. But I'd be really pissed-off if you didn't use anything at all because all there was was Saran Wrap and you were too sentimental about us to use it. I want you to keep well. That's more important these days than being sentimental."

"I'm not sentimental, anyway."

"Bullshit." She put out the cigarette.

"You should quit smoking."

"So should you."

"Yeah," I said.

"David doesn't smoke."

"Bully for him."

"But he's not snotty about it. As long as he doesn't get snotty about it, it should help me quit."

"Fine."

"I feel like we're sending each other off to school," she said.

"Some school. Do you remember when I got picked up for drunk driving?"

She made an "Argh" sound in her throat. "How could I forget that?"

"And you bailed me out."

"Yes. I bailed you out."

"With your money."

"Yes, with my money." Suddenly she sat up. "Which I don't think you ever paid me back." She stared down at me. "You never did pay me back."

I laughed.

"What's funny?"

"I think I'm about to get socked for that again." I said. And I told her about Sam Hauser's hitting me up for it.

"Gene again. That was just like him, wasn't it? If there was pocket change around, he'd go for that, too." She frowned at me. "What were you doing talking to Sam Hauser?"

"Just checking around."

"Damn it, Mel. You've got to stop this. You're playing around where you don't have any business."

"Yeah. I think I have stopped," I said, and went on with, "How come, back then, you and Grace were so buddy-buddy with Elaine? Even though Elaine had been screwing Grace's husband? And kept wishing she still was?"

"Oh, for God's sake!"

"It's just curiosity. That's all."

"Curiosity. Fine. Okay. By that time who cared who Gene screwed? And Elaine was having a bad time. She was Grace's friend before Gene went after her, anyway. Now can we really stop this?"

"Stopped. But there's something else. It doesn't have anything to do with Gene getting killed. It has to do with us. And maybe we ought to figure it out before you marry somebody else. How come we broke up?"

I expected her to be really angry now. Maybe I was trying to push her into it.

But all she did was stay neutral and act as if she hadn't heard me. "I think it's time for us to go to sleep for a while. Maybe later I'll be ready to cry." She gave me a quick kiss. "I'm sorry I barked at you a minute ago." She chuckled. "And I'm sorry I snore."

"You don't snore," I said. "I was just being a shit when I said that."

She laughed.

I said, "Don't go to sleep yet. I did something else. I saw Roy Purdy today."

"You what?"

"I picked him up when they let him out, and gave him a ride to town."

"My God, Mel! Why didn't you tell me?"

"There's not much to tell. He's not any kind of werewolf any more. He's an old puppy is all."

"Is he angry?"

"I don't think so. He's religious now."

"Roy Purdy?" She sat up with her back against the headboard and lighted two cigarettes this time. "Do you think he really is?"

"I think so. He's got all the talk and the Bible and the personal Savior. I think it's real."

"What about revenge? Some of those people can get awfully serious about revenge, right along with their religion."

"I asked him if he was angry that he was framed. He said no—that was how he found the Lord."

"Oh, God, Mel. What's he going to do?"

"I don't know exactly. I took him to this mission downtown. I guess he's going to do that. Feed homeless people. Things like that."

"I don't know if I can quite see him like that or not."

"I believe him," I said, realizing suddenly that I did. "I

think he's had to face a lot of things. He's aged a lot. He's had a lot whipped out of him. He's got no money. Nowhere to go but there. But I think he's found a way to accept it."

"You sound like his mother."

"He beat Elaine sometimes—did you know that? And he was stupid to let Gene cheat him. But he's paid for that."

"I guess so," Jane said.

I said, "I don't want to talk about any more of this. I want you to make love with me again."

We did.

This time she was ready to cry. She buried her face in my throat and said, "I've loved you for such a long, long time," and then she cried herself to sleep.

I did a little crying, too.

Then she started to snore and gently I shifted her onto her side and she stopped.

I held her for a long time.

Then I eased out of bed and pulled on a pair of gym shorts and went into the office.

It was amazing! CHAPTER TWENTY-THREE sprang onto the screen like Cracker Jacks. I almost didn't have to think about it. About the only thing I thought about was that it was hell that my mind kept racing ahead of my fingers, and I should have cut Miss Breswick a little slack in Typing I and let her really teach me how to do it, instead of spending so much time wondering why she didn't use deodorant.

I thought there'd surely be a hitch when it was time to slog some spaces and begin CHAPTER TWENTY-FOUR. It was still raining and, two feet from my face, water dribbled down the glass wall and drizzled messily on the plants in the patio, but this chapter went just as quickly and easily as the one before it.

Next time I noticed, it was after two. And still raining. I had been sitting here for over two hours and had whanged out something like 5,000 words and was ready for more. What the hell was wrong with me?

Who cared?

The next chapter went, and it was next-to-last, and I couldn't believe any of this. No way was I going to sit here and finish this book like this.

But maybe I was, after all.

Jane was with me, I realized after a while, leaning against me, her hands down on my chest. There's nothing quite like bare breasts on your back to keep up your energy level. I listened to her soft, soft breathing while I finished the book.

"I can't believe you did that," she said, when I typed "END—Draft One," and took my hands away from the keyboard and put them on hers.

"I can't, either."

"Will you come back to bed with me now?" she asked.

"Yes."

She kissed me and went back to the bedroom, and I went back to the first of the book and made one quick addition. Then I set it up to print and closed the office door and went back to bed with Jane.

"Who does Roy think did it?" she asked.

"I don't think he cares," I said.

She turned into my arms.

When I woke up, it was morning, and the rain had stopped, and she was gone.

Zoe called.

When the telephone rang, I didn't want to bother with anybody. Except Jane. Maybe it was Jane.

It wasn't, and I found I was almost as happy it was Zoe. I felt as if I needed an old friend right now.

She invited me to breakfast.

It was our favorite place for the breakfasts we had gotten in the habit of having together every month or so—but usually we planned at least a half hour or so in advance. The pancakes and waffles were magnificent. The place was more than okay. The menus went a little far in describing the glories of their secret batter, claiming rather too explicitly that they did something to it to keep it from making you fart, but otherwise, it was a very pleasant place.

Zoe looked great. She must have gone to the hairdresser yesterday afternoon because her hair looked terrific. I wondered if there was any slightest possible way that she was going to the same hairdresser my grandmother did. I kept my mouth shut, though, and promised myself that the only way I'd ever find out was to follow her.

I was ready to spring it on her that I'd finished the new book. And she'd run an item on it. It was a little premature, of course, but in a time when the publishing companies ate up their entire promotion budgets pushing the big guys like Stephen King and Robert Ludlum, we little guys needed all the help we could get—or generate ourselves. Besides, it would tickle her to know that I'd made it through another one.

She didn't give me a chance to say anything about the book, though.

She had a thin eelskin clipboard with her, and as soon as the waitress went away with our orders, she opened it and pushed a newspaper clipping across the table to me. "Is this what you were talking about?"

"Yeah," I said, surprised.

It was an actual clipping—not a photocopy.

"You keep files of the other paper, too?" I asked.

"Of course. That's what makes it fun."

"This is the one," I said. Jane's face was blurred in the photocopy in Gould's file. This original wasn't blurred at all. At the moment I kind of wished it was. She was something, all right. If I looked up and saw her at this moment, I'd jump up and run after her just as I had way back in the eleventh grade.

Zoe's patronizing tone pulled me back. "Peggy Cheatham's usual sloppy work."

"What?" I said.

She ignored that. Pulling a sheet of typing paper from the clipboard, she set it down and hid Jane's face with it. "I wanted to show you this myself. Not have you read it in the paper."

It took me a moment to focus on what was typed on the paper:

> We hear there'll be wedding bells at any moment—if not sooner—for beautiful sculptress Jane Saunders and that very eligible attorney, David Perryman.

I pushed it all back to her. "Yeah," I said. "I heard something about that."

"Oh, Mel. I'm sorry."

"No big deal." I looked to see if the food was coming. It wasn't.

She hadn't put away the clipping.

I wished that she would.

"That woman can't get anything right," she said.

"What?"

She pushed the clipping back toward me. "They're not arriving."

I said, "The only thing about this place is they're so damned slow with the food."

"I think you're not very interested in this clipping, after all."

"I think I'm not."

She started to replace it in her clipboard.

Finally I heard what she had said a few moments before. "Not arriving? What do you mean, not arriving?"

"They must be leaving after breakfast. Certainly not arriving for brunch."

"How can you say that?"

"Well, the time on the clock—about a quarter to ten. So, of course, they could be arriving for brunch." She looked and sounded very superior. "But they're not."

I waited for the rest of it.

Zoe waited, too. I had stepped on her production a couple of minutes ago, and it was payoff time.

For a moment I was irritated enough to wonder if maybe it was time to ask her about my grandmother's hairdresser, after all.

I saved myself the guilt and said, "How can you say that?"

She was enjoying this; I let her. "The roses, of course," she said.

"The roses?"

"Of course. Jane's holding a rose. And Elaine has one. I'm sure Grace has one, too, but she's holding it down, so all you can see is the end of the stem. Everybody knows about Dino's roses." She sniffed. "Except it certainly seems that Peggy Cheatham doesn't." She relented somewhat. "She does, of course. She'd have to. But it shows the kind of sloppy work she does. Someone told her they were arriving, and she took it for granted."

"What are you talking about, Zoe?"

She had her payoff. She leaned forward and sweetly patted my hand. "A man wouldn't notice it. But it's one of Dino's traditions, and it's so sweet."

Our breakfast arrived. I've never hated blueberry waffles and Belgian pancakes so much in my life.

But finally the waitress went away.

"Dino's tradition," I said, prompting.

"He always gives roses to the ladies, Mel. But it's when they leave. Never when they arrive."

I pushed my plate aside and tapped the newspaper

clipping. "Are you saying that Grace and Elaine and Jane weren't arriving at Dino's at a little before ten on 27 October 1986? But that they're leaving at fifteen minutes before ten?"

"Of course. Leaving after breakfast. With Dino's sweet roses."

"Of course!" I said, and suddenly things were tumbling into place in my head. Tumbling hard—crashing. . . .

Zoe said, "Mel? Are you all right?"

Absently—"I don't know." Then I pulled myself back. "Sure. I'm fine." I picked up my plate and brought it within operating range. "How's your Belgian pancake?"

"Oh, it's wonderful."

I got into eating so I didn't have to talk. I was thinking ahead. It looked as if there was some more of this detecting stuff to be done, after all.

The Merciful Lord Mission was located in an ancient building which had started its existence as a cotton warehouse and sometime later had been used to store tires. It was cavernous. It had been badly used. With probably not much more than a couple of million dollars of heavy fix-up, it could have been brought up to modern standards, but no one wanted to do that because who needed another warehouse? As it was, the Historical Buildings people weren't interested enough in it to put a plaque on it, but they wouldn't let anybody tear it down, either.

It was perfect for a homeless shelter.

Most of the furnishings and equipment had been donated by various businesses around town. Most of the donations, it appeared, had been motivated not so much by the warmth of charity as the prospect of getting rid of the odds and ends that were cluttering up their back rooms.

The floors were covered with odd widths and lengths of vinyl floor covering in wildly varying patterns. The cots that were ranked and rowed along the left two-thirds of the space ranged from standard wooden fold-up camping cots to hotel rollaways to the five or six iron double-decker army bunks that sat against the wall. They were all neatly made up. Some of them were covered with good old Army O.D. green blankets, but there were also colors and plaids and patterns and a Donald Duck and Roger Rabbit blanket or two.

The only thing that was coordinated in the place was the oilcloth coverings on the tables that occupied much of the rest of the space. The tables themselves were as mismatched as everything else, ranging from metal-legged, fold-down office tables to all-wood picnic tables. But some lucky merchant must have got stuck sometime with a mile of oilcloth patterned in yellow and white, because all of the tables were covered with it. It was a bit of coordinated cheeriness so out of place here that it pointed out more clearly than anything else just what this really was. An old, abandoned place for people who had nowhere else to go.

It was about eleven o'clock, and slack time at the Mission. Breakfast and supper were served there, but not lunch. The rest of the time was for cleaning up and getting ready for the influx as night fell. There were just a couple of people sitting at the tables with mugs of coffee. In the back, past the walls whose roughness was partly obscured by signs bearing religious slogans and the rules of the establishment, which included, in both English and Spanish, "NO PROFANITY; NO CHEWING OR SPITTING; NO CROSSING OUT OF YOUR BED ZONE; NO FIGHTING," and a big American flag, I presumed there were the rest rooms and the kitchen and the office where the head of the mission spent his or her days praying for guidance.

Roy Purdy was sweeping the floor in the bed area. When I walked up to him, he gave me the same closed, blank look he had given me yesterday when I pulled my car up beside him.

I said, "Hello, Roy. Just wanted to see how you're getting along."

"Why?"

That struck me as funny. "Why not? Can you take a coffee break?"

He went to the back and returned with two mugs of coffee and we sat down at one of the tables.

"The police had you wired yesterday when I picked you up, didn't they?" I said.

He nodded. "Yes."

"Damn," I said.

"They wanted me to do it. I wasn't sure what was really going on. You get not to expect much. And I wasn't sure but what I had to do it, or they wouldn't let me out."

"It doesn't make any difference."

The oilcloth was old and much-scrubbed, but it still had a lot of that funny sticky-oily surface left. The design was yellow daisies. Nothing else. Just lots of yellow daisies.

Roy put his fingertip on a daisy and dragged his fingernail along to another one. "Don't look now," he said. "But follow that line in a minute."

I did. Sitting at another table, clutching a coffee mug, seeming completely unaware of us, was a man wearing shower shoes and dirty black wool pants and a leather jacket that had started scabbing about two years before the Korean War. He was stubbly and needed a haircut.

"Cop," Roy said.

"I figured there'd still be at least one around. He doesn't need to be here. He could be out raiding dirty bookstores."

Roy shrugged.

"You going to be happy here?" I asked.

"It's the Lord's will."

"That money I gave you—did you send it off to Jim and Tammy Faye yet?"

He gave me a disgusted look, and I privately gave him points for it. Then I said, "Did you give it to the mission?"

"Part of it."

"'Part of it.' But you've still got the rest."

He looked at daisies. "Yeah."

"What about your boy?"

"What about him?"

"Are you going to see him?"

He looked around the Merciful Lord Mission. "I don't think so. I don't think I'd want him to see me like this."

I started to get up.

"Why're you asking things like that?"

"Turns out I've still got a story to finish, after all."

He flicked a quick look over toward the cop, as if he was wondering if he might need him, after all.

"Not that story," I said. "It's not a very happy one, but it's not that one."

CHAPTER 12

Gould was at his desk, eating his lunch in today. It was all fixed up in Tupperware shapes and looked terrific. There was a smothered steak and home fries that he had warmed up in the microwave down the hallway, and salad with a great-looking dressing and a wonderful slab of cheesecake and a couple of deviled eggs and three crescent rolls that must have been microwaved, too, to make all that butter run like it did.

I set a box down on his desk between the cheesecake and the salad.

"What the hell is this?" he asked.

"You'd just completely freak out if it was my confession, wouldn't you?"

He flipped off the lid and stared.

"Well, sorry to disappoint you. It's just a manuscript. The new Mel Morris Great American Science Fiction Novel. Give it to Celeste, if she wants to read it. It's just the first draft, so it's rough and there's mistakes—typos and everything else. But most of it's there. The title probably won't hold up, but a lot of times they don't. I'll think of a better one, or they will."

"Geez," he said. "She'll be tickled as hell."

"Did you tell her why you were talking to me?"

"What do you mean?"

"What do I mean? Did you tell her you were talking to me because you thought you might pin a murder on me?"

"No. I wouldn't tell her something like that."

"Good. I wish you wouldn't. Whatever your private opinion may be. I'd kind of hate for her to think that of me."

"No problem."

"You still think I killed my brother, don't you?"

He raised his hands. "That's ancient history, isn't it? Like I told you it was." He leaned back and gave me the tough, unflinching eye contact they teach them in Interrogation 143 at the Cop Academy. "What's this 'finishing a story' stuff you were telling Purdy?"

"Jesus, Gould! He's still wired. When are you people going to give up?"

He raised his hands again.

I laughed. Then I said, "Do you ever get your blood pressure and cholesterol checked?"

He ran his tongue over his braces without opening his lips. "Well, they run a little high now and then. You know how it is. This is a stress job."

"The job's not half as stressful as that food is."

He looked apologetic. "The wife's a good cook. If I tried to get her to change her cooking, she'd think I didn't like it any more. Hurt her feelings."

He looked at the steak.

"Eat," I said. "It's getting cold."

"What about that goddamned story stuff?"

"Private joke. That's all. Scout's honor."

He tapped the manuscript. "Thanks again. She'll just freak out for sure when she sees this."

"Hope she kind of likes it, too."

He took a closer look at the title page. "I'll be damned!

This is that sequel she was talking about, isn't it? You must have been working on it all along."

"Kind of," I said.

I was halfway through the doorway when I heard him say, "I'll be damned!" again, as he lifted up the title page and saw the next one.

RETURN TO
VARIG'S WORLD

by
Mel Morris

For Celeste— keep thinking—
but kind of take
it easy with the
gum. Okay?

"Hello."

"Jane. Good. I was afraid I'd just get your answering machine. Listen, stay at the studio. I'll see you there at three."

"Why? What's going on?"

"Three o'clock, Jane. Serious."

"Crenshaw Corporation."

"Tom Crenshaw, please."

"Just a moment."

"Executive offices. May I help you?"

"Tom Crenshaw, please."

"May I tell him who's calling?"

"Mel Morris."

"Just a moment, sir. I'll see if he's in."

"Morris?"

"Hello, Mr. Crenshaw."

"What can I do for you, Morris?"

"I said I'd keep you informed. I'm doing it. I'm about to call Elaine. To tell her to be at a meeting at three o'clock this afternoon. You and Lupe aren't invited, but you're welcome to wait outside. Outside. Not inside."

"What the hell are you talking about?"

"The address is 2502 West Alabama. It's Jane Saunders' studio. Sign on the gate. Got the address?"

"Yes—2502 West Alabama. What meeting?"

"A pretty damned important one. I'm calling Elaine as soon as I hang up. Good-bye, Mr. Crenshaw."

"Hello."

"Elaine, this is Mel Morris."

"Mel? What . . ."

"Is Maria on the line? If you are, Maria, hang the hell up!"

"She was! I heard the click. What in the world was she . . ."

"That's your problem, Elaine. There's a meeting this

afternoon at three o'clock, and your presence is required. At Jane's studio."

"A meeting?"

"You know where her studio is."

"I . . . well . . . I think so."

"You know so. Be there. Three o'clock."

"Rand residence."

"Grace, please."

"I'm not certain if Mrs. Rand is available. Who may I say is calling, please?"

"She's available. Tell her that her ex-brother-in-law says she is."

"Well . . ."

"Do it."

"Mel Morris, is that you?"

"Yes, Grace, it is."

"What in the world do you mean, calling and terrifying my housekeeper?"

"Sorry. But it worked, didn't it? I'm inviting you to a meeting. Three o'clock today. At Jane's studio."

"A meeting? Whatever are you talking about? Why should I come to a meeting?"

"How about to reminisce over some old times? Like 'Arriving For An Elegant Monday Brunch At Dino's' on 27 October 1986? How does that grab you, Grace?"

"I haven't the slightest idea what you're talking about."

"Sure you do. See you at three."

"Yeah. This is Gould speaking."

"This is Mel Morris."

"Sure, Mr. Morris. What's up? You forget something?"

"Not exactly. I just wasn't completely sure about the time when I was in your office. Now I am."

"What's this time you're sure of?"

"Four-thirty this afternoon. My place. Can you make it?"

"Why?"

"What if I told you I'd have that confession for you then?"

"I'd be there."

"Okay. That's all I wanted. Four-thirty."

"Is that all you're going to tell me?"

"Yeah. It is. Except for one thing. That dedication. That gum-stuff'll sound cute to Celeste right now, probably. But a year from now, when the book comes out, she'd probably just practically freak out over something like that. The dedication'll be there. But it won't say anything that'll embarrass her."

"Jeez, Morris. Sometimes I think you're crazy as hell."

"So do I, Lieutenant. So do I. See you at four-thirty."

CHAPTER 13

Gould had turned out to be a little more interested in things than I liked, so I drove around some. After I circled the Galleria a couple of times, I drove under the Loop on Richmond and then cut off and zigzagged over to West Alabama. Picking a moment when there wasn't a car heading in my direction for as far as I could see, I drove in behind a closed-up restaurant that still hadn't gotten the word about prosperity and left the car there.

Three minutes later, feeling very Mike Hammer, I was sitting in outdoor dining with my back to the street and ordering a cup of coffee, at a trendy restaurant that had definitely heard about prosperity coming back, to judge from the prices on its menu.

Reflected in the plate glass window was a terrific view up the street, featuring the brick wall and gate at the front of Jane's studio.

It was a beautiful blue sky and white puffy cloud afternoon. The temperature was down some from the long, sweltering summer which, around here, stretches from mid-spring just about all the way to the fifteen minutes of winter we get in January or February. But it was still very pleasant shirtsleeve weather, and it was okay for a jacket if you didn't get too active. A lot of people found our weather dull and oppressive, and I bitched about it a lot. But today people in Buffalo were shoveling snow.

Nothing was happening in front of Jane's studio.

A darkly tanned young man wearing nothing but gym shorts and sweat zipped athletically past on a bicycle. Across the street, a woman who wasn't as young as she wanted to be, judging from the tight shorts she was wearing and the shirt with the tails knotted high up over her navel, was watering her lawn. In Buffalo people would be shoveling snow tomorrow, too.

A bottle-green Rolls sighed past. I watched its reflection as it slowed and parked just past the studio. Grace got out of it and went to the gate and rang the bell and in a moment went inside.

It was six minutes before three.

At 2:57, a black Lincoln Town Car with opaque windows and Lupe driving came from the other direction and stopped almost directly across the street from Grace's Rolls.

Elaine and Tom Crenshaw got out, and I wondered for a moment if I was going to have to hassle him to get him to stay with the car. But Elaine went on to the gate alone, and he got back into the car and sat beside Lupe.

At 2:59 I dropped a five-dollar bill on the table in commemoration of the fact that I'd used it for the one and only stakeout of my private eye career, and walked up the street and hit the bell button.

"Yes," Jane said.

"It's Mel."

The gate clicked, and I went in.

I stopped in the workroom and got a can of beer from the refrigerator. Then I walked through to the middle bay.

Three pissed-off ladies.

I sat on a stool and got comfortable and drank a little beer and looked around while they yelled at me.

Jane was just as pissed-off as the others. She had worked some more at the piece she was welding on yesterday. But it looked as if she had cut it all to shit instead of finishing it. I was damned glad I wasn't a chunk of steel plate at the moment.

She had had time to tidy up the place. Those tools of hers were all hung up, and the hoses of the welding torch were coiled and neat. She had even swept the floor. That was characteristic of her. We'd be working up to an argument, and I wouldn't be available right then, and she'd neat things up like crazy until I turned up. That sounds chauvinistic as hell. It isn't. I used to do the same thing.

When they started to run down, I said, "Don't give me all this protest. All three of you know exactly why I asked you to come here."

"Told us to come here," Grace corrected.

"Whatever you're happy with."

They looked at each other now. Jane was in working dress—jeans and T-shirt, with her hair loose, but with the crimping of the ponytail rubber band still showing. She didn't seem quite as angry as the others. How could she when we had held each other and cried last night?

Grace was severe, in a very pale gray silk pantsuit that must have been just about exactly the color of Gene's eyes, and a purse that I'd have bet your left one she had a gun in. Even severe and pissed and stressed, she still was a good-looking woman. Gene had outdone himself and hadn't even cared.

Elaine was wearing a soft-looking orangy-pink skirt suit with a frilly silk blouse under it. The color worked well somehow with her pale orange skin, and she had done makeup today. She, too, was still more than almost beautiful. Even compared with Jane.

After they were quiet for a moment, I leaned back and

pulled the .38 out of the breast pocket of my jacket. "My gun. Not quite as big as the .45 that killed Gene, but it'll do."

They looked at me warily.

"For demonstration purposes only," I said. I smiled at Jane. "The one I keep in the car. Do you have any idea how many times I've sat in front of your apartment at night and talked myself out of shooting out the tires of whatever damned car happened to be sitting in that damned guest parking spot of yours?"

"Don't, Mel," she said softly.

That rocked me.

But I had told myself that everything couldn't go according to my script, so I just went on. Lifting up the gun, I ejected the clip and put it into my pocket. Then I ejected the bullet from the chamber and put that away, too. Turning, aiming the gun at the sky, I pulled the trigger.

Nothing but a click. And a gasp, probably from Elaine.

"Just guaranteeing it's empty," I said.

Next exhibit, forgetting about the gun for the moment, was that newspaper clipping. I read the caption aloud: "'Three Girls About Town Arriving For An Elegant Monday Brunch At Dino's.'"

They looked at each other.

"Monday brunch on 27 October 1986," I said. "The day Gene was killed."

"What does this have to do with anything?" Elaine asked.

"Except that it's your alibi? Well, it wouldn't have much to do with anything at all. Except for one or two minor things."

"Oh, please," Grace said with infinite disgust.

I continued. "There's the clock. And those nice, sweet roses. The clock tells us you were standing in front of it fifteen minutes before Gene was killed. And the caption says you were just getting there."

They looked at me blankly and innocently, but with just a bit too much intensity.

I said, "There's only one little problem. Dino's very careful with his nice little special, personal touch with the roses. I have it on very good authority that you can't pry 'em out of his hands unless you've paid your tab and you're on the way out. I've got it on good authority, too, that Peggy Cheatham isn't nearly that careful about what she says in her column. Buy her a martini now and then, and she'll repay you with about any little item you suggest."

"Just get on with it, Mel," Jane said. "Just please get it over with."

Elaine cried, "Jane!"

"Stop playing. He knows."

"I know," I said. "I know you were leaving, instead of arriving. It all worked great, except the roses. But that's such a small thing that, if you're kind of preoccupied about what's coming next, you wouldn't be expected to think about it."

I figured we needed a little drama, so I took some time lighting a cigarette.

Elaine looked for a moment as if she was going to jump me for it. But she couldn't quite face going back out to the Lincoln and breathing tobacco all over Tom.

For consolation I puffed a little smoke in her direction and said, "Jane had my Mustang that day because I banged her car up on Friday afternoon when I went barreling over to Gene's office to yank him across his desk and slap him around for trying to rape her, so I was putting it in the shop."

Grace said, "I'm not going to listen to any more of this."

"Yes, you are." I gave them a little dramatic pause, and said, "You damned well are going to listen to me. You and Elaine and Jane planned Gene's killing. And one of you did it while the other two helped."

There was a big dramatic pause now.

Finally, in a very small voice, Elaine said, "You can't prove a thing."

"I don't have to prove it. I know what happened."

I picked up my gun again. "Figure it's bigger. Like Roy's .45. A .45's kind of a big gun for a woman—and a lot of men—to handle. That's something I was too dumb to think of myself, and it didn't get pointed out to me for a long time. But when it did, it certainly made a lot of sense. Jane's got strong hands. She might be able to use a .45 with some practice, but I don't think she's ever had the practice."

I stood up from the stool and went toward the wall. "But that's the way people are. If you can't do it all by yourself, you call in the machinery."

Jane whispered, "Please, Mel. Do you have to do this?"

"Yes," I said.

I took down one of her homemade clamps. "This handling tool isn't it, of course. I figured the real one got cut down and stuck onto some nice piece of sculpture. Probably that one that your ferns are trying to eat, Elaine—that'd be a nice touch, for you to have it. But this'll do for demonstration purposes."

I pulled the steel rod handles of the clamp apart and opened the jaws a couple of inches. They were flat on the inside, with three or four beads of metal sticking to them for purchase. I stuck the grip of my gun between the jaws and squeezed the handles of the clamp together.

"Gun-holder," I said, brandishing the clamp with the gun held firmly in its jaws.

I reached onto the wall again and brought down a pair of tongs that were maybe ten inches long and slender. "Then you use something like this and pull the trigger. In a minute Gene's dead, and no human hands have ever touched the gun. You don't even have to wipe the fingerprints off it."

I disassembled everything and put the tools back in their places. "Actually, I'm sure that it got a little more elaborate than that. Once in a while Jane makes a tool that fits against her shoulder so that she can use both hands to manipulate whatever it is she's working with. I figure she did that. Made a tool that, in effect, turned Roy's .45 into a rifle, without any need to touch it with the human hand.

"In fact, I'm just about certain of it. You'd have to have some kind of rifle-type holder for an inexperienced person to be able to put four .45 shots that close together." I looked out into the sunlight. "If I tried to plug Jane's car from here with a .45, I'd be lucky if more than two shots out of four even hit it."

"None of this means anything," Elaine said. "None of it can be proved. Not even if it were true. You're just guessing."

I ignored her. "We had lots of people who wanted Gene Morris dead. But let's cut it to three. You three. Jane made the gun holder. One of the three of you used it."

"This is preposterous. I never heard anything so preposterous in my life," Grace said.

Elaine said, "It's stupid. It sounds like something you'd make up for one of those silly books of yours."

They waited for Jane to chime in.

She didn't.

For a moment they were as angry with her as with me. Then they swung back to me as I continued. "The way it worked was that you left Dino's together, sure that the big going-away party for the maître d' would make enough confusion to cover exactly when you were there—that was why you picked that particular day, of course.

"You stayed together. You left my Mustang in the Galleria parking garage, along with one of your cars and took the other one and drove to the side street by Morris, Purdy Properties, Ltd. There were only about a million big gray cars in town, and the fact that it was raining made it even better.

"Then one of you took Jane's clever gun-holding tool, stuck it under your raincoat, and slipped into the back door of the office."

I let them have some more pause.

They used it.

"Stop this," Grace commanded.

"I can't stand any more of it," Elaine said.

"Please, Mel," Jane said. "For God's sake, let it go."

"I'm not going to stop, and you know it," I said. "When you get that far, it looks pretty obvious. All three of you wanted Gene dead. The thing is that there's only one of you who wanted Roy blamed for it."

Elaine's skin now was of a color that clashed sickeningly with her orangy-pink outfit. She was chewing the lipstick from her mouth. She stared at me as if she were thinking about hyperventilating. But she didn't. She knew I would have let her. She was afraid Grace and Jane would, too.

I stared at her. "That one's Elaine, of course. Roy was broke. Her old boyfriend, Tom Crenshaw, wasn't, and he was freshly divorced. Besides that, Roy was a wife-beater.

"So all that had to be done to take care of everything was a little twist on the basic plan, which was to get the gun out of Roy's desk, wipe it off, fit it into Jane's handy art-quality gun-holder, and walk ten steps over to Gene's office and blow him away. Then the gun would be tossed into the Dumpster down the block, where it would be found sooner or later, whether somebody saw it get tossed or not, because the cops would be sure to check around the neighborhood, looking for it. There'd be no fingerprints on it. Anybody at all could have gone prowling into the offices, been surprised by Gene, and shot him."

Grace stared at Jane. "You told him, didn't you. You told him because . . ."

"I didn't tell him anything. I didn't have to. He figured it out," Jane said, cutting her off abruptly with as much anger as I had ever seen in her.

I was glad that she did, because I wasn't ready to deal with what Grace had probably intended to say.

I said, "She's telling the truth, Grace. She hasn't told your little secret. Neither has Elaine. It just all got more and more obvious to me what really happened."

Grace went to Elaine and held her comfortingly. "It doesn't make any difference. He can't prove a thing. It makes no difference at all. There's no proof whatsoever. And you know that Jane and I will never say anything. We couldn't. There's too much to lose. He's playing detective and making a fool of himself. That's all. There's nothing at all he can ever do about it."

Elaine pulled herself up. She patted Grace's hand and spat at me, "I hate you, Mel Morris!"

"The breaks," I said, and left them there and went to the front and got another beer. I wanted to stay there, leaning against the refrigerator and rubbing the cold can against my eyes.

But I popped the tab and took a big drink and walked back out into the bay.

Elaine looked much calmer. She sat on her stool with her back stiff and straight and stared at me. Jane was full of pain. I wanted to leave it there and then, but I couldn't.

Grace said, "Not that anyone's admitting a scintilla of this, but just what's your game, Mel?"

"Game? Goddamn you, Grace, this is no game."

"None of this can be proved. The only thing you could do if you tried would be to make a fool of yourself. And look at who we're talking about—Gene Morris." She snarled the name. "If anybody ever deserved what he got, he did."

I looked at Jane.

She said, "You know, don't you?"

"Yes," I said.

"What are you talking about?" Elaine said, lapsing suddenly out of her calm.

I ignored her. "I have no interest in trying to prove what really happened. There's no point. The trail's too cold. The gun-holder's chopped all to hell. Any lawyer would make horse manure out of anything the cops could dig up now. It'd just be a big waste of the taxpayers' money. If there's such a thing as a perfect crime, this could be it. I'm just glad that the victim was Gene and not somebody who didn't deserve killing."

"Then what's all this about?" Grace said.

"Roy Purdy."

"Roy?" Elaine said. "Roy? He beat me! He abused me!"

"Bring him up on charges for that, then. But don't, for Christ's sake, hang murder on him. Who the hell do you think you are? If the goddamned beatings were so bad—and they undoubtedly were—why didn't you press charges against him?"

Her face looked doughy.

"Because he still had some money then," I said. "That's why you didn't. And you thought that he and your lover, Gene, would make you some more. So you put up with it. Until he was broke."

"Money doesn't mean that much to me!"

"Oh, yeah? Your dad went broke when you were a kid, and your mother stopped throwing parties and went to work in a drugstore. I imagine even thinking about being broke again gets you crazy. I suppose you married Tom Crenshaw and Lupe and the Immigrant of the Month for love."

I thought she was going to faint. But she didn't. She did stay quiet for a while, though.

"I'm going to play King of the World myself," I said. "Just for a little while. Just this once. Right now."

They looked confused.

I cleared it up somewhat by issuing an edict. "As the one act of my short reign, I'm telling you to make things right with Roy Purdy."

I had to get off the stool and walk around now. Kings

must have a rather tough time of it, just sitting there in one place all the time.

I went to one of Jane's few remaining stainless steel pieces and put my hands against it. It was an abstract bust consisting of part of a woman's face and one breast. It felt like smooth, cool skin.

I said, "Gene screwed Roy out of about a million and a half, I figure. Elaine, you and Tom are going to kick in $750,000. To Grace. And she's going to turn that over to Roy, along with $750,000 of her own. There ought to be a half dozen lawyers you can convince to handle it with the story that it's funds recovered that he lost. I don't care if he ever knows about your generosity or not."

"That's stupid!" Grace said. "What would Roy want with money now that he's gone religious?"

"That's not your problem, is it?"

"My God! Tom will go crazy!" Elaine said.

"Tom won't mind at all. You're his childhood sweetheart, and you give him the respectability he wants above all, whether he gives you anything but money and committees to go to, or not."

I turned to Grace. "It isn't stupid. It's only right. If you weren't damned near as greedy as Gene was, you'd have set some things right with people he screwed long ago."

"I've heard enough," she said. She stood up. "I won't have anything to do with any of this."

"Let's talk about Hugh," I said, and she stopped as if she had been struck.

I let her stand there staring at me for a moment before going on with, "I've always thought Hugh looked like a nice guy to drink a couple of beers with. Hey, Hugh, let's talk architecture. Now that prosperity's coming back, do you think there's any way we can get 'em to knock some of that crap off those buildings downtown so they wouldn't look so damned silly when it's not raining or dark? Sure, I'll have another one. Next one's on me. By the way, how's old Grace doing? Does she ever talk in her sleep about how she and her buddies planned her first husband's killing? You don't listen? Well, start listening, fella. Or just out-and-out ask her. Better yet, take her over to Dino's for breakfast and, just for kicks, ask her if she's figured out how to knock you off yet."

"You wouldn't dare!"

"In a fucking instant, Grace. In half that."

She looked tough and mean and angry. "Damn you, Mel Morris! Don't you try to blackmail me. He'd laugh at you. Anyone would."

I lowered my voice so that she had to lean to hear better. Elaine was staring wide-eyed, one hip still on the stool, the other half off, so that her foot was on the floor. The rubber band crimping was almost gone from Jane's hair, and it was loose and free. I hoped to hell it would be a long time before there was another thunderstorm.

And I hoped I'd learned something about timing since I screwed things up when I was talking to Elaine and her jumpsuit. There was only one way to find out.

I said, "Even if Hugh and I had three beers, Grace? Here you go, Hugh, old buddy. Cheers. And listen, don't bother asking good old Grace about her planning to kill her first husband. Go all the way. Get her to tell you what really happened."

I did a huge pause now. The biggest one I could work up.

When it ran out, I said, "Get her to tell you how she stood there, dripping with rainwater, and blew him all to hell herself."

Everything was suddenly new and different.

Grace sagged backward, got her hand on one of the stools, and held to it to keep her legs from buckling under her.

She was suddenly the old mousy Grace of Gene-time again. At any second he was going to come rushing in demanding to know why the hell she'd blown twenty dollars on tea goodies yesterday on somebody as unimportant as his brother.

She pulled herself closer to the stool and leaned against it. "But you said . . . Elaine . . . you said she was the one . . ."

"I said she was the obvious one, Grace. But you and I and everybody know exactly what would have happened if she'd gone in there to kill Gene. He wasn't stupid. Far from it. He'd have looked up at her and known immediately what was happening. And he'd have cut loose with that big smile of his and said, 'Elaine, honey! I was just this minute sitting here missing you,' and Elaine would have thrown down that gun contraption and ripped off that wet raincoat, and you and Jane would have sat out there in that car waiting for her until the sun came out."

Grace gave in all the way and sat on the stool, looking shrunken and gray-skinned and old.

"You engineered the whole thing," I said. "All the way. Gene was starting to put the money out of reach, and by the time somebody else got mad enough to kill him, you'd have ended up with pocket change.

"So you went to work on Elaine and Jane. Jane had lots of motive to kill him. Probably you even engineered that last visit of his to her studio, just to jack up her resolve a little. All it would have taken was a remark to him that Jane was pissed-off at me, or something, and he'd have been hot to go after her again.

"Elaine was easier. She was pissed-off and hurt. And she was going to be broke along with Roy, with hell to go through before she could get loose from him and marry Tom. With Jane, you just worked up a scheme to kill Gene. With Elaine, you worked up a private deal to kill Gene and frame Roy.

"And Elaine was going to be the hit lady. Jane believed that. Elaine probably even believed it herself. But Grace, you knew exactly what would happen if Elaine tried to kill Gene. First, she'd be too scared even to try it. Second, she wouldn't be able to do it, even if she did get brave enough to try to.

"So you drove to the office. Elaine went into a panic. You grabbed the raincoat and the gun-holder—as you'd known you were going to do all along—and you went in and killed Gene. I don't know, but he may have tried to work you out of it, too. No good—you blew him away.

"You had no reason to go ahead with framing Roy, but you did it, anyway, leaving his fingerprints on the gun, because, if you hadn't, there was too much chance Elaine would have been so pissed-off and scared about being broke that she would have talked."

I stared at Grace until she raised her head and looked at me. Then I said, "Do you have anything to add?"

She shook her head wearily. "No. You're right. Damn you. But they'll never do anything about it. Even if all of you talk. There's no evidence. There's just two scared women and somebody playing detective. I'll hire lawyers that'll make this all a joke."

"I'm not going to the cops," I said. "You're right—it'd be stupid. But you and Elaine are going to turn that cash over to Roy."

There was a flicker of continuing defiance on Grace's face.

"Just remember me and my old buddy, Hugh," I said.

The defiance died.

I said, "While you're making it up to Roy, why don't you drop a little cash on Sam and Bella Hauser, too? They don't deserve it—they were about as scummy as Gene was, only classier and not as smart—but it'd give you that nice, warm Lady Bountiful feeling. 'Grace-Aid'—that has a real nice sound to it."

Elaine was feeling defiant now. "That money—Tom will never let me do anything like that. How could I explain it to him?"

"There's not a damned thing to explain, Elaine. Tom knows exactly what this meeting's about. He figured things out yesterday afternoon at my house. Long before I did. He's sitting out there in his car right now, waiting to find out how much it's going to cost him to keep things looking good and acceptable."

Elaine wasn't quite finished. She pointed toward Jane. "What about her? Why should Grace and I do all the paying?"

"It's cost me more than both of you," Jane said. She walked out into the afternoon sunlight and turned toward us so that her face was in shadow. "And now, will you please leave? All of you. I want all of you to get out of here."

Grace came down off her stool, told herself that she could stand up all right, and did so. "Damn you," she said to me.

"I want Roy to have that money by noon tomorrow, Grace. Don't try to screw me around."

"He'll have it," she said lifelessly.

"Just get out of here," Jane said, her voice sounding thin and desperate.

Grace and Elaine did. I didn't.

"Please go, Mel," Jane said.

"Not just yet."

"You know, don't you?"

"I just guessed it, Jane. This morning, when I was staring at that clipping, wondering why you and Elaine went along with it." I went back to the stool and said, "I was pretty much right about what went on in the car, wasn't I? Elaine panicking, and Grace grabbing the gun-holder and doing the job herself."

"Yes. You were right."

"The only thing I missed on, probably, was where the

pieces of the gun-holder are. They're in that sculpture in Grace's house, aren't they? Not in Elaine's sunroom."

"Yes."

"And I wasn't exactly right about why you kept quiet."

She took a deep breath and said, "I kept quiet for my own personal reasons, Mel. Because of you."

"That's what I thought," I said.

I threw my beer can at the metal trash barrel as hard as I could, and missed, and walked out of the bay.

It was the-hell-with-beer time, and I went into Jane's workroom to the refrigerator, and dropped a couple of ice cubes into a couple of glasses, and filled them up with scotch, and went back to the bay.

I gave one of the glasses to Jane and lifted mine to hers and said, "Damn it!" and then we took a drink.

She said, "Why did you do that? Make us think you thought it was Elaine?"

"To soften up Grace and let her get feeling victorious for a while, before I told it as it really was. Because if I'd just come right out and accused her, she'd have been angry, instead of beaten. And I'd have had to take it a whole lot further before she finally gave in."

Jane leaned wearily back against the wall. "Oh, Mel. Why did you have to mess into this? You could have just let it go. We'd all have been so much happier if you had just let it go."

"Roy Purdy wouldn't."

"Is that money going to make him happy?"

"It may not. But it'll help him start feeling like a man again."

She set her glass on a ledge. "I still want you to leave."

"Not yet. I haven't told all of it yet."

"You don't have to do that."

"Yes, I do."

She walked over and leaned against the side of the door opening, not caring or not noticing that the rail on which the big sliding door rode was smearing her shoulder with grease.

"That day I caught Gene leaving here," I said. "I rode up on my bicycle, and he was charging out with his clothes torn and steel-smear on his face. And I came in here, and you said he'd been after you again, trying to force you this time. That wasn't exactly how it was, was it?"

She turned around. She looked lost and alone. Her hair fell around her face, and I wanted to brush it back. But I didn't.

"He didn't try to rape me," she said. "Not exactly. I had the cutting torch going, and he left it at suggesting that we do it. He wasn't going to force when I had the torch in my hand."

"He threatened you, though, didn't he?"

"He threatened me."

She raised her face to look at me. Tears were in her eyes, and there were great dark shadows in the soft skin beneath them. "He said that if I wouldn't, he'd tell you that we had."

"God—damn him!" I said. And then, very softly, very painfully, said, "It wouldn't have been a lie, would it? Grace was about to yell it out, but you cut her off by yelling at her that you hadn't told me anything."

She kept looking at me. She wasn't going to hurt me the worst way she could hurt me without looking me in the face when she did it, so I'd know how much it was hurting her, too. "No. It wouldn't have been a lie."

"Jane, damn it, Jane."

"It was stupid, Mel. It was the most stupid thing I ever did to you." She stopped and took a deep breath for strength before she could force herself to say it all. "I went to bed with him. I was angry with you when it happened. That was all it was. Just stupid anger, and wanting to get even, and knowing exactly the best possible way to get even with you.

"And then I knew that everything was ruined, because how could you ever stand to touch me if you knew Gene had? I wanted to kill him then. But I'd still know what I'd done to you. Damn it! Why was I so goddamned stupid! You could have slept with other women, and I'd have forgiven you somehow. And you'd have forgiven me. Except for Gene."

I said, "That's when it all started falling into place in my head. When I was staring at that clipping because I'd found out the caption was a lie, and I was trying to figure out, not why you had been a part of killing Gene, but how you could possibly have been forced to keep quiet about framing Roy.

"They kind of had you over a barrel, didn't they? Not they—Grace. She got Elaine into it by figuring out a way to frame Roy so she could live happily ever after with Tom. She got you into it because you wanted to kill Gene because you'd slept with him. And they both kept you quiet about Roy's being framed by threatening to tell me about you and Gene."

Lifelessly—"Yes."

"But after he was dead, and I'd never need to know about it, your knowing it still soured our marriage."

"Yes."

"I never could figure out what happened to us. I thought of everything but that. I couldn't think that."

I walked over and picked up the beer can and dropped it into the trash barrel, and damned near missed from that close.

Then I said, "That day when you and Elaine and Grace made your appearance at Dino's—I've been remembering a couple of things about that day.

"I had your car so I could take it to the shop. But I waited around at home because I had that damned phone call coming up with Joel Younger, arguing about the corrections to that book.

"You called me, and it must have been just before you left Dino's. I remember your calling, beeping-in with call-waiting.

And I thought it was kind of a funny call. All you said was, 'Hi. Are you okay?' And I said, 'Yeah, I will be if I don't crawl up this phone line and strangle this son-of-a-bitch.' And you said, 'You always say he's the best editor in the world, except at galley proof time. And you can't have everything. Get back to him and be nice. I love you.' That was so you knew I was covered while Gene was getting killed, wasn't it?"

"Yes."

"Thank you," I said.

"It's over now. Isn't it, Mel?"

"Yes."

"It isn't right," she said. "Nothing's happening. Just some money that they're paying. That's all. It just doesn't seem right."

"Don't include yourself with them. You've already paid. If losing our marriage hurt you anything like it's hurt me, you've paid too much."

She didn't have an answer to that. But her eyes went huge and wet.

"What Grace said was true," I said. "Trying to prosecute her would just be a waste of time and money. Elaine? She's already paying. Her marriage is punishment enough for her."

"But there's Grace."

"Grace is going to have it hardest of all."

Jane stared at me.

"Worse than if the cops went after her and tried to prosecute. If they did that—if outsiders came after her—Hugh would just rally around her. He wouldn't believe strangers, and he'd help her fight them."

"But you . . ." Jane began.

I chuckled. "He'd laugh at me, Jane. But Grace's getting upset about the possibility of my talking to him just points up what a hellacious time she's going to have."

Jane shook her head in bewilderment.

"The worry about Hugh's finding out won't ever leave her

mind again. He'll make some offhand remark about an item on TV about some woman somewhere killing her husband, and Grace will think he's saying it to her. She'll get up in the night to go to the bathroom and come back to bed and find him awake, and she'll think he's watching her. It'll get worse and worse.

"Her nice life in Piney Point with Hugh is finished. She'll always be rich. But she's always going to be scared and miserable and lonely now, too."

Jane said, "What happened to me because I slept with Gene is going to happen to Grace."

"Yes. But she deserves it. Not so much because she killed Gene, but because she used so damned many people doing it. Gene would be proud of her, you know. She turned out just like him."

Jane turned away from me for a moment and then turned back, her face a mask as hard as the steel with which she worked.

"That's all, isn't it?"

"Yes. That's about all."

"Then just go, Mel. Please."

I did.

I got home at 4:25. Gould was already there waiting.

"What the hell now?" he asked, as I unlocked the door and we went inside. "What's this confession-shit?"

"Sit down," I said, and pulled off my jacket and threw it onto the sofa. Then I pulled off my shirt.

"What the hell?" he said. "What the hell is all that shit?"

"Tape." I pulled it off my belly. It hurt!

"A recorder!" he said. "And what the hell kind of rig is that?"

I ground my teeth a little as I pulled loose the tape from the microphone leads that ran down my arms and up my neck to where my shirt collar had been. "I wasn't sure about the pickup. I wanted to make sure I could pick up from two or three directions."

"You wired yourself? What kind of crazy shit have you been up to? If you wanted a wire, we could have done it a hell of a lot less sloppy than that."

I pulled my shirt back on and set the recorder down on the coffee table by the stainless steel egg and started Rewind. "I figured I could do it. I figured you were still probably using all your equipment on Roy Purdy."

"Shit! What's on this thing?"

Rewind was done. I hit Play.

"That's the refrigerator door in Jane's workroom," I said, as sound started. "That's me opening a can of beer. Picks it up pretty good, doesn't it?"

It had picked it up pretty good.

We listened to the tape play on through.

Pretty soon we were getting close to the place where I threw my beer can at the trash barrel.

JANE: You know, don't you?

MEL: I just guessed it, Jane. This morning, when I was staring at that clipping, wondering why you and Elaine went along with it. I was pretty much right about what went on in the car, wasn't I? Elaine panicking, and Grace grabbing the gun-holder and doing the job herself.

JANE: Yes. You were right.

MEL: The only thing I missed on, probably, was where the pieces of the gun-holder are. They're in that sculpture in Grace's house, aren't they? Not in Elaine's sunroom.

JANE: Yes.

MEL: And I wasn't exactly right about why you kept quiet.

JANE: I kept quiet for my own personal reasons,
        Mel. Because of you.
MEL: That's what I thought.

Then there was the sound of the beer can crashing against the side of the trash barrel.

Gould gave me a curious look.

More noise from the recorder.

"That's the refrigerator again," I said. "I was getting ice this time. For something a little harder than beer."

Then there was just white sound from the empty tape.

"That's all of it?" Gould said.

"That's all—I turned the recorder off then."

"What did she mean, 'personal reasons'?"

"That's not important." I picked up the recorder. "It's not important to anybody but Jane and me. That's why I stopped recording then."

"Okay. Fine."

"What's important is that I wanted you to know I didn't kill Gene."

He laughed, flashing those damned braces. "What difference does that make? I thought I made it pretty clear I couldn't do anything about it, anyway."

"You scared me, Lieutenant. The more I got to know you, the more you scared me."

He laughed at that, too, and watched me eject the cassette. "There's not even anything I can do with that tape. Not even knowing about that clipping. That was three years ago, and nobody could prove now whether they were really there or not."

"You could sweat 'em some. Raise hell with them."

"It'd be a waste of time. And the taxpayers' money."

"I'm glad you agree," I said.

I set the cassette on the coffee table. Then I picked up the egg and mashed hell out of the cassette with it. Scooping up the mess, I dropped it into the ashtray and held my lighter to it. The tape didn't burn well, but it melted very nicely.

"What the hell did you do that for?" Gould asked.

"Like I told you before, I'm through with this shit," I said. "I just write a little science fiction sometimes and try not to mess around with people's lives. That's all."

CHAPTER 14

I wanted it to rain again, but it didn't.

This would have been a good time to drive down to Galveston and shiver in the cold rain and sea spray and watch that old woman fish, and drink whiskey. But it didn't rain.

I ran for a while.

I came home and showered off the sweat.

There was a lot of work to be done on the new novel. Lots of pruning and correcting and tidying up. I didn't go to work on it.

I could go someplace.

Australia was still there where it had always been. Where I'd never been. Where Jane and I should have gone as we planned, even though it would have eaten hell out of the nest egg—that we didn't need anyway.

I could go to Australia now. Except what the hell would Ayers Rock be without Jane there with me to wish that she could cut and torch and weld a piece of steel that big?

I could go out for a drink or two and try to find a woman who looked like Jane, and pretend that she was.

Goddamn you, Gene! Why didn't I work on that brake line better? Why did you have to live long enough to spoil the only thing I ever really wanted?

Goddamn you! Why do you always win?

I had to get out of the house, and I did.

I sat by the fountain in the park by Allen Parkway. I loved this fountain. It was made of hundreds of tiny metal stalks that made a sphere about six or eight feet across that put out fine sprays of water so that it looked like a huge dandelion head shedding with the wind.

But I wasn't there for the fountain tonight; I was begging for a mugger to come at me.

No luck.

It started to rain. Finally.

I didn't go to Galveston. I walked in the rain because you can't tell you're crying when it's raining.

Then I went back to the car and drove some more.

The rain stopped.

Finally there was that goddamned brown BMW parked in Jane's guest parking spot.

I stared at it for a while.

Jane.

Because I saw Jane that day in the school library in the eleventh grade, I didn't get to read *Way Station* for a whole other six months. And even now, after all these years, it's still the one book I'd die to write.

But it was okay. Because it was for Jane.

Damn you, Gene!

I started to drive away. And then slammed on the brakes and sat there in the car, trying to think. I was missing something somewhere. I figured Elaine out, and I figured Grace out. Why couldn't I figure out some things about my own damned life?

It all came down to Gene, didn't it?

Hell, yes! Gene.

But wait a minute, Gene-Who, for Christ's sake?

Gene-Dead, and -Gone, and -Finished! That's who. Finished!

I sat there and considered that for a while. The son-of-a-bitch was really dead and gone, wasn't he?

For some reason it felt like a whole new idea to me.

He was really gone.

And he'd damned well tried to screw up my life long enough! He wasn't going to keep on doing it from his damned grave.

I sat in the car and thought about it some more.

It kept on coming out the same way—Gene was dead, and I wasn't. And it was time for me to start acting like it.

I got the .38 out of the glove compartment and buttoned down the window and shot the shit out of the tires of that goddamned BMW.

Lights came on all over the place.

I put the gun away and got out of my car.

David Perryman came stumbling out of Jane's front doorway, trying to get his slacks pulled up and zipped.

"Mel?" he said, as he ran past me toward his car. "What are you doing here? What the hell happened?"

Jane stepped into the doorway, her hair down, looking out into the rain. She was naked under a pale green robe that she held closed over her breasts.

She stared at me.

"Gene's dead and finished," I said.

I caught her arm and pulled her toward me, out of the doorway.

"What are you doing?"

"Taking you to Australia."

She wasn't ready to go.

I lifted her up, started down the steps with her.

"Stop it, Mel! What are you doing?"

"Taking you home so we can have our babies. Serious."

David came running back up the steps. His mouth dropped open when he saw us.

I said, "You're a lawyer. When the cops get here, take care of 'em."

"Mel's taking me home," she said.

What Is the Supreme Court?

by Jill Abramson

illustrated by Gregory Copeland

Penguin Workshop

For Linda Greenhouse, whose coverage of the US
Supreme Court is nonpareil—JA

To a great American, my dad—GC

PENGUIN WORKSHOP
An imprint of Penguin Random House LLC, New York

First published in the United States of America by Penguin Workshop,
an imprint of Penguin Random House LLC, New York, 2022

Visit us online at penguinrandomhouse.com.

Library of Congress Cataloging-in-Publication Data is available.

Printed in the United States of America

ISBN 9780593386781 (paperback)   10 9 8 7 6 5 4 3 2 1 WOR
ISBN 9780593386798 (library binding)   10 9 8 7 6 5 4 3 2 1 WOR

Contents

What Is the Supreme Court?

Washington, DC

In December 1953, a lawyer named Thurgood Marshall climbed up the many stairs outside the US Supreme Court Building, upon which is engraved the phrase "Equal Justice Under Law." He was there to put those words to the test.

Marshall was going to present a case before the nine justices of the Supreme Court—the highest court in the country. This case would become

one of most important ever in the history of the United States—one that could forever change life in America.

The case was about children and schools. At that time, public schools throughout the South and in some other states were segregated. It

meant children of color had to go to separate schools from white children. Since an 1896 court decision called *Plessy v. Ferguson*, segregation had been the law of the land, as long as the separate schools for students of color were equal to those of white schools.

Linda Brown was a Black third grader in Topeka, Kansas. Her school was miles from her house. To get to the school bus stop, she had to walk several blocks, passing over dangerous train tracks. Then she had to wait for the bus. In cold weather her tears sometimes froze. There was a school just seven blocks from where Linda lived.

But it was for white children. When her father, Oliver, tried to enroll Linda there, the school said no. Other Black families with school-age children got the same answer.

The families banded together to try to change this, and Thurgood Marshall was their lawyer. They hoped he would convince the Supreme Court to get rid of the law about segregated schools—to rule that it was illegal.

Marshall planned to use some of the same arguments that had helped him in a California case eight years earlier. In that case, Mexican American schoolchildren won the right to enroll in previously all white schools. But that case never went before the Supreme Court, so the stakes in the 1954 *Brown* case were much higher.

Thurgood Marshall was Black. In the 1950s, very few Black lawyers had presented cases to the Supreme Court. The justices at the time were all white. Some were from the segregated South.

Marshall would need a majority of votes—
votes from at least five justices—to win the case.
(In Supreme Court cases, there are no juries.)

When Marshall spoke, the justices, in their
black silk robes, listened from above him on a tall
platform called the bench.

Would Marshall be able to convince the court?
It would take many months to find out.

CHAPTER 1
What Is the Judiciary?

The Supreme Court is the most important court in the judicial branch of the US government. It is known as "the court of last resort." That means it has the final say on all legal matters. It decides if laws that have been

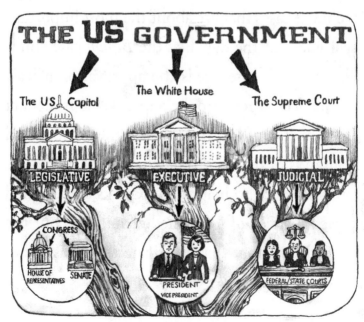

THE **US** GOVERNMENT

The US Capitol — LEGISLATIVE — CONGRESS — HOUSE OF REPRESENTATIVES — SENATE

The White House — EXECUTIVE — PRESIDENT — VICE PRESIDENT

The Supreme Court — JUDICIAL — FEDERAL/STATE COURTS

passed are constitutional. If they aren't, the laws must be eliminated or changed.

As written in the Constitution, the other two branches of the government are the executive (the president and advisors) and the legislative (Congress, in which laws are passed).

The Supreme Court cannot hear every appeal. The justices accept about eighty out of more than seven thousand requests (called petitions) each term. They meet as a group (called a conference) to choose cases that are about the most important legal issues of the day, like the *Brown* case about schools. Each case needs the approval of at least four justices to get onto the Supreme Court docket (the schedule of cases). How can the justices read thousands of requests? They have clerks, who are young lawyers, to help them. Clerks are assigned to each justice's office (called chambers). But the justices meet together in private to discuss what cases to hear.

Justice Sonia Sotomayor (right)

The "Triangle"

The judicial branch of government is responsible for the courts of law. And it is made up of a system of courts called the judiciary. Think of the judiciary as a triangle with three layers.

The first and lowest layer is composed of federal district courts. These courts decide all kinds of cases, from some types of murder trials to bankruptcy (when people or companies run out of money and can't pay their bills). Cases across the country are tried in ninety-four federal district courts. Federal cases are usually decided by juries, but sometimes by a judge alone. (States, counties, and cities have their own courts as well.)

If one side in a trial thinks the federal court decision is wrong, it can appeal. That means the case may be heard again by a panel of judges who serve on the next level, the US Circuit Courts of Appeals. There are thirteen regional appeals courts, and their decisions can be appealed as well. The case then may go to the Supreme Court. But that's the last stop.

When a case is picked, lawyers for each side usually get only thirty minutes to speak before the justices. Although there are limited seats inside the court, the arguments are open to the public (but they aren't televised).

The justices ask the lawyers questions and sometimes make comments about the case. Among the justices on the court in 2021, Stephen Breyer, for example, talked a lot while Clarence Thomas mainly stayed quiet on the bench.

Stephen Breyer   Clarence Thomas

The justices do not issue their decisions right away. After hearing the lawyers, the justices sometimes meet afterward to discuss the case further. Then they each decide on their own how to vote. The majority—five or more of the nine

justices—wins the case. Justices in the minority
can write dissenting (opposing) opinions, but
that will not change the court's decision.

The chief justice is called "First Among Equals." The chief justice does not have any special powers, but when he votes with the majority, he decides which justice gets to write the opinion. The chief justice also swears in each president on Inauguration Day at the Capitol, and leads them in reciting their oath of office.

Learn to Speak Legalese

The legal terms, often in Latin, used by the Supreme Court can sound unfamiliar. Here are some translations:

Stare Decisis: This means "to stand by things decided." In other words, a decision made by one court is rarely overturned by a later court.

Precedent: How an issue was decided in an earlier case

Opinion: A Supreme Court majority decision

Dissent Minority: Statements of disagreement by justices issued alongside majority opinions

Counsel: What a lawyer is called

Petition: A legal filing asking the Supreme Court to hear a case

Oath: A promise to tell the truth in court

Chambers: A justice's office

Habeas Corpus: A requirement that a prisoner must be brought to court to determine whether their imprisonment is lawful

Capital Offense: A crime that is punishable by death. The Supreme Court sometimes hears appeals from death row inmates.

CHAPTER 2
The First Monday in October

Everything about the US Supreme Court is formal. By tradition, the justices all wear long black silk robes. The chief justice sits in the center of the bench. The longest-serving justices sit on either side of the chief justice, with newer justices at the ends of the platform. Old-fashioned feather quill pens are given to the lawyers who argue cases before the justices as souvenirs from the days that all lawyers needed quills and inkwells to take notes.

Every year, the Supreme Court starts hearing cases on the first Monday in October. It's been that way since 1917. The court's schedule (or term) ends in June. That's when decisions in the most important cases are announced.

Every morning the justices shake hands before going on the bench. They also do this at the start of private meetings when they discuss and vote on cases presented to them. Shaking hands shows their respect for one another even when they disagree about cases.

An officer of the court calls it into session by saying: "The Honorable, the Chief Justice and the Associate Justices of the Supreme Court of the United States. Oyez! Oyez! Oyez! All persons having business before the Honorable, the Supreme Court of the United States, are admonished to draw near and give their attention, for the Court is now sitting. God save the United States and this Honorable Court."

Oyez (say: OH-yez) means "hear ye," and has been a call for silence and attention since medieval times in England and France.

Most Supreme Court justices are trained as lawyers, but being a lawyer isn't a requirement. In fact, *you* could become a Supreme Court justice!

That's because there are no age, education, or work requirements for the position. You don't even have to be a US citizen. There is only one rule: The president chooses nominees to the Supreme Court and then a majority of the one hundred members of the US Senate must approve (confirm) the nominee. Sometimes the Senate

votes a nominee down. Since 1789, twelve out of 164 Supreme Court nominees have been rejected by the Senate.

Politics is not supposed to influence the justices' decisions. They are supposed to be guided only by the Constitution. A Supreme Court justice is appointed for life. There is only one way to remove a justice—a guilty verdict in a trial in the Senate. If the senators vote to convict, the justice would be thrown off the court. So far, that has never happened.

Justices leave the court after they retire or die. The longest-serving associate justice was William O. Douglas, who retired after thirty-six years, seven months, and eight days, from 1939 to 1975.

Associate Justice
William O. Douglas

Where the Supreme Court Meets

The US Supreme Court has had its own building located across First Street from the Capitol in Washington, DC, since 1935. With its Corinthian columns and imposing staircase, the courthouse looks like an ancient Greek temple. However, in the nineteenth century, the court met on the bottom floor of the Capitol building.

CHAPTER 3
Beginnings

According to the Constitution, the president proposes laws and the Congress passes laws. But what power exactly does the Supreme Court have? That was not very clear in the late 1700s, the earliest years of the government.

It wasn't until John Marshall became the chief justice in 1801 that the Supreme Court grew in power and made decisions about important issues of the day.

Marshall was a close friend of George Washington and served thirty-four years as chief justice, from 1801 to 1835. He guided the other justices to vote with him and make unanimous decisions. *Unanimous* means everybody has voted the same way.

The Marshall Court's first really important case was *Marbury v. Madison*. Why is it so important? Because the decision gave more muscle to the Supreme Court. It was the first time the court had struck down a federal law as unconstitutional. From then on, it would decide on what the words of the Constitution meant. It would decide whether Congress or the executive branch had violated the Constitution. This power is called judicial review, and it made the court a coequal branch of government. In the cases brought before the Supreme Court, it was "the duty of the judicial department to say what the law is," Marshall wrote.

Marshall also changed the way the court operated. In its earliest days, each associate justice and the chief justice wrote his own separate decision in every case. After Marshall arrived, he wanted to give decisions greater authority. So he had the court issue a single opinion reflecting the majority's view of the law. That's how decisions are made now.

John Marshall is considered by many lawyers to have been the court's greatest chief justice. The decisions made by the Marshall Court helped shape the nation and clearly defined the three coequal branches of government. A giant statue of him is located inside the Supreme Court building today.

JOHN MARSHALL

Marshall was born in Virginia and his wealthy family owned large farms called plantations with hundreds of enslaved people. In Marshall's lifetime, Virginia had more enslaved people, eventually some 300,000, than any other state.

Enslaved people were the greatest source of wealth for white Virginians who clung to the institution of slavery, along with white people in other southern states. Northern states ended slavery between 1774 and 1804.

As chief justice, Marshall's pro-slavery views influenced the court's decisions. The Marshall Court decided a group of cases that denied enslaved people any rights as citizens. As the nation grew bigger, with many people moving west, the Supreme Court allowed slavery to expand, too.

"The Marshall Court heard fourteen cases involving freedom claims. The chief justice wrote an opinion in seven cases," according to legal scholar Paul Finkelman. In all of these, no enslaved person won freedom.

CHAPTER 4
The Worst Decision Ever

When Marshall died in 1835, another Southerner, Roger B. Taney, became chief justice.

Roger B. Taney

He served until he died in 1864, during the Civil War. Taney believed in slavery even more strongly than Marshall had. He said that each state should get to decide many issues—such as slavery—for itself. The federal government had no business butting in.

In 1839, however, a case before the Taney

Court was decided in favor of a group of enslaved Africans. They'd been kidnapped and put on a Spanish ship called *Amistad*.

Amistad

The plan was to sell them when the *Amistad* docked in Cuba. But the Africans rebelled and killed the ship's cook and the captain. Eventually, the ship arrived in New London, Connecticut.

That's when the owner of the ship sued to reclaim them as his property. The case went before the Taney Court in 1841. Former president John Quincy Adams represented the Africans in the case. Associate Justice Joseph Story wrote the decision, which sided with the Africans. They were now free. Many had already been taken in by Connecticut missionaries. Later, they returned to West Africa.

In 1997, the event was made into a popular movie, *Amistad*. In it, a modern associate justice named Harry Blackmun played the role of Justice Story.

The case that Taney is probably best known for is the *Dred Scott* case. Taney wrote what is widely considered the worst decision in the history of the US Supreme Court.

The case involved a fifty-eight-year-old enslaved man named

Dred Scott

Dred Scott. In 1846, Scott was living in the state of Missouri, where slavery was legal. Earlier, though, he and his wife had been taken by their enslaver, John Emerson, to Illinois. Illinois had been a free state since it joined the union in 1818.

Later, back in Missouri, the Scotts went to court. They said that because they had once lived in a free state, under the law they were free citizens.

The case went all the way up to the Supreme

Court. Would the court decide in Dred Scott's favor or side with his enslaver?

The decision, made in 1857, was written by Chief Justice Taney. It denied the Scotts any rights of citizenship. Anyone born in slavery remained enslaved no matter what state they were in. The decision applied not just to the Scotts but to all enslaved people in the United States.

It is chilling to read Chief Justice Taney's words. Citing the country's founders, he wrote

that Black people should be "regarded as beings of an inferior order . . . who had no rights which the white man was bound to respect."

The court decided the *Dred Scott* case in a 7–2 majority. One of the two justices who ruled against the decision was so angry that he resigned from the court.

Dred and Harriet Scott

The Scotts were sold to a new owner soon after the decision. The new owner paid for the couple so he could grant them their freedom. Sadly, Dred Scott lived only a short time as a free man. He died of tuberculosis in 1858.

Abraham Lincoln, who would become president in 1861, thought the *Dred Scott* decision was all wrong. He saw it as an effort to expand slavery and make it legal everywhere.

The court's decision so outraged people in free states that it brought the divided nation closer to war—the Civil War between the North (the Union) and the South (the Confederacy).

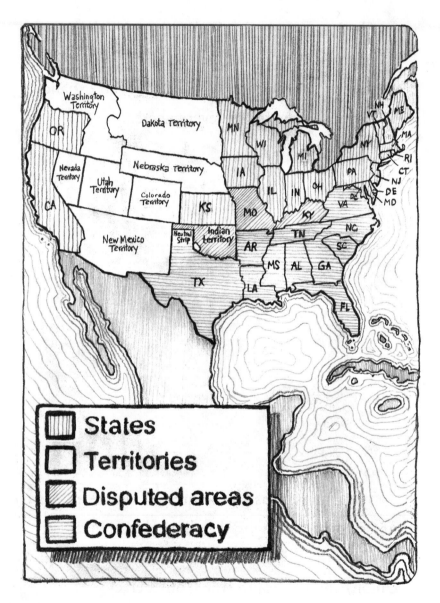

How war divided the US in 1861

The Union victory in 1865, and the passing of the Thirteenth Amendment to the Constitution afterward, ended slavery once and for all everywhere in the United States.

After the war, men who had been enslaved won the right to vote. Would this bring in a new day for the United States where all people, no matter their color, would be treated as equals?

Oliver Wendell Holmes Jr.

Some members of the Supreme Court actually fought in the Civil War. One was Oliver Wendell Holmes Jr., a brilliant lawyer from New England. He was wounded in several battles fighting for the Union.

As a Supreme Court justice, Holmes believed that no justices should try to make new laws based on their own personal beliefs. Passing laws was up to Congress. This view is called "judicial restraint." (To restrain means to hold back.) Holmes was also a champion of free speech—that people had the right to say what they believed, even if their beliefs were hateful. He ruled that only a "clear and present danger," like shouting "fire" falsely and causing a panic in a public place like a crowded theater, was a reason for banning speech.

After Holmes retired, President Franklin D. Roosevelt visited the ninety-two-year-old Holmes and found him reading Plato in Greek. Why was he reading the ancient philosopher? the president asked. "To improve my mind, Mr. President," Holmes responded.

Louis Brandeis

Louis Brandeis served on the court with Holmes. He was the court's first Jewish justice. His views on interpreting the law as laid out in the Constitution were different from Holmes's. Brandeis believed the Constitution to be a "living document" that has to be interpreted in light of changing times. Sometimes justices who follow Brandeis's view are called judicial activists.

CHAPTER 5
Separate but Equal?

The Civil War ended slavery, and for a short while in the South, Black people were able to make better lives for themselves. Hiram Revels and Blanche Bruce—two Black men—became

Hiram Revels

Blanche Bruce

US senators. Bruce had been born into slavery. This period of American history is called Reconstruction. (To reconstruct something means to rebuild or put it back together.)

Sadly, this time of hope did not last long—only from 1865 to 1877. Beginning in the 1870s, governments in the former Confederate states saw to it that Black people were totally segregated (kept apart) from white people.

In Louisiana, a Black man named Homer Plessy was fed up living under Jim Crow laws. He took a seat in a train car for white people but was soon told to move to the "Blacks only" car. When he refused, the conductor had him arrested. Plessy's case went all the way to the Supreme Court.

Thurgood Marshall (center) after winning
Brown v. Board of Education in 1954

Justice Sandra Day O'Connor in her Supreme Court chambers in 1981

The Supreme Court building in Washington, DC

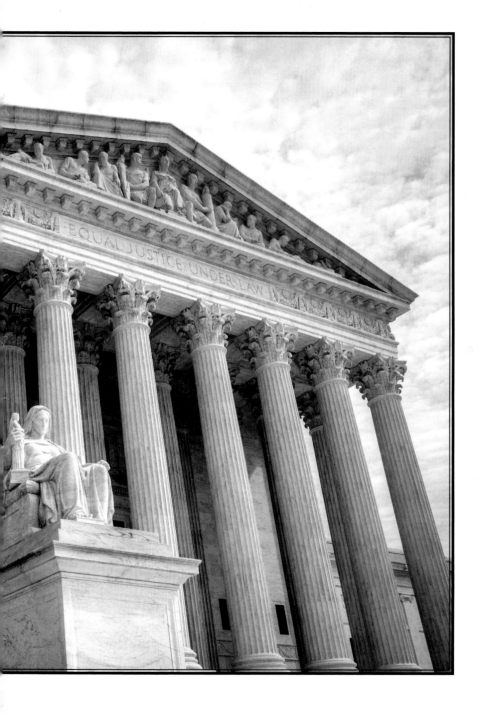

Ruth Bader Ginsburg is sworn in as a justice of the Supreme Court in 1993.

Dred Scott in 1857

Chief Justice Roger B. Taney in 1850

George W. Bush (left) and Al Gore debate during
the presidential election of 2000.

Ernesto Miranda (right), of *Miranda v. Arizona*, speaks with his attorney.

Mildred and Richard Loving of *Loving v. Virginia*

Siblings Mary Beth and John Tinker hold the armbands they wore to protest the Vietnam War in 1968.

Norma McCorvey (left), also known as Jane Roe of *Roe v. Wade*, and her lawyer Gloria Allred (right)

Supreme Court justice William O. Douglas, who spent thirty-six years on the court

A child holds a picket sign outside of the Supreme Court during *Bush v. Gore* in 2000.

People await the Supreme Court's decision on legalizing same-sex marriage in 2015.

Louis Brandeis, the first Jewish Supreme Court justice

Future Supreme Court justice Oliver Wendell Holmes Jr.
in his Union Army uniform in 1861

Linda Brown in front of segregated elementary school in 1953

Justice Thurgood Marshall (top right) with his fellow justices after joining the Supreme Court in 1967

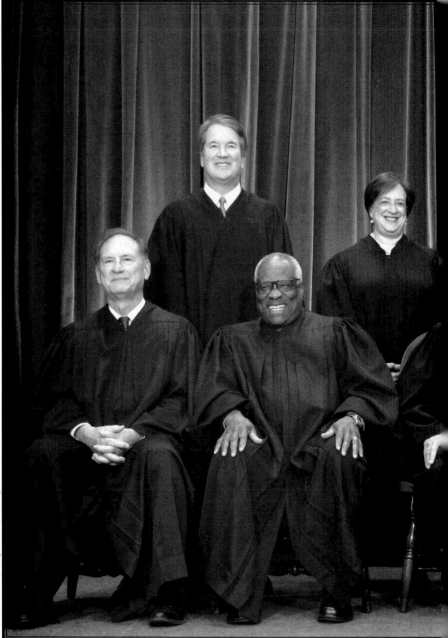

The 2021 Supreme Court justices

Justices Ruth Bader Ginsburg (center, holding fan) and Antonin Scalia (right of her) with the Washington National Opera in 2009

Ketanji Brown Jackson, with President Biden, speaks at the White House after her confirmation to the Supreme Court, 2022

In 1896, the court upheld the Jim Crow laws. In a famous case called *Plessy v. Ferguson*, the justices ruled that segregation was legal as long as separate places for Black people were as nice as those for white people. This court decision became known as "separate but equal." Of course, in reality, this was false, because separate was never equal.

For example, schools for white children were in nicer buildings and had more spacious classrooms, libraries, and gymnasiums. Teachers in all-Black schools had to buy their own supplies and use tattered, often out-of-date textbooks. The inequality of white and Black schools was the issue, decades later, that would bring Thurgood Marshall and the Brown family to the court in Washington, DC.

As for Homer Plessy, he ended up paying a twenty-five-dollar fine for breaking the law.

Jim Crow Laws

Laws known as Jim Crow laws made it illegal for Black people to eat in the same restaurants as white people or stay in the same hotels as them. Black people had to sit in the back of public buses and drink from water fountains that said "Colored."

On trains, Black passengers had to sit in separate cars. And Black children could not attend schools for white children.

CHAPTER 6
Packing the Court

Many presidents have been frustrated by rulings of the Supreme Court. None fought

Franklin D. Roosevelt

harder to change it than Franklin D. Roosevelt.

From time to time in its rulings, the court strikes down what the president and Congress agree should be the law of the land because it runs contrary to the Constitution. That's what happened when Roosevelt wanted, and Congress approved, new ways to fix the economy.

Roosevelt became president in 1933 as the Great Depression worsened. The country was in crisis. Millions of Americans had lost their jobs and homes. Banks were running out of money and about to shut down. That would cause more panic and deepen the Depression. Roosevelt was determined to get the country back on its feet. "The only thing we have to fear is fear itself," he told Americans, who indeed feared the terrible times would never end.

Roosevelt sent a lot of bills to Congress. His policies were known as the New Deal. One bill was called the National Recovery Act. It provided government jobs to people out of work, including artists and writers. They painted murals in public buildings; they wrote guidebooks to various

states. Roosevelt also intended to control parts of the economy, like farming and coal mining, to set prices to what he believed to be fair.

The Supreme Court stood in the way of some of Roosevelt's programs. It believed that Roosevelt was going outside the powers of the presidency and meddling in the economy in ways beyond his legal power. The justices began striking down key parts of the New Deal. The Supreme Court said what Roosevelt was doing was unconstitutional.

What could Roosevelt do in response?

He hatched a plan to "pack the court" and increase the number of justices to as many as fifteen. (He wanted one new judge for every justice then on the court who was older than seventy.) He planned to pick judges who would agree with his policies. This was a way to stop the Supreme Court from overturning New Deal laws. Roosevelt was feeling bold after winning the 1936 presidential election in a landslide.

Six of the nine justices at that time just happened to be older than seventy. If Roosevelt appointed six more, he could count on a majority of the Supreme Court ruling the way he wanted. His New Deal programs would no longer be in danger.

As often happens in politics, things did not go as Roosevelt planned. Newspapers were against Roosevelt tinkering with the Supreme Court.

And it turned out Americans did not want the popular president to pack the court, either. After all, what would prevent another president, with very different ideas—maybe very bad ideas—about government from doing the same thing?

Congress refused to approve the bill the president proposed. Since then, no president has attempted to fiddle with the makeup of the Supreme Court. It is what it is.

The nine seats of the current Supreme Court justices

CHAPTER 7
A Decision for Linda Brown

Have you been wondering if Thurgood Marshall won his case before the Supreme Court?

So much was riding on *Brown v. Board of Education*, because if the court decided that Thurgood Marshall was right, then Linda Brown and the other schoolchildren would be admitted to the white schools they wanted to attend. The Supreme Court would be throwing out the old "separate but equal" decision from 1896.

Plessy v. Ferguson had been enforced for sixty years. It's rare for one Supreme Court to reverse (change) a decision made by an earlier court. Instead, the court usually follows precedent (past decisions). While they are on the court, justices use past decisions to guide them on the meaning of the law and what is constitutional. That's how they reach decisions on new cases. In *Brown v. Board of Education*, Thurgood Marshall was asking the court to throw out precedent.

Marshall knew all about the importance of precedent. Since boyhood, he wanted to become a lawyer. His father, a railroad worker in Baltimore, would take Thurgood and his older brother, William, to the courthouse to watch trials and then quiz him about them at dinner.

Marshall knew the sting of school segregation firsthand. The law school he wanted to attend, the University of Maryland Law School, would not admit him because it was whites-only. (He attended Howard University School of Law in Washington, DC, instead and became its most famous graduate.)

Marshall became the top lawyer for a civil rights group, the NAACP Legal Defense Fund.

Marshall at Howard University

(NAACP stands for the National Association for the Advancement of Colored People. *Colored people* was once a polite term for Black people but is not considered one now.) This national civil rights group got parents like Oliver Brown to challenge school segregation. The goal was to overturn *Plessy v. Ferguson*. Five similar cases about Black children attending white schools were combined into *Brown v. Board of Education*.

The case was listed on the Supreme Court's docket in October 1953.

As important as Marshall was to *Brown v. Board of Education*, its outcome rested more on the brand-new chief justice, Earl Warren. He had been elected governor of California three times before being appointed chief justice. No one really knew much about his beliefs on civil rights.

Earl Warren

Marshall had begun working on civil rights cases in the late 1930s. On December 8, 1953, his biggest moment had finally come.

Crowds had started lining up for a seat inside the court at sunrise. Those who gained entry watched Marshall make his argument before Chief Justice Warren and the other eight justices.

Marshall's style was calm and easy. His wife, Cecilia "Cissy" Marshall, said her husband would talk to the Supreme Court justices like they were "old friends."

Marshall ended his argument by saying that the object of school segregation was to keep "people who were formerly in slavery . . . as near that stage as is possible." Black children deserved an equal education.

It took six more months for the court to announce its decision. Earl Warren was indeed in favor of civil rights and ending school segregation. He had meals with each justice and tried to convince them to vote in favor of Brown.

Chief Justice Warren felt it was crucial for the court to decide the case unanimously and to speak with one voice on such an important and divisive issue.

A lot of white people in the South clung to segregation. And some of the associate justices came from southern states. However, through gentle persuasion, Warren did get to a unanimous decision, an incredible feat considering he was so new at his job as chief justice. He decided to write the decision himself, his very first one.

Copies of Warren's decision in *Brown v. Board of Education* were locked away in the court's safe. Except for the nine justices, no one knew the outcome of the *Brown* case. Copies would be given out only after Chief Justice Warren began reading the decision from the bench.

On May 17, 1954, in the early afternoon, Warren read in a firm voice, "Does segregation in public schools solely on the basis of race . . .

deprive children of the minority group of equal educational opportunity? We believe that it does."

As Warren continued reading, it became clear that *Plessy v. Ferguson* was being thrown into history's dustbin.

In "the field of public education, the doctrine of 'separate but equal' has no place," Warren said. "Separate educational facilities are inherently [basically] unequal."

The _____ Bee.

For all departments call
4500

SEGREGATION IN PUBLIC SCHOOLS ENDED BY COURT

Ruled Unconstitutional
By Supreme Court; Date
To End Practice Not Set

Firm Entered
Raid is made;
Any Wounded

Painted Slayer
Captured After
Bizarre Death

McCarthy-Army
Hearings' Future
Thrown In Doubt

When Thurgood Marshall heard those words, he said, "I was so happy I was numb." Linda Brown's mother was home in Topeka ironing when she heard the news. Oliver Brown did not hear about the decision until he came home from his job as a welder for the railway that night.

With the *Brown v. Board of Education* decision, the Supreme Court was once again changing the course of American history.

But change would not come quickly or easily, something Thurgood Marshall knew. The night of the decision, after celebrating briefly, he told coworkers, "I don't know about you fools, but I'm going back to work. Because our work has just begun."

Although the Supreme Court said schools should integrate "with all deliberate speed," many states, including Kansas, dragged their feet. As it turned out, Linda Brown was already in junior high school when the elementary school she wanted to attend finally allowed Black children to enroll. (Her younger sisters did attend a formerly all-white school.)

As a grown-up, Linda Brown often spoke about how long it took for segregation to actually end. "It's disheartening that we are still fighting," she said in 1994. "But we are dealing with human beings. As long as we are, there will always be those who feel the races should be separate."

Thurgood Marshall himself was appointed to the court by President Lyndon Johnson in 1967. Marshall became the first person of color to wear the black silk robes of a justice. He remained on the court for twenty-four years, always voting to ensure the rights of all Americans.

Thurgood Marshall, Cecilia Suyat Marshall, and President Lyndon Johnson

CHAPTER 8
Rights of the Accused

In 1961, Clarence Gideon, a homeless man, was arrested for theft at a pool hall in Panama City, Florida. He was poor and wanted a lawyer to defend him in court, but he couldn't pay for one. The state of Florida, however,

only paid for court-appointed lawyers when people had been charged with murder. So Gideon's only choice was to represent himself—to act as his own lawyer. Did he have any training in law? No. None. At the end of the trial, he was convicted of theft and sent to prison for five years.

In jail, Gideon spent every hour he could in the prison library to learn all about the law.

Eventually, he wrote to the Supreme Court, asking the justices to hear his case. Gideon believed that the Constitution said that all poor defendants in state court cases deserved to have the free services of a lawyer. It was only fair.

Did the handwritten letter from someone in jail get the court's attention? Indeed it did. The Supreme Court, led by Earl Warren, agreed to hear Gideon's case. His lawyer—appointed by the Supreme Court— was a man named Abe Fortas, who would later

Abe Fortas

become a Supreme Court justice himself. In a unanimous decision, the court agreed with Fortas and Gideon that a person could not get a fair trial without a lawyer.

After that, two thousand prisoners in Florida alone who had not had a lawyer at their trial were freed. Clarence Gideon was not among them.

Instead, he was given a new trial. This time, with the help of a lawyer, Gideon was acquitted. (That means he was found not guilty.)

Robert F. Kennedy, the US attorney general at the time, was inspired by Clarence Gideon. He said, "If an obscure Florida convict named Clarence Earl Gideon had not sat down in prison with a pencil and paper to write a letter to the Supreme Court; and if the Supreme Court had not taken the trouble to look at the merit in that one crude petition among all the bundles of mail it must receive every day, the vast machinery of American law would have gone on functioning undisturbed."

Gideon became something of a hero after the book *Gideon's Trumpet* was published and made into a movie. A famous actor named Henry Fonda played Gideon.

The Warren Court also granted other rights to people accused of crimes. Before, a person could be arrested and questioned without a lawyer present and without being told they could remain silent. Why is remaining silent important? Without thinking, people who are arrested could say something that makes them look guilty. But if they hear that there's the choice to remain silent, it protects them.

Sometimes, suspects are treated unfairly by the police and forced into making false confessions. That mostly changed in 1966 when the Warren Court heard the arguments in *Miranda v. Arizona*.

Like the *Brown v. Board of Education* case, the *Miranda* case was really four cases combined into one, all about the same issue. The defendants had been questioned by local police officers, by detectives, or by a prosecuting attorney (that's the lawyer who will present the case against them in court). They were held in a room, cut off from the outside world. Before being questioned,

Ernesto Miranda

they were not warned of their rights or told they could call a lawyer. All of them but Miranda signed confessions.

Accused of rape and kidnapping, Ernesto Miranda was badgered into confessing to the crimes. He was convicted and sentenced to a long prison term. His name appears in the name of the case that the Supreme Court heard in 1966.

Ernesto Miranda (right) with his lawyer, John J. Flynn

This time, the Warren Court was far from unanimous. However, in a 5–4 decision, the justices ruled in favor of Miranda. So from then on, any accused criminal was to be given a card before being questioned. The card said:

"You have the right to remain silent. Anything you say can be used against you in a court of law. You have the right to the presence of an attorney to assist you prior to questioning and to be with you during questioning, if you so desire. If you cannot afford an attorney you have the right to have an attorney appointed for you prior to questioning. Do you understand these rights? Will you voluntarily answer my questions?"

If these words sound familiar, it's probably because your family watches crime dramas on TV or in movies. These famous words are known as Miranda Warnings, named after Ernesto Miranda.

As with Gideon, the ruling of the Supreme Court meant Miranda got a new trial. His original confession could not be used against him. However, the new jury also found him guilty and he was sent to prison in 1967. He was paroled in 1972. (To be paroled means a person is freed from prison after serving part of their sentence.)

In 1976, Miranda was killed during a bar fight in Phoenix, Arizona. Police found autographed Miranda cards in his pockets. Miranda was selling them for $1.50 apiece, which was his right. To this day, many accused criminals have gone free because they could prove that they were not read their Miranda rights.

In 1967, Earl Warren was getting ready to retire from the court. There was another important civil rights case, however, involving an issue close to the hearts of so many Americans: marriage.

More than half the states in the country, including every state in the South, still made it illegal for Black people and white people to marry each other.

Was that about to change?

CHAPTER 9
Marriage and Protest

In June 1958, Richard Loving and Mildred Jeter fell in love and got married. He was white and she was Black. The Lovings lived in Virginia, where marriage between white and Black races was against the law. A couple like the Lovings could be sent to jail for anywhere from one to

Mildred and Richard Loving

five years, just for being married.

The Lovings were arrested and, to avoid jail, they moved north. They were very sad to be away from their families. But finally, in 1967, another 9–0 ruling by the Warren Court erased their conviction. Not only that, but laws against interracial marriage were also struck down in fifteen other states.

After Warren retired in 1969, his successors as chief justice were not expected to make as many landmark rulings. But it was an era of social protest, including marches against the Vietnam War and for women's rights. Important cases about the rights of an individual came before the court.

In 1968, there was a case involving a brother and sister in Iowa—Mary Beth and John Tinker. They were part of a group of five public school students who had been suspended from school in 1965. Why?

They had worn black armbands to school to protest the Vietnam War. The suspended teenagers stayed home for a week. Then they returned to school without armbands but wearing all-black clothes—a sign of mourning.

The Vietnam War

In the early 1960s, the country of Vietnam in Southeast Asia was split in two—the Communist North and the US-allied South. The two sides were at war with each other. The United States decided to help the South Vietnamese government. At one point, there were 500,000 US military personnel fighting in Vietnam. Many people, especially young people, thought the war was wrong; that the US government had no business taking part in it. The war ended in 1975 with the North winning. During the war, more than 58,000 American military personnel died.

Four years later, the court ruled that students could mount political protests during school hours. They were entitled to because of their constitutional right to free speech, as long as they were not being disruptive.

In *Tinker v. Des Moines Independent Community School District*, the court said that students do not leave behind "their constitutional rights to freedom of speech or expression at the schoolhouse gate." The decision was written by Justice Fortas, the man who had once been Gideon's lawyer.

Women were also demanding more rights, including on issues concerning when or whether to have a baby. This brought another extremely divisive issue before the court in 1972. This case, *Roe v. Wade*, was about whether women had the right to abort an unwanted pregnancy.

Many believed what a woman did about her own pregnancy was up to her and her alone. On the other side were many people who believed that before a baby was born, it had the right to life. So they thought deciding to end a pregnancy was wrong.

The US Constitution was written in the late 1700s and said nothing directly about this issue. Still, the Supreme Court agreed to hear a case called *Roe v. Wade.* (*Roe* was not the woman's real last name. Henry Wade was the district attorney in Texas responsible for enforcing the state's law.)

The court's decision made front-page headlines in newspapers all across the country. In a 7–2 decision, it ruled that women had a right to privacy. That right included deciding whether or not to continue a pregnancy. But there were some restrictions—for example, for women who were in the final months of pregnancy.

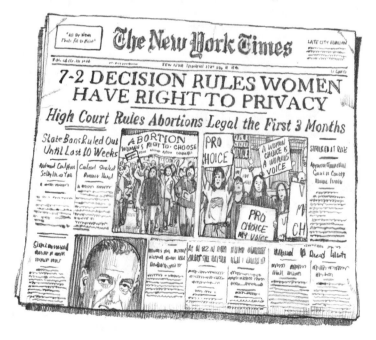

Justice Harry Blackmun was asked to write the decision. He did research going back to the ancient Greeks and Romans. The Blackmun decision said that states could pass laws that restricted women from ending a pregnancy too close to when their baby would be born. Many states did do that. There was wide disagreement in each state over how to balance a woman's right

Harry Blackmun

to end a pregnancy and the desire to protect the lives of unborn children. Those disagreements rage to this day. Your own family may have strong opinions about this issue.

CHAPTER 10
The 2000 Presidential Race

Believe it or not, for five weeks after the presidential election in 2000, a winner was still not declared. In modern times, the results are usually known late on the night of the vote or early the next morning. In 2000, the race was too close to call.

The Republican candidate was George W. Bush, who had been governor of Texas. (His father, George H. W. Bush, had been president from 1989 to 1992.) The Democrats' candidate was Al Gore, who had been vice president under Bill Clinton.

In the end, it all came down to the state of Florida. The results there would tilt the victory to either Bush or Gore. Because the results were so close, there were recounts. Then fights over whether the recounts had been fair.

Both political parties went to court, the case going all the way up to the Supreme Court in *Bush v. Gore.* Although the Supreme Court prefers to stay out of politics, a winner needed to be declared.

On December 11, 2000, two lawyers, Ted Olson for the Republicans and David Boies for the Democrats, had their day in court. They had both argued Supreme Court cases before and were among the most skilled and famous lawyers in the country. Each made strong arguments for his candidate. The court promised to decide the case quickly. And it did.

The very next night, December 12, the justices reached a decision. It was close—as close as could be. The court said, 5–4, that there would be no more recount. From the evidence presented, George W. Bush had won and would become the next president.

One night later, Al Gore said he would accept

the court's decision. "Now the US Supreme Court has spoken," he said in his televised speech.

"Let there be no doubt, while I strongly disagree with the court's decision, I accept it. . . . And tonight, for the sake of our unity as a people and the strength of our democracy, I offer my concession."

Because of the Supreme Court's decision, Al Gore didn't get to be president. (You may be surprised that Gore actually received almost 550,000 more individual votes than George W. Bush. But the results of presidential elections are counted in a different and very complicated way by a group called the Electoral College.) Gore valued the way the US government works over his own ambitions. The Supreme Court had ruled against him and he accepted that.

In 2020, Republican president Donald Trump wanted the Supreme Court to rule that he had won the election and would get to serve a second term. But the court refused to hear the case. The

majority in the court decided to stay out of politics this time; Joe Biden had already been declared the winner and certified by Congress. He was sworn in as president on January 20, 2021.

Other decisions about elections also reached the court. There are complicated rules about the amount of money that presidential candidates can lawfully receive as campaign donations. This issue may not sound important, but it is. The more money candidates raise, the more advertising their party can place in newspapers, on social media, and on TV. It helps pay for signs people put in their front yards saying who to vote for. This is a way to reach millions of people and try to get their support. More money means a candidate can open more offices in different states and hire more workers on the campaign.

But suppose a rich person gives a ton of money to help one candidate in a presidential or congressional election. Is that fair to the other side? There were laws that attempted to restrict what a rich person could give to a campaign.

The case before the Supreme Court was named *Citizens United v. Federal Election*

Commission. It was about a documentary movie about a politician (Hillary Clinton). It portrayed her in an unflattering way. The money for the movie was given by a private group. Making a movie costs a lot of money.

Hillary Clinton

The court decided narrowly (5–4) that saying something positive or negative about politicians was a form of free speech, protected by the First Amendment in the Constitution's Bill of Rights. The movie was expressing personal opinion and that fell under the right of free speech. Placing limits on this went against the Constitution.

The result meant that candidates and political groups more or less got to raise and spend as much money as they could. Campaigns cost more and more. The 2020 presidential election (Trump versus Biden) cost $14 billion, the most expensive in history.

Do you think the Supreme Court was right or wrong in its decision? The *Citizens United* case is still hotly debated among people who care about politics.

CHAPTER 11
No Longer a "Men's Club"

In 1981, history was made when Sandra Day O'Connor became the first woman to join the Supreme Court. This didn't happen until nearly two hundred years after the first Supreme Court was formed.

Sandra Day O'Connor

O'Connor grew up on a ranch in Arizona, riding horses, and had served in state government. She was selected for the court by President Ronald Reagan.

During O'Connor's twenty-four years on the court, there were 360 Supreme Court cases decided 5–4 in which she cast the deciding vote. She was called "the swing justice" because her vote so often swung a decision one way or the other.

A second female justice, Ruth Bader Ginsburg, joined O'Connor on the bench when President Bill Clinton appointed her in 1993. Before Ginsburg became a justice, she had argued many important cases before the Supreme Court to get equal rights for women.

Although O'Connor was appointed by a Republican president and Ginsburg by a Democratic president, the two women became close friends. They both had been brilliant students in law school. O'Connor went to Stanford and Ginsburg studied at Harvard and Columbia. Yet, after graduating, they each had a very difficult time getting a job. "We don't hire women," each was told repeatedly. Both as a lawyer presenting a case to the court and then as a Supreme Court associate justice, Ginsburg helped make that kind of talk (and action) illegal. She became a celebrity, especially beloved among supporters of women's rights. Her nickname was the Notorious RBG.

Justice Ruth Bader Ginsburg working out

Justice Ginsburg also was friends with Antonin Scalia when they served together on the Supreme Court. They both enjoyed good cooking and loved the opera. They even appeared together as extras on opening night of the Washington National Opera in 1994!

After Justice Ginsburg's death in September of 2020, Amy Coney Barrett became the fifth woman to serve on the Supreme Court. She joined Elena Kagan and Sonia Sotomayor, the court's first Hispanic justice. Only a year and a half later, upon Justice Stephen Breyer's announcement that he'd retire, again there was historic news. In April 2022, Ketanji Brown Jackson was confirmed by the Senate, making her the first Black woman on the Supreme Court and changing the balance of justices so that there are four women to five men.

Ketanji Brown Jackson

The Supreme Court has changed and now better reflects the makeup of the people in the United States.

CHAPTER 12
It Is So Ordered

The right to marry a person of a different race was the issue in the *Loving* case. That case involved the marriage of a man and a woman. But what if people of the same gender identity wanted to marry each other?

By the end of the twentieth century, many felt this should be a legal right. The country was changing. Indeed, several states began allowing people of the same gender to get married in "civil unions." However, Congress passed a law in the 1990s called the Defense of Marriage Act (DOMA). DOMA said marriage was only between a man and a woman.

LGBTQ+ activists were strongly against DOMA. It was unconstitutional, they said.

It should be struck down. They also wanted LBGTQ+ couples to have the right to marry anywhere in the country, not just in certain states.

In 2013, the Supreme Court heard a case involving the marriage of two women. It was about whether one of them was entitled to the government benefits of the other. This would include receiving money for health care.

How did the court rule?

The slim majority (5–4) voted to strike down DOMA. Ted Olsen and David Boies, the lawyers who had opposed each other in *Bush v. Gore*, now both argued against DOMA.

But the decision did not make gay marriage legal everywhere. That issue had to wait until the end of the court term in 2015. Two men who had married asked that the Supreme Court rule that same-sex marriage was legal everywhere in the United States.

Jim Obergefell was one of the men who

originally filed the case, which was called *Obergefell v. Hodges.* He came to the court early on the day the decision was to be announced. He wanted to make sure to get one of the seats reserved for the public. Retired justice John Paul Stevens also came back to hear the decision in the groundbreaking case.

Why was it such a landmark case?

Jim Obergefell (right) and his partner, John Arthur

Justice Anthony Kennedy's decision—which resulted in the legalization of gay marriage—was written in words that stressed the dignity of all human beings and what marriage means.

Justice Anthony Kennedy

Without legal marriage, Kennedy wrote, same-sex couples are denied "the recognition, stability and predictability marriage offers, their children suffer the stigma of knowing their families are somehow lesser." His language echoed Warren's in the *Brown* decision so many years earlier, when he said that "separate but equal" made Black children feel "inherently inferior."

A network news producer was inside and described the atmosphere in the court as Justice Kennedy was reading. "It felt in the room as if a wave of emotion was rising and had nowhere to break," she said. "No one could stand, or clap, or hug or yell in the court. Some quietly cried. Some quietly beamed."

Chief Justice John Roberts wrote a dissenting opinion. He believed that marriage always had a "universal definition" as "the union of a man and a woman" and any other kind of union was harmful to child-rearing.

But four justices sided with Justice Kennedy, convinced that there was a moral and legal basis for gay marriage.

"No union is more profound than marriage," Justice Kennedy said, "for it embodies the highest ideals of love, fidelity, devotion, sacrifice, and family. In forming a marital union, two people become something greater than once they were. . . .

The Constitution grants them that right. . . . It is so ordered."

Those last four words sum up the Supreme Court's authority to interpret the Constitution in our democracy. This will continue long into the future.

Timeline of the Supreme Court

1789	George Washington signs the Judiciary Act on September 24, establishing the Supreme Court of the United States
1790	The Supreme Court holds its first session
1803	The Marshall Court hears *Marbury v. Madison*
1857	The Taney Court rules on *Dred Scott v. Sandford*, denying Dred Scott citizenship
1896	In *Plessy v. Ferguson*, the Supreme Court decides that "separate but equal" is fair
1954	In *Brown v. Board of Education*, the court strikes down segregation in public schools
1966	"Miranda Warnings" are established to protect the rights of suspects in a crime
1967	*Loving v. Virginia* rules against laws prohibiting interracial marriages on June 2
	Thurgood Marshall is appointed to the court and becomes the first Black Supreme Court justice in October
1973	In *Roe v. Wade*, the court rules that women have a right to decide whether or not to continue a pregnancy
1981	Sandra Day O'Connor becomes the first woman to join the Supreme Court
2015	The Supreme Court strikes down laws against same-sex marriage everywhere in the United States

Timeline of the World

1793 — King Louis XVI is beheaded in the aftermath of the French Revolution

1803 — The Louisiana Purchase more than doubles the size of the United States

1865 — Days after the Civil War ends, President Abraham Lincoln is assassinated; Vice President Andrew Johnson becomes president

1892 — The Nutcracker ballet premieres in Saint Petersburg, Russia

1909 — Robert Peary claims to have reached the exact spot of the North Pole

1921 — Band-Aids first appear in stores

1947 — Jackie Robinson of the Brooklyn Dodgers becomes the first Black baseball player in the Major Leagues in modern times

1975 — The war in Vietnam ends with a North Vietnamese victory

1980 — The Rubik's Cube puzzle first hits stores and becomes a worldwide craze

1990 — The Hubble Space Telescope is launched

2008 — Barack Obama becomes the first African American president of the United States

2020 — The COVID-19 pandemic spreads around the world

Bibliography

*Books for young readers

Dellinger, Walter. "SCOTUSblog on Camera." *SCOTUSblog*, August 14, 2015. https://www.scotusblog.com/media/scotusblog-on-camera-walter-dellinger-complete/.

*Giddens-White, Bryon. *The Supreme Court and the Judicial Branch*. Chicago: Heinemann Library, 2006.

Greenhouse, Linda. *The U.S. Supreme Court: a Very Short Introduction*. New York: Oxford University Press, 2012.

Kluger, Richard. *Simple Justice: The History of* Brown v. Board of Education *and Black America's Struggle for Equality.* New York: Alfred A. Knopf, 1975.

*Kolpin, Amanda. *Understanding Supreme Court Cases*. New York: PowerKids Press, 2018.

*Panchyk, Richard. *Our Supreme Court: A History with 14 Activities*. Chicago: Chicago Review Press, 2007.

Paul, Joel Richard. *Without Precedent: Chief Justice John Marshall and His Times*. New York: Penguin Publishing Group, 2018.

Shesol, Jeff. *Supreme Power: Franklin Roosevelt vs. the Supreme Court*. New York: W. W. Norton & Company, 2010.

Toobin, Jeffrey. *The Nine: Inside the Secret World of the Supreme Court*. New York: Doubleday, 2007.

Website

https://www.supremecourt.gov/